# TAKE ME

# TAKE ME

## SHELLI STEVENS

APHRODISIA

KENSINGTON PUBLISHING CORP.

http://www.kensingtonbooks.com

APHRODISIA BOOKS are published by

Kensington Publishing Corp.
119 West 40th Street
New York, NY 10018

All Kensington titles, imprints and distributed lines are available at special quantity discounts for bulk purchases for sales promotions, premiums, fund-raising, and educational or institutional use.

Special book excerpts or customized printings can also be created to fit specific needs. For details, write or phone the office of the Kensington Special Sales Manager: Kensington Publishing Corp., 119 West 40th Street, New York, NY 10018. Attn: Special Sales Department. Phone: 1-800-221-2647.

Aphrodisia and the A logo Reg. U.S. Pat & TM Off.

ISBN-13: 978-0-7582-3528-2
ISBN-10: 0-7582-3528-3

First Trade Paperback Printing: August 2009

10  9  8  7  6  5  4  3  2  1

Printed in the United States of America

# Acknowledgments

Thanks to all the readers who've picked up my books! Without you I'd be writing stories and reading them to myself. Your support is priceless and I can't thank you enough!

And thanks to Deanna Lee for having so much faith in this story and convincing me not to give up on it. To Emma Petersen and Lacy Danes for convincing me to send this to Kensington. Thanks to Susan Lyons, Bonnie Edwards, Kate Pearce, and Jaid Black for reading my book and giving me such fabulous quotes!

I'd also love to thank the ladies at my group blog Naughty and Spice: Lilli Feisty, Amie Stuart, and Karen Erickson. To my beta readers; Jo Starkenburg and Danielle Redmond. To the GSRWA and Romance Divas for your support and info.

A HUGE thanks to my editor Peter Senftleben and my agent Laura Bradford. Peter, I truly feel blessed that you picked up my book and believed in it enough to take a chance on me. I love working with you and am convinced I got hit with the lucky stick! And Laura, I'm so excited to be a client of the Bradford Literary Agency and I'm thrilled you believed in my writing and signed me on. I look forward to continuing to work with both of you!

Finally, a big thanks to my family and friends for being so patient with me and supportive of my writing. And to Cherry Adair for your *Write the Damn Book* challenges and your belief in me through the years!

For anyone I forgot (because of course I forgot someone—and why wouldn't I?) thanks to you as well!

# 1

---

By the gods, she was late. Talia stepped off the walkatron, ignoring the electronic voice that blared a reminder that she was tardy for her next scheduled meeting with the Council. Dragging a towel across her forehead, she headed toward the bathing room.

The physical wellness hour was the one time during her day that she absolutely savored, that she considered her hour. Complete isolation and privacy, taking out her frustrations and wants in the only way she was allowed. Forty-five minutes of running on the walkatron, until her legs were sore and her mind rid of all the dreams that could never be.

She could simply be Talia, a twenty-two-year-old woman blessed—or cursed—to be one of the few dozen women alive and well living on the planet. She was no longer Natalia, the well-pampered and well-used commodity of the Council. A highly educated, groomed plaything for the most powerful men on the planet. In here she could escape the reality of her life as a Rosabelle.

Her mouth tightened and she shook her head.

*Stop feeling sorry for yourself. Every woman blessed to be alive on this planet bears the same reality as you. Only most do not have your luxuries.*

She was envied by the other Rosabelles, as well she should be. Though every woman alive was groomed and sold to the highest bidder, she was the only woman who now kneeled at the feet of the Governing Council.

Pausing to look in the mirror, she toyed with a strand of red hair that had escaped the severe knot on top of her head. Her lips twisted downward. Such freedom that strand of hair had. A freedom that was never to be. She pulled the hair taut and tucked it back into the expected knot on her head.

"Mistress Natalia, you must begin your bathing ritual." The male voice rang out through the bathroom.

Her stomach dropped as she met the bored obsidian gaze of her male servant who waited in the corner. *And now the return to reality.* She turned around and approached the large basin, already filled with near-scalding water.

"Did you enjoy your run?" Dane asked, taking her arms and urging them above her head.

"It was quite lovely as always, thank you." She waited as he unfastened, then unwound the strip of fabric that bound her breasts.

"You always seem to look forward to that hour." He grimaced. "I don't tolerate exercise, or sweating. The physical wellness hour would be my least favorite time of the day." He dropped to his knees in front of her and untied the fastenings at each side of her hip, plucking the fabric away and leaving her completely naked. "Then again, I see nothing wrong with being surrounded by the most powerful men on the planet who want only for me to please them."

"Yes, now why doesn't that surprise me?" Talia rolled her

eyes as he cupped the mound of her sex and ran a thumb down her slit.

He nodded in approval. "Still smooth. The treatments last summer appear to have killed the hair follicles in this region." Standing again he gestured toward the bath. "Let us begin."

Talia climbed into the basin, wincing as the water stung her legs. Protesting the temperature would only gain her disapproval from her owners. As with every Rosabelle, she was to be cleansed with the hottest of water that would not damage her skin, but would leave it pink and clean.

She sank all the way under, rinsing all the sweat off her body and wetting every square inch of flesh. When she sat back up, Dane held a sponge drizzled with honey and a creamy, moisturizing soap.

"Hands in the air, please," he ordered.

Raising her hands above her head, she laced her fingers and closed her eyes. The first stroke of the sponge moved over her breasts and her nipples tightened. She went through the bathing ritual daily, with a man who would never be aroused by her, yet her body continued to respond to the silky touch of the sponge on her flesh.

"Jeez, Talia, you're so damn responsive. The Council members must love you."

She bit back a sigh. Yes. The Council members did indeed love her. Although, love was probably a poor choice of words. They loved her body and her skills as a Rosabelle. Never had she, nor would she likely, feel the warmth of another's love.

Her gut clenched and the familiar sense of despair and feeling trapped washed over her. The recurring *this can't be my life* moment that threatened to rip apart her soul.

Dane moved the sponge between her legs and heat speared through her body.

3

"No, love, don't get yourself aroused. That's the Council's job. It will only anger them if you arrive already prepared."

A spark of irritation ran through her. Of course it would. Gods help her if she were to be aroused when she wasn't in the Council's presence.

Every moment of her life revolved around pleasing men, but only the select three men who owned her. Anyone outside the Council and Dane was forbidden from ever touching or even gazing upon her naked flesh.

And never was she allowed to touch herself. A Rosabelle caught touching herself was to be punished in the most severe manner, where she would only begin to wish for death. Though never would she actually be killed, for to do so would mean one less woman on a planet where there were already so few.

Her expression turned bitter. Life on the endangered species list could be a real pain in the ass.

"Close your eyes while I wash your hair."

She obediently closed her eyes and enjoyed the moment where her hair was let free down her back. So rarely was that allowed; only if one of the Council members requested it. Otherwise, she was to wear it in a knot atop her head.

Dane massaged her scalp and worked the cleanser in her hair into a lather.

"Rinsing now. Keep the eyes closed."

Warm water sluiced over her head, down her face, and over her breasts.

"Very nice, love. All done. You can get out now."

Talia stepped out of the tub and into the fluffy soft towel that Dane held. He wrapped it around her, patting her down. Once she was dry he pulled her hair again into the severe knot atop her head, and then began oiling and lotioning her body.

A half hour later her body was dewy and perfumed. Her lips were topped with shiny pink gloss and her lashes curled and inked. She donned a pale blue silk dress with sleeves to the wrists, an empire waist, and a low bodice.

Dane gave her an appreciative glance. "Look at how nicely you've cleaned up."

"Only with your help, as always." She gave a slight smile; the movement felt awkward as the muscles around her mouth stretched. When was the last time she'd smiled?

"Well, I do try. Now, we should go, because I have a lunch date with a certain warrior in training."

They left the bathing chambers and she cast him a sideways glance. "I take it things are well between you and Thomas?"

"Quite well." The slight flush in his cheeks and brightening of his eyes surprised her. Perhaps Dane was developing an attachment to the younger man?

On a planet with so few women, it was not uncommon for men to take other men as lovers.

They moved into a busy corridor, passing a general.

"Good day, mistress." He bowed slightly, his hungry gaze moving over her.

Talia curtsied and lowered her eyes demurely. The general was just one of the many men who would never be allowed to touch her.

"The Council has already begun meeting for the day." Dane cast a nervous glance her way. "They will not be pleased to find you late."

"I'm sure they will not," she agreed mildly and glanced through the window in the corridor down to the city below. Men roamed the streets, their clothes tattered as they begged for handouts. They would not be outside for long, though; the air outside was not safe to breathe for long periods of time.

She bit back a sigh. Even with the dangerous environment, she wished just once to be able to experience life outside the Council's headquarters. Once, as a child, she'd been taken outside, but the memory was so vague she couldn't tell what was real and what was simply made up in her head from watching the teletron.

*But that is not your life, it never will be.* She lifted her chin, squelching back the bite of loneliness. Turning her gaze back to the corridor, it locked on a pair of dark brown eyes.

She had no idea who he was, yet he watched her rather intimately. Irritation pricked her. The man leaned against the corridor a few feet ahead of them.

He was quite attractive. Tall, dark hair, broad shoulders, and a predatory stillness in him that sent a frisson of alarm through her. Alarm and . . . heat. She felt a warm flush steal into her cheeks. But why? She was no virgin unused to a man's sexual interest.

Dane escorted her closer to him, and the breath in her throat seemed to lock. He did not bow, she realized in shock. With so few women in existence, all Rosabelles were held in the highest regard. It was required that every man bow in the presence of one. Instead his gaze moved over her slow and thorough, to the point where she wondered if he might have the impossible ability to see beneath her dress.

Her pulse, which had already begun to race, throbbed for a different reason now. How dare the man? Had he no respect?

He straightened from the wall as she came abreast of him, but instead of bowing as she assumed he'd do, he gave her a mocking smile and lifted one eyebrow as if to challenge her. She jerked her gaze away from him, her heart thudding like mad.

How foolish he was to stare at her so, to not bow. If she were smart she'd report him. It was no less than he deserved.

Even after she'd passed by him, she could feel his gaze burning into her back. She was accustomed to being stared at, but never had it unsettled her so. Never had something as common as a man's stare created heat that spiraled throughout her body and settled low in her belly.

Her nipples tightened and she groaned in dismay. This was not good. Her arousal was now blatantly apparent, and the Council would note as much the moment she entered the room.

"Come." Dane punched in the code that opened the automatic doors, and they hissed open.

Talia took a deep breath and, unable to resist, glanced back at the man. He continued to watch her, but his eyes were now narrowed and his mouth drawn tight.

He didn't appear pleased with her being led into the Council's chamber. The thought perked her spirits a bit and she raised a mocking eyebrow back at him, before turning to enter the chamber alone.

Ryder watched the doors to the Council's chamber slide shut and clenched his fists. Fuck. She was the target Rosabelle? He shook his head and walked to the window that overlooked the city. Now this was just a complication that he didn't need.

What should have been a simple plan had just become a helluva lot more complicated. The last thing he needed was his dick rock hard when he set the events in motion. *As long as you think with the right head you'll be fine.*

And they would be blindsided if all went well. He rocked back on his heels and envisioned the Rosabelle who'd just passed by. Like all Rosabelles he'd encountered on this planet, she had been beautiful. With lush breasts, a small waist, and slender thighs that he already imagined spread wide for him. But there had been more about that woman. A fire he'd seen within those pale blue eyes, where as in most Rosabelles he had encountered there was simply a flatness, a resignation to their lives.

The blood in his cock stirred and his breathing grew heavier. He would have her. Hot and willing when the time was right, but now . . . now he needed to stick to the plan.

Talia entered the Council's chamber, pushing aside the familiar despondency and apprehension. She walked with her head held high and her shoulders back, allowing her breasts to thrust against the fabric. *Always present your body's curves in the most provocative manner.* She'd learned the manner of walking from the day she was first groomed to become a Rosabelle.

The room was cold with steel walls, circular in structure with each of the Council members' desks spread throughout. In the middle of the room was the couch that could be altered into a bed. Just looking at it brought a cold trickle of sweat down her spine.

"Natalia, my dear. You're late, but have impeccable timing. We were about to begin our first break of the morning." One of the Council members, Victor, arose from his desk and approached her. His gaze moved over her possessively. "You look absolutely stun—"

He broke off and the sudden silence in the air was wrought with tension. Oh gods. He'd sure noticed quickly enough. She'd hoped he'd not see it, be too preoccupied.

"Take notice, gentlemen," he said and closed the distance between them. Reaching out he cupped her breast through the dress, capturing the tight nipple between his fingers. "It appears our Natalia has found something to be aroused by outside our chamber."

"And I apologize, sirs," she murmured uneasily and lowered her gaze. "It was simply the thought of you three that has put me in such a state."

The lie was reasonable enough, but would they believe it?

"Really?" Victor's tone indicated his doubt. "How aroused have you allowed yourself to become? Shall we check, my dear?"

She kept her gaze lowered and gave a submissive nod. Her pulse quickened with trepidation. She heard the scrape of the other chairs across the hardwood floor and knew that Ramirez and Franklin were approaching her.

The warm air tickled her ankles as one of the men lifted her dress. With her gaze still downcast, she recognized the age spots on the hand that held the fabric. It was Ramirez, the eldest of the men, who was somewhere in his mid-fifties.

The dress was raised past her knees, up her thighs, and then over her hips. Her naked pussy was revealed to the men in the room. Men who knew every inch of her body the way a painter knew every detail in his painting.

Ramirez's fingers slipped between her legs and rubbed over the lips of her cunt. She closed her eyes, knowing her body would respond at this point. Heart and emotions out of the equation, her body knew pleasure.

"She is already wet." His disappointment was evident.

And her body also knew pain. She knew what would come next. She bit her lip and a tremble shook her body.

"I see." Victor sighed.

Her dress was once again lowered. She heard the rasp of a zipper and opened her eyes, lifting her gaze to the men. Franklin had his cock out, and was stroking the thick purple erection as he leered at her.

"Remove your dress, Natalia," Victor commanded.

Without hesitation she undid the single button in the back and let the dress slide off her body and onto the floor.

"Now you will assume the position for punishment." Victor glanced over at Ramirez. "You may participate if you wish."

The older man nodded and went and sat upon his desk, hastily reaching for the fly of his pants.

Talia took a deep calming breath, walked to the desk, and leaned forward, thrusting her ass out toward Victor. She placed her palms on either side of Ramirez, watching as he freed his erection and lifted it eagerly toward her lips.

"Take him within your mouth," Victor commanded. And then the first stinging slap of his hand rained down on her buttock.

She barely flinched and parted her lips, allowing Victor to press his erection into her mouth. The slaps continued, harder as she suckled upon Ramirez's flesh. She went into her zone, the only way in which she got through these moments. Not thinking, only performing.

His fingers clenched in her hair, holding her mouth to his cock as she brought him to orgasm. He spilled his seed into her mouth and she swallowed automatically, trying not to focus on the hot burning of her buttocks.

Ramirez released her just as an arm wrapped around her waist and pulled her upright.

"You are forgiven, my dear." Victor turned her around, his gaze full of lust.

Ramirez slipped off the desk, which allowed Victor to lay her down upon it. The wood was hard upon her spine, but she offered no protest as he stepped between her thighs.

He ran his hands over her body, squeezing her breasts and then moving down between her legs. He thrust two fingers inside her and wiggled them around.

"Wet indeed. A woman's cunt is like the rarest fine wine. So few can afford it. We are entitled, we are blessed." He fell to his knees and buried his face against her pussy.

His tongue moved over her, rough and eager. He found her clit and lapped at it, at her, devouring her like a man deprived.

The warm arousal she'd felt when she'd seen the man in the corridor returned. His image instantly embedded itself behind her closed lids, and suddenly it was not Victor pleasuring her, but him. The dark-eyed man in the hall, sucking and licking her flesh.

The pleasure spiraled until it seemed to spill over in waves. Her body trembled. She blinked. What had just happened?

Victor stood and ran his hands down her thighs. "How interesting. I do believe our Rosabelle just had a small orgasm."

An orgasm? She had not thought it possible. Confusion swept over her. The pleasure had built while she had thought about that man in the hall.

"Do not get a swollen head over it. I am sure it was an accident," Franklin grumbled. "I believe it was decided that I was to have her during the morning break?"

"Yes, that was what we agreed upon this morning." Victor's reply sounded reluctant.

She opened her eyes, watching Victor step away from her and Franklin move between her thighs. Since the day they'd purchased her when she'd turned eighteen, never would they take her one after another, always spreading out the actual act of sex throughout the day.

"Hello there, baby." Franklin grinned, pinched her nipple to the point of pain, and thrust his erect cock hard inside her. "I've missed you."

Victor climbed atop the desk and straddled her chest. He freed his own erection and rubbed it across her lips.

"If you don't mind, my dear?"

She opened her mouth and took him inside. Why did he ask her when they both knew she had no choice? This was her life. Yesterday, today, and tomorrow.

Ramirez leaned over the desk and a moment later his fleshy lips closed over her nipple and he began to suckle.

What if there was some way to have more? If there was an out from her life as a Rosabelle. *Don't be a fool. You know it's impossible.* Yes. Completely impossible. She bit her lip, squelching back any hope, and went back into her zone.

Two hours later Talia was in what she liked to refer to as the midday lull. Where the three men had been pleasured, and her only duty was to sit with them while they discussed business. Or perhaps serve them food or beverage if they so desired.

"Ramirez, what is the course of action we have lined up against the planet of Belton?" Victor asked while she sat on his lap. The hand that rested around her waist slid upward to idly fondle her breast. "Are the troops prepared to be deployed?"

Talia lowered her gaze, all too familiar with this topic. The Council was organizing an unplanned assault on a nearby planet that they had a supposed alliance with. The reasoning behind their plan was to gain resources that were dwindling upon their own planet.

"Indeed they are. The preliminary attack is scheduled for the fifteenth of next month. By all accounts Belton's government has no reason to suspect we have anything but good intentions."

Their discussion might have unsettled her, yet she'd heard enough in previous talks to not be bothered. The planet Belton was nothing but a wasted planet run by violent barbarians. She sighed and pressed a hand to her head. How long until she could leave?

"My dear, are you well?" Victor turned his attention to her fully.

Talia saw her opportunity and jumped on it. The men would be in discussion for at least another hour.

"I fear I am on the verge of a headache." She ran her tongue across her lips. "I would request a few minutes to return to my bedding unit and lie down?"

"Oh. Well, I suppose there's no harm in it." His tone was reluctant as was the arm that left her waist. "So long as you return by the two o'clock hour. And make sure you summon Dane to accompany you."

"Of course." She lowered her gaze and slipped off his lap, stepping into her dress again.

At the door she glanced back into the room and found Franklin's gaze on her. She could sense the lust and cruelty radiating off him from across the room.

For the most part she was treated well and never harmed. Yet Franklin possessed a cruel side that he on occasion let loose on her when they were alone. Fortunately, they were rarely allowed in that situation.

Suppressing a shudder, she turned and exited through the door. She made her way to Dane's chambers, reluctant to interrupt him during his time with Thomas, yet knew there was no choice. A Rosabelle was never allowed to be alone in her bedding unit.

She reached the corridor that led to his chamber; a glass window above looked down upon his room. Spotting Dane and Thomas in bed together, her heart sank. She sighed, hoping he'd forgive her.

Truly there was no privacy in this community. The entire building that housed the Council and its staff was made up of mostly windows.

Sex was nothing to be ashamed of within these walls, therefore was never hidden—with the one exception being with a Rosabelle. The Council's chambers and bedding units were equipped with privacy shields that would slide down to cover the windows. No man, save the three Council members, was allowed to watch her in any sexual act.

She clasped her hands in front of her and glanced down

13

again at Dane and Thomas. It was time; she could avoid the interruption no longer.

Talia stepped toward the stairs to his chamber, but hesitated as the men exchanged a long kiss. Rarely, if at all, had she ever seen two people so completely besotted by each other.

She watched as Dane urged Thomas onto his hands and knees. He kissed the younger man's neck, wrapping his hand around Thomas's cock. The trembling in the other man was visible even from where she stood.

*You should not watch this.* A hot flush made its way through her body. It was not the first time she had seen two men make love, but she had never seen her assistant. She would almost consider Dane a friend, and to watch this intimate moment felt awkward. But the obvious love they shared held her entranced.

Dane now stroked his fingers between the younger man's buttocks. He picked up a small bottle that sat next to them on the bed and squirted lubricant over his fingers. Talia's breath caught while she watched him press two fingers into Thomas's asshole. He moved them in and out, while continuing to stroke the other man's cock.

"Oh . . ." She bit her lip, cutting off her husky groan.

Dane removed his fingers and lined his cock up with the small hole, then pressed steadily inside the other man. His thrusting started slow and then grew faster, while still he continued to stroke Thomas's cock.

Talia shifted her stance, trying to ease the pressure of the slick cream that gathered heavy in her cunt.

Minutes passed and she continued to watch them make love, transfixed by how both men's passion seemed equal and was not feigned, forced, or even lukewarm, as was the life she was accustomed to.

Dane thrust deep and stayed within the other man. She could swear she heard them both cry out. Then he pulled out of the younger man and kissed his shoulder. Thomas rolled over onto his back, reaching his arms up and drawing Dane down for a deep kiss.

Talia closed her eyes. How was she supposed to walk back into the Council's chambers in such a state of arousal? How would she explain it? They would never believe the same excuse twice in one day.

She stepped back, hitting something hard. Steel-like arms slipped around her waist, wringing a gasp from her and holding her immobile.

"Release me." She struggled, attempting to twist her head to see who held her.

"Interesting. A Rosabelle who not only likes to perform, but enjoys watching as well?"

Though she had never heard him speak and could not yet see him, she knew it was he. The man she'd seen in the corridor earlier. Blood raced through her veins and heat spread throughout her body.

"Do you have a death wish, sir?" She clenched her teeth and attempted to pry his fingers away from her waist. "No one outside the Council is allowed to touch me. To do so is grounds for immediate execution—"

He spun her around, his hands gripping just above her elbows. He backed her up against the wall in the empty corridor, his dark eyes boring into hers.

Her back slammed into the cold metal wall and her eyes widened when his head dipped just inches above hers.

"Well, if I'm going to die, princess, I think I should do so having gotten to know you a little better."

His breath feathered over her cheek, sending shivers of awareness down her spine. So new was the sensation that all protests died on her lips. She met his gaze, her own eyes wide.

No man had touched her outside of the Governing Council.

15

Now this man, a stranger with eyes that burned like the devil, touched her as if he had every right to.

"What is your name?" he asked, his lips nearly touching hers.

Her knees felt oddly weak and she gripped his solid forearms. "Talia."

His mouth closed over hers, confident and demanding, sending shock waves of pleasure through her body. His tongue pressed past her lips and delved into her mouth, rubbing slowly against hers. The onslaught of sensation and emotion was confusing, yet pleasing.

The Council rarely kissed her and when they did the gesture was hurried and sloppy. It was nothing like what this man was doing to her. Even knowing that if discovered he could be put to death and she would be severely punished, having this one chance at an unusual type of freedom was suddenly worth the risk.

He pressed her harder against the wall, sliding his hand beneath her dress and up her leg. The pleasure of his rough hands upon her was so intense her body shook. He moved one finger between her thighs and honed in on her clitoris.

The first touch sent her onto her tiptoes, pleasure spearing every inch of her body.

He lifted his mouth from hers and whispered, "Do you like me rubbing your hot little clit, princess?"

*Yes. Oh gods yes.* She gripped his arms to keep her knees from giving out.

"All slick and swollen." He dropped another hard kiss on her mouth, his finger rubbing harder against her clit. "Just waiting to be licked."

She moaned, and his tongue stroked deep into her mouth, taking control of hers as the finger on her cunt worked her harder and faster. The pleasure built, spiraling up higher than ever before. Lights flashed in her head and she cried out sharply into his mouth. Her legs gave out, but his arm around her waist kept her from falling.

The explosion he'd given her was ten times more powerful than the orgasm she'd had earlier just imagining his touch.

"Talia . . ." He lifted his mouth from hers. "You are so sexy when you come."

# 2

*When you come.* Oh gods! What had she done? Had she completely lost all sense of reality? Her pulse jumped frantically.

"Is there a place we can be more private, princess?" He kissed her cheek.

She pushed his hand away and smoothed her dress back down. She had to stop this before it went further; it had already escalated to a deadly dangerous level.

"No. There is not. This will go no further, and let me advise you to forget that this ever happened."

His smile was slow. "Forget? We both know that's not likely, Talia."

Why would he not back off? Did he not realize what was at stake? *His life?* The thought of him being killed sent a cold wash of fear through her. She had to dissuade him, remove any hope he had of her being with him.

"I don't know who you are, but let me assure you that you will never touch me again," she said stiffly. "I am no common Rosabelle that might be shared amongst friends. I am Rosabelle to the Governing Council. And you, sir, are a nobody."

"Is that so, princess?" His grip on her arms tightened and she reluctantly turned her gaze back to him.

"Stop calling me a princess when we both know I am not one."

"No." His mouth grew tight. "You're just a slave forced to act as a whore."

Her face burned with anger and humiliation and she raised her hand to slap him. He caught her wrist mid-swing, his grip tightening painfully around her smaller bones.

"Not your smartest move," he warned and drew her toward him again.

A series of beeps signaled someone was punching in the code to enter the corridor.

"This shall be continued later." He released her and strode down the hall in the opposite direction, just as someone else entered the corridor.

Later? Gods. The man was audacious. Talia leaned heavily against the wall, the breath leaving her body in one ragged sigh. What had she just done?

"Mistress Natalia? Do you fair well?"

She opened her eyes and smoothed her dress over her body, before acknowledging one of the guards that routinely patrolled the Council's headquarters.

"I am well, thank you," she lied. "Just a bit of a head cold."

He nodded and then bowed. "I wish you well, mistress. Have a nice day."

She curtsied and remained where she was until he'd passed. Her heart still raced from her encounter with that man, and her nipples stabbed against the silky fabric of her dress. She must not walk back into the Council's chamber in this state. Her bottom still smarted from the punishment she'd received earlier.

She walked to the window in the corridor to look down into Dane's chambers. The couple was no longer inside. Her sigh of regret rang through the again empty corridor. There would be no brief nap today. She would simply run to the toilet chamber before heading back to be with Council. Hopefully that would be enough time for the physical effects of her encounter with the stranger to abate.

Ryder strode through the corridors of the Council's head-quarters, his blood pounding through his veins. *Damn.* He had not intended to touch her. Had known the minute he did so that all rational thought would be history.

Then he'd come across her, and she'd been watching the two men fucking below. Her lips parted in wonder, large breasts pressed up against the glass window as she strained to see the couple. His control had snapped, and he knew he wouldn't leave that corridor without having tasted the sin behind her lips.

He shook his head, as if the harsh movement would rid her from his thoughts once and for all. The next hour would be the true test. Once he met with the Council and—if all went well—he had Talia alone, then he could begin retribution of her abrupt and callous dismissal of him. Then she would realize he was anything but a nobody.

"You are an outsider. Please present your badge, sir."

Ryder glanced up and met the empty gaze of one of the corridor droids. He pulled his visitor's pass from the pocket in his suit and allowed the droid to scan it.

"Alan Worthington. Thank you. Enjoy your visit to the governing headquarters."

The droid's buttons lit up as he floated past him and down the corridor.

21

Ryder slipped the pass with the fake identity back into his pocket. So far the initial phase of the plan had gone smoothly, but the real test was what he was about to do.

As he wandered the headquarters to pass the time before his appointment, he felt no fear, only confidence and the knowledge that his planet's survival rested on the success of this mission.

Talia entered the Council's chamber one hundred percent in control of her emotions again. Ramirez and Franklin sat on the couch with mugs of coffee in their hands, while Victor paced in front of the windows that looked out over the city park.

"The amount Mr. Worthington is willing to invest in the weapons program is astronomical," Ramirez was saying. "I feel it is in our best interest to encourage him by any means necessary."

Victor sighed and then nodded. "Yes, yes, I quite agree."

"I don't know." Franklin stood, having caught sight of her, and crossed the room toward her. "I'm still not certain we can trust this man."

Tension ran through her body as he suddenly pulled her hard against him. The breath caught in her throat as he grabbed the hem of her dress and jerked it above her hips. His fingers plunged between her legs.

A slow satisfied smile spread across his face. "You are dry."

She swallowed hard, grateful that she'd taken a few moments to compose; and clean herself after the intimate moment with the strange man in the hall.

She lowered her gaze. "Of course. Did you think I would not be? I was away from you three."

"Yes, you were." Franklin's tone indicated he didn't trust her, and his fingers moved a bit more roughly inside her.

"Franklin," Victor's voice held a warning. "We agreed to

keep things on a lighter note this afternoon with Natalia, due to our meeting."

"Yes. So we did." Franklin released her with narrowed eyes and the hem of her dress fell back to the floor.

She was unable to stop her shoulders from sagging with relief. His touch, even as he'd stroked her clitoris, had failed to bring forth any arousal.

Had he kept his fingers within her long enough to discover her lack of desire, there would have been anger and endless questioning.

Fortunately, "lighter note" meant keeping their attention above the waist. There would be no more little tests any time soon.

"How did Mr. Worthington come about his riches?" Franklin queried. "Surely he is not old money?"

Ramirez made a loud snort. "Old money? I think not." He patted the couch and gestured for Talia to come sit beside him. "The man has made an obscene fortune as an oil tycoon on the planet Earth."

Automatically she crossed the room and sat down on the white leather couch, curling her legs under her bottom.

"Earth," Franklin grumbled. "That shithole? Now I really don't trust him."

"What's not to trust?" Ramirez reached behind her and unbuttoned her dress, pulling the fabric down to bare her breasts. He caressed the right breast, toying with the nipple. "If the man is willing, then by gods we should do it."

"It doesn't seem odd to you?" Franklin demanded, but his glare was targeted on her.

Talia lowered her gaze. It was apparent he wasn't pleased that he'd been forced to release her, yet Ramirez took the liberty to fondle her breasts.

Her stomach knotted and heaviness settled in her heart.

How many more hours were in this day until once again the men had taken their pleasure with her and she was granted the freedom to sleep? To drift off into that alternate reality where she could be free for the six hours of sleep—monitored by Dane—that she was allotted.

"Look, gentlemen, the bottom line is Mr. Worthington is considering making an offer to back our expansion in our weapons and military." Victor shook his head. "Without that backing, the planet's deficit will quadruple by the time our attack on Belton is complete."

"Yes, but what does Mr. Worthington gain by doing this for us? Surely he wants something in return."

Victor was silent for a moment. "He would like to become the fourth member of the Governing Council."

"Have you lost your fucking mind?" Franklin demanded. "No. Absolutely not. We make the attack with the resources that we have—"

"I agree with Victor," Ramirez interrupted quietly. "We have little choice."

The intercom buzzed, stopping any response Franklin may have had.

Victor walked around to his desk and pressed a button. "Yes?"

"Alan Worthington has arrived for your meeting," a gruff voice announced.

"Give us two minutes and then send him in."

Victor walked back to the center of the room and looked at the other two men.

"Are we agreed that we will do whatever it takes to gain Mr. Worthington's backing?"

"Reluctantly," Franklin muttered. "You know my thoughts."

"I am in agreement." Ramirez nodded and squeezed her

nipple between his fingers one last time. "Cover yourself, Natalia."

She nodded, closing her eyes against the threat of tears. Why was it so much harder today to bear the Council members' touches? She slipped her arms back into the sleeves of the dress, and the door swished open as she reached behind her to button it.

"Welcome, Mr. Worthington," Victor boomed in a bright voice. "Thank you for coming today."

"No big deal, boys. I wouldn't be here if I didn't want to be."

Talia's muscles tensed and the blood drained from her face. *He* was Alan Worthington? She lifted her gaze and saw it was indeed him: the man from the hallway. But his voice was different. He had an accent that she hadn't noticed earlier. He still wore the suit, but now had some strange-looking hat on his head. It looked familiar, like the same style she'd seen in old Western movies.

He was watching her in such an intimate way that she was certain the Council would notice. Would he expose the two of them? Terror clawed at her throat and her nails dug into the arm of the couch.

"Well, aren't you a pretty thing?" he drawled and winked at her.

She was as good as dead! It was a miracle she hadn't fallen to the ground in a faint. Her pulse throbbed. She was sure the frantic beat of her heart could almost be seen through the silk of her dress.

"Yes, she is." Victor's voice held a bit of an edge, but then he smiled. "Natalia, please bring in more coffee for the Council and our guest."

She gave a jerky nod and stood, her legs wobbly as she made

her way out of the chamber. In her mind, she prepared for the severe punishment that doubtless would come.

Ryder watched her leave the room, her head held high and her ass swinging lusciously. His eyes narrowed when the doors swished shut behind her.

Talia. Or no, *Natalia.* It took everything in his power to not allow himself to get a mammoth-sized hard-on. He knew his interest in her was not discreet, but then that was not necessarily a bad thing. Though the sensual Rosabelle had no idea, she would be the key game piece in his plan.

"You seem quite interested in Natalia."

*Yes, I am.* He turned to face the man who'd spoken. Victor Owens. One of the Council members and the man behind so much destruction and violence. It would be all too easy to simply kill the man now—all three of the men, actually.

He had officially infiltrated the highest-ranking form of government on this small planet; the opportunity was perfect. But it would also diminish his chances of leaving this building alive.

"She's a hot filly," Ryder replied with a broad grin.

"Hot filly?" The man on the couch—Franklin, he knew from the file they had on him—stood and approached him.

"Well, sure. Meaning she's a beauty." Ryder scratched the back of his neck. "We got the same problem back home that you folks got. The women all started dying off 'bout a couple hundred years ago. Sure, we got a few. But I don't think I've ever been with a woman who didn't look like horse manure."

Franklin's mouth twisted with obvious disgust. Good. It meant they believed him to be what he portrayed: just a horny, dumb, oil tycoon.

"Why don't we get down to business, gentlemen?" Ramirez

spoke from the couch. "Have you considered our offer, Mr. Worthington?"

"Yeah, I've been considering it." He shook his head. "But I'll be real honest with you boys. I'm not so certain that I won't be getting the short end of the stick."

"We have agreed to your terms. What more could you possibly want?"

Ryder's lips curled into a smile and he glanced toward the door Talia had just exited. "Well, now that you're asking . . ."

Talia took a deep breath as she made her way back down the corridor. Her pulse still raced, her stomach felt all fluttery.

Would the man—Mr. Worthington—have told them what had happened between the two of them? Surely he wouldn't be that stupid. She had warned him that his punishment could be death. And if they were to learn that their precious investor had forced a kiss on her . . . by gods it would not be pretty.

She balanced the four mugs on a tray with one hand and used the other to press the code to enter the Council's chamber.

The doors slid open with a hiss and she stepped into the room. Immediately she noticed the change in dynamic. It was uncomfortably quiet, and all eyes focused on her as she made her way across the floor.

"Your coffee," she murmured, lowering her gaze as she set the tray down on Victor's desk. "Mr. Worthington, do you take cream and sugar?"

"Always with cream."

She looked up. The way he'd said that made the word cream seemed dirty. His gaze bore into hers, and her hand that held the pot of coffee trembled.

"Do we have a deal, boys?" He spoke to the other men, but never took his eyes off her.

His question was met with a heavy silence. She paused in the midst of pouring the coffee and glanced over at the Council. Something was wrong. All three appeared reluctant to answer, but Franklin appeared absolutely livid as well.

Victor finally gave a terse nod. "Yes, Mr. Worthington. You have a deal."

The words chilled her and a sense of foreboding took root.

"That's right decent of you." He grinned and then crossed the room toward her. "Oh, and I should warn you, I like things a bit rough."

A strangled gasp escaped her throat as he reached out and cupped the back of her neck. Her gaze flew to the Council, sure they would be reaching for their weapons.

Ramirez nodded. "You may use her as you wish, but do not leave lasting marks."

*Use her as you wish.* The words spun in her head. *Use her as you wish.*

"Victor?" Her voice cracked as she turned to the head Council member.

He ignored her, instead keeping his focus on Alan Worthington. "The agreement is for two hours."

"Sounds great, boys. And we can use her bedding unit?"

"Ramirez?" She tried to get the older man's attention, but he lowered his gaze. "What is happening? Please, someone explain."

"I'll explain, princess." Mr. Worthington touched her cheek, his face so close to hers she could see the mocking amusement in his eyes. "I get to do whatever the hell I want with you for the next two hours."

The room spun and she was unable to breathe. No. . . . He had permission to bed her? Heat spread through her body as she thought of that moment they'd shared in the hall. How firm and confident his mouth had been on hers, how knowing his fingers. How he'd coaxed a fire within her that she had never experienced.

That one encounter had lasted less than ten minutes, yet had subtly changed her ability to respond to the Council's touches. Two hours with him would ruin her for good, which could only lead to the most hellish of punishments.

"No." She shook her head and fled across the room, falling at Victor's feet. "Please, no."

"Stand up." He jerked her to her feet, looking annoyed. "You're disgracing yourself."

"Please. You cannot mean to do this. . . ." She was babbling, tears in her eyes now.

Never had they given her away for another man's personal use. The thought of it sickened her, validated the term of whore Alan Worthington had called her earlier.

She shook her head. "I can't do this. I won't."

A hand gripped her elbow, spinning her around. She noted Franklin's furious glare before his palm slapped across her cheek. Her head snapped to the side, the sudden stinging pain shocking her into silence.

Her gaze connected with Alan's and she didn't miss the anger that flashed in his narrowed gaze or the tightness around his mouth.

"Franklin," Victor protested.

"No, she must learn." Franklin gripped her shoulders and glared down at her. "You have no freedom, my dear. You are our *possession*. And if we decide to lend you out for a business deal or even to the Council's entire army, you will spread your legs without protest."

Everything inside her went numb. Her emotions went strangely flat. She was a whore. She was. Stick the term Rosabelle on her all you want, she was a whore.

"I will take Natalia to her bedding unit now," Alan said and crossed the room, sliding an arm around her waist.

She didn't protest; was almost grateful for his strength that held her upright.

"Now?" Victor's voice rose. "What guarantees do we have that you will not take use of Natalia and then go back on your word to back us?"

Almost to the door, he stopped them and turned around. "I have instructed my accountant to transfer five million tremas to your account in one hour as a gesture of goodwill."

Victor gaped, practically salivating. "I see. Well—"

"If you haven't got the money after one hour, then come get me." His grip around her waist tightened. "But only if it hasn't arrived. I plan to have the fuck of a lifetime with this little filly, boys."

*Little Filly?* Some of the numbness dissipated and Talia blinked. *Fuck of a lifetime?* Anger filtered through her blood and she clenched her teeth. She would not make this easy for him. To hell with the punishment she'd receive later.

"So unless you boys have any more protests, I'm going to make use of my gift here." Alan smacked her ass and then squeezed the flesh, his palm nearly covering an entire cheek.

Her blood burned hotter. What weapons were in her room? To be more exact, what would be best to gouge his eyes out?

"No, no more protests, Mr. Worthington." Ramirez went back behind his desk and began toying with his computer. "Enjoy your time with Natalia. You'll find her quite agreeable."

"Thank you much, boys." Alan tipped his hat and then led her out the doors into the corridor. He leaned down, his quiet voice tickling her ear. "I promise that he will pay for hitting you. Lead me to your room, princess."

Why did he care if the Council hit her? "Do I have any choice?"

"No, Talia. You don't." All lightness in his tone vanished and it almost sounded as if his accent had disappeared for a moment.

But wait, that made no sense. Confusion warred with her frustration.

"Don't call me Talia," she muttered, attempting to pull away but his grip simply tightened.

"In the corridor you told me that was your name."

Her laugh rose to semihysterical. "In the corridor I was out of my mind."

"Perhaps you were in the state of mind you have always deserved to be in."

What did he mean? And yes. The accent was gone, and his words were more formal now than that bizarre slang he'd been speaking to the Council with.

They arrived outside her chamber and she turned to him, her brows drawn together in a frown. When she hesitated to open the door, he grabbed her hand and placed it on the palm recognition security box. A few men passed by them in the corridor casting curious glances their way.

The door slid open and he pushed her inside.

She stumbled to the middle of the chamber, swinging around to face him. Her breasts rose and fell beneath the fabric. "You need to explain."

A predatory smile crossed his face and he reached for the tie around his neck. "I don't need to explain anything, princess."

His voice was cold, not even a trace of the accent. Who was he? A shiver ran down her spine and she took a few steps backward.

He pulled off his suit jacket and dropped it to the floor. "Take off your dress."

31

Her pulse slowed and then accelerated right back up into double time. The heat that spread throughout her brought a flush to her body.

She ran her tongue across her lips. "No. I will not."

"Agreeable indeed." He raised an eyebrow. "All right. If you will not remove it, then I will do so for you."

He lunged and her scream reverberated through the chamber. Her dress ripped as he caught the hem and jerked.

"No!" She twisted away, causing the dress to split halfway up her hip.

He jerked hard on the fabric he held in his fist, catching her off balance and sending her sprawling to the floor.

"Barbarian!" she screamed, trying to scurry away.

He fell to his knees and straddled her, grabbing her wrists in one hand and forcing them above her head. With his other hand free, he grabbed the bodice of her dress and ripped hard. Her breasts spilled free and she closed her eyes with a groan.

The room went quiet, with only the sounds of their ragged breathing to break the silence.

"By gods, Talia," he rasped. "You're more beautiful than I imagined."

She shook her head and tugged at her wrists. She tried to hold onto the anger inside her, but there was a more dominant emotion fighting to take hold. Hot fire spread through her body, locking the breath in her throat and hardening her nipples.

"Oh gods. This makes no sense," she confessed huskily. "I should not want this."

His eyes darkened. "But you do." The calloused pad of his thumb smoothed over one nipple and she gasped, heat moving between her legs. "You do, princess."

He lowered his head and nuzzled her throat, kissed the

pulse that beat there before sliding up toward her ear. His palm, wide and rough, cupped her breast. He caught her earlobe between his teeth and bit gently.

Talia's hips arched off the floor, a guttural cry escaping past her lips. It was back, this strange heat and almost drunken state of arousal she got when he got near her.

He rolled her nipple between his finger and thumb. Another tremble rocked her body and hot cream gathered in her pussy.

"I can smell your desire for me." His fingers moved between her legs and rubbed lightly between the folds, the sensation so intense the muscles of her cunt clenched. "Unfortunately, fucking you will have to wait."

"I . . . I don't understand." She squirmed, desperate with the need for him to press his fingers inside her. "Alan . . . please."

His lips moved against her ear, his words just a whisper. "My name's not Alan."

The odd response brought her up from the thick depths of desire. "W-what?"

His hand moved away from her pussy and slid over to wrap around her right thigh. His expression turned somber, hard. "I'm sorry, princess."

She saw the flash of the needle, just before it swung down and jabbed painfully into her thigh.

"No!" She struggled again, panic slicing through the fog of desire, but it was too late. Her flesh burned from whatever he was injecting into her.

Oh gods! What had he just done? She struggled harder, managing to free one wrist because of the terror-induced adrenaline.

"Hold still." He recaptured her wrist and held her down, kissing the tears that rolled down her cheek. "Just relax."

She shook her head, but the movement made her dizzy. The

lights above her head left tracers. Opening her mouth to speak, she found her tongue thick and the words stuck in her throat. Why? Why had he done it?

"That's it, princess. Close your eyes," he whispered and smoothed his thumb over her lips.

Her eyelids grew heavy, too heavy, and finally she closed them, almost certain she would never wake up.

Ryder waited until she was limp on the floor and then glanced around the room. He reassured himself there were no cameras, even if the room was almost certainly bugged for audio. It was the reason he'd told the Council he liked it rough, so her screams would be taken as a woman in pain. Not as a woman being abducted.

He hadn't expected her to succumb to his touch so quickly, to be trapped under the web of arousal. He'd only spoken in whispers, so low the bug would not suspect anything more than whispers of passion. Her moans had been real, and thankfully aided him in his quest. Surely the Council would have no doubts that she'd been a willing lover enjoying a moment of passion with a stranger.

He'd wanted to give her the injection when her mind was clouded by passion, and it had worked. She had not even realized his intent until the needle had already pricked the skin of her creamy thigh.

Ryder turned his glance back down to her. She was lying on her back, with her knees bent to the side and her arms limp on the ground above her head. Her thigh bore the small red mark where he'd plunged the needle. He kissed two of his fingers and then pressed them against the inflamed flesh.

Now came the final part of the mission. He glanced at his watch to assure himself he was on schedule. He was, though just barely. He'd taken the seduction stage just a little further than intended. *She goes to your head, be careful around her.*

He stood and went into the bathroom, kneeling down near the east wall and prying open the grate over the heating vent. Inside was the bag he'd stored earlier. He picked it up and went back into her room.

She was still on the floor, out cold just as he'd left her. Unzipping the bag, he pulled out the small incision knife and another syringe already loaded with the numbing agent.

Only a few minutes had passed since she'd been injected, but too long of a period of silence might raise the Council's suspicions.

He cleared his throat, infusing a bit of huskiness into his voice. "That's right, princess, use your mouth on me. Oh . . . yes . . . just like that."

Gods, he sounded like an idiot.

Lifting her foot onto his lap, he traced the pad of his thumb over her heel. The skin was buttery soft, no calloused skin anywhere. His mouth drew tight. Obviously she was a pampered, kept woman. He kept searching until he felt it. The slight ridge under the skin.

He grabbed the syringe, inserted it into her heel, and pressed the plunger. She groaned loudly. Fortunately, it sounded a bit sexual. He glanced at her, making sure it had just been a reflex. Yes, she was still out cold.

He recapped the syringe and dropped it into the bag, then grabbed the small incision knife. He tapped the point of the knife lightly against her heel, watching her face to see if she'd react. Nothing. She was completely numb.

He pressed the knife into her heel, cutting a small square around the area of the ridge, wiping away the blood that appeared. Peeling back the skin, he found it. The tiny tracking device that was so carefully implanted.

Using the tip of the knife, he lifted the plastic device out of her foot and set it in the bag. He pulled a small bottle out and removed a capsule, breaking it over the wound, knowing the gel inside would stop the bleeding within minutes.

He quickly bandaged her heel and then grabbed a small cotton jumpsuit—common dress for a male on this planet—from his bag. He quickly dressed her in it and then glanced at his watch again. His pulse sped up. A half hour had passed since they'd entered the room. The clock was ticking.

Time to appease the Council again, play up the dumb cowboy image.

"All right, princess. We've still got plenty of time. Let's have some good old-fashioned shower sex." He whooped. " 'Cause, whoooeee, did we get sweaty."

He slid his arms under her limp body and scooped her high against his chest. After walking them into the bathroom, he laid her on the carpeted floor and turned on the shower.

He took the tracking device and placed it on a high shelf in the shower where it wouldn't get wet, but would give the illusion of Talia taking a shower with him. He stripped off the rest of his suit and changed into the lightweight clothes he'd packed.

Grabbing his transmitter mobile, he punched in the code to signal for the pickup. A few seconds later the confirmation signal came through.

A light sweat of sheen broke out on his forehead as he went to work removing a metal panel from the wall.

The Governing Council on Zortou had let the planet enter a state of poverty and near decay. Bribing a guard to create an escape route from Talia's chamber had been easy enough. The offer of money and asylum had been all the convincing he'd needed.

The metal finally fell away, leaving a short and narrow tunnel in the wall. Almost there.

Ryder walked back into the bedroom, checking to see if he'd left anything behind and then went back to the bathroom.

He picked up Talia and slung her over his shoulder, then hunched down and moved into the tunnel. He ran the few steps and kicked out the panel of metal on the other side. Blinding sunlight filled the tunnel and he blinked, searching for the escape pod.

Nothing. His blood pounded harder. Where the fuck was it?

He coughed, the air from the atmosphere already clotting in his lungs.

There was a whirl of noise and then the black, spherelike pod pulled up front. The door slid open and Dillon stood with his arms outstretched. Ryder handed Talia over, waited as Dillon settled her in, and then climbed in after them.

They'd done it. A small smile played around his mouth as the pod shot straight up and into the atmosphere of the planet. The skin on his body went taut at the speed they moved.

"Everything go well, my friend?" Dillon asked, casting him a sideways glance.

"Very well."

"Did the Council suspect anything?"

Ryder's mouth twisted. "No. They were too focused on the expansion of their money accounts. In about fifteen minutes they'll figure it out, though."

"I imagine they'll be fairly enraged."

"Most likely." Ryder glanced back at Talia. She was slumped over in the back. "But worse will come when they realize their precious Rosabelle is gone."

"I'll bet. Losing your personal whore can really shit on your parade."

Ryder's jaw clenched and he resisted the urge to defend her. But why? She was exactly that. Whore to the Governing Council that was planning an attack on his home planet. No. She didn't need his defense. If anything she would need protection from him by the time he finished with her.

"When will we arrive on Belton, Lieutenant?"

"Approximately two hours of travel and then the half hour of detox after arrival."

He nodded and closed his eyes. "Good. She'll be out for at least the next five hours."

# 3

---

"The money has not arrived." Ramirez glanced up from the computer, his expression worried.

"Son of a bitch." Franklin pounded his fist into his desk, his blood pounding as he stood up. Gods, he had known from the beginning what a shit idea this was. "I told you we could not trust him. We must bring them back at once."

"Wait." Victor paced the floor and glanced at the hologram clock on the wall. "It is only a few minutes past the hour. Perhaps we should give him the grace of a few minutes more."

"No, perhaps we shouldn't," Franklin snapped harshly. "There was never going to be any money transfer, it was all just a ruse to convince us to offer him a complimentary hour-long fuck with our property."

"We don't know that for certain." Victor hesitated and looked out the window. "If we interrupt him and he becomes angry, he will likely withdraw all support."

"You idiot, surely you cannot be that naïve," Franklin snarled. Gods, he regretted the day he'd signed on as one of three members in the Governing Council. Victor was often too soft, and Ramirez was growing weak as the years passed. His eyes narrowed. But that would all change soon. Being one-third of the highest power just wouldn't do anymore.

"Franklin may have a point." Ramirez sighed and stroked his chin. "Worthington did tell us we may come get him if the transfer had not gone through."

Franklin strode to the middle of the room. "Yes, he did. And as we speak that filthy Earthling is probably tainting our Rosabelle."

Having to share Natalia with Victor and Ramirez was maddening as it was, but to have given her over to some filthy Earth pig brought his blood to boiling point. Natalia was his, and when the day came when he became the absolute power she would be touched by no one save him.

Already, he intended to bring her to his chamber tonight and spend time alone with her. He had not missed her reaction to the foreigner—she had been attracted to him. His fists clenched at his side. That was completely unacceptable and she needed to be punished. The blood in his cock stirred as he imagined the marks he would leave on her skin, right before he fucked her sweet ass.

"I must agree with Franklin at this point," Ramirez finally agreed wearily. "We should speak with Mr. Worthington."

"All right. We should go speak with him." Victor nodded. "But if this deal goes bad—"

"It will not go bad." Franklin strode toward the door, confident the other two men would follow.

He walked through the corridor, heading straight for Natalia's chamber. Perhaps the rich Earthling should be taught a lesson in what consequences could come from lying to the Governing Council of a planet.

Franklin pressed his hand against the palm recognition security box and waited until the doors slid open. He strode into the room, but one glance around showed it was empty.

"I hear the shower running." Ramirez spoke from behind him. "Should we wait for them to finish?"

Irritation pricked at Franklin and he swore under his breath. The last thing he wanted was to walk in on the two of them going at it. He growled and strode forward, pounding on the door.

"Mr. Worthington, we must speak to you."

There was no answer, nor did the shower turn off.

"Mr. Worthington." He pounded again and the door slowly swung inward. "*No.*"

From the gaping hole in the wall it was obvious that Alan Worthington had disappeared and taken Natalia with him.

Ramirez stepped past him and then paled. "Oh gods, this is not good."

Victor stood in the doorway, shaking his head but remaining silent.

"Trust the oil tycoon?" Franklin snarled and spun around, grabbing Victor's jacket and shaking him. "Do you realize what you've done?"

"What *we* have done." Ramirez pried him away from Victor. "We will take equal responsibility for the error in judgment."

"Error in judgment? Talk about the understatement of the fucking millennium." Franklin pressed his palms to his throbbing head. Gone. She was gone. There'd never been any money, and now Natalia had been taken.

Unless . . . His body shook and a growl or rage grew thick in his throat. Unless Natalia had left willingly, had known of the deception.

"I will send trackers to Earth to locate them." Victor thrust a shaking hand into his hair. "We will fix this."

"There is more to this." Franklin shook his head and left the bathroom, yelling over his shoulder, "Send your trackers, but I will be searching for other leads. I don't believe for one minute Alan Worthington is who he seems."

Ryder stepped out of the detox chamber and stretched, attempting to ease the stiffness of his muscles.

Intergalactic travel was more sophisticated than it had been years ago, but it still had its drawbacks.

He walked back to his office with just a towel slung around his waist and went to his desk, pressing the button that would summon his assistant.

Going to the closet, he pulled out another uniform. It would not be wise to stay in a near-naked state this evening, not with Ines on her way.

His mind conjured up the image of the rather plain, olive-skinned soldier whom he'd indulged in a brief love affair with. He cringed, slipping his arms into the sleeves of his shirt. It had not been one of his wiser moments.

She had been forward in her interest in bedding him, had ultimately been the one to initiate the affair. In the bedroom she had been an aggressive lover, one who had enjoyed anything and everything.

Initially he had enjoyed the affair, but soon the constant demands and growing possessiveness grew tiring. What had eventually ended the relationship was the day Ines had arrived with another man, intent on a ménage à trois. Ryder was not one to share his women in general, let alone in bed with another man.

He'd ended things with her shortly after and she'd seemed to take it in stride. Last he'd heard she was dating a sergeant in another unit.

There was a knock on the door and he glanced at it, fastening his trousers. He walked across the room and opened it.

Ines stood on the other side, giving him her usual sultry smile before striding into the room.

"You called?" She raised an eyebrow and went to his desk, sitting down on the edge.

*Damn. And this is why you did not fuck your subordinates. They showed you absolutely no respect afterward.*

"I was curious about the status of our prisoner. Have you checked on her?"

Ines's eyes narrowed and she crossed one leg over the other, the skirt rising high on her thigh.

"I did a check a few minutes ago. She has been removed from the detox chamber and is still unconscious."

"Excellent."

"She is very attractive, sir."

Well, at least she still called him sir. Ryder fastened the cuffs of his shirt and glanced up at her again.

"Is she?"

"Of course you have noticed."

"Perhaps she is," he admitted. "But she is a prisoner, nothing but business. She will provide me with the answers we have been seeking."

"Just business? Does that mean you have no desire to bed her?"

"And what concern of yours would it be if I did?" Ryder's temper flared and his gaze hardened on her. To question him in such a manner was not only disrespectful, but completely out of line.

"I suppose none, seeing as we're no longer together." She shrugged and slid off his desk, approaching him with a slow sashay. "Unless . . . you have changed your mind?"

Gods. His fists clenched at his side and he glanced over her shoulder. "No, Ines, I have not changed my mind."

"Well," her fingers straightened the lapel of his shirt. "If you need an outlet for any sexual frustration, you know where to find me."

"I have a few errands to run before I check in on the prisoner myself. Thank you for your time, Ines." He dismissed her with a nod, stepping away and seating himself behind the desk.

He could see the annoyance and hesitation on the woman's face, before she gave a brief nod and left his office.

Gods. It was useless. He had not thought it would be necessary, but it appeared it might be best to inconspicuously transfer her to another unit.

The trick would be pulling it off without offending her. A promotion might be the only way.

He sighed and shook his head, logging onto the computer.

There were rocks in her head. There had to be. Why else would it feel so heavy and throb so fiercely?

"Oooh." Talia pressed the back of her hand to her forehead and opened her eyes just a crack, so the light wouldn't hurt them.

Her heart leapt and her brows drew together. Surely she was seeing things. She lay on her side, and directly in front of her gaze was a large glass window. Beyond the window was lush foliage and a colorful sort of flower that she'd never seen before.

She bolted upright in the soft feathery bed, not caring that it spread the throbbing fire in her head through the rest of her body.

Oh gods. Where was she? What had happened? She looked around the room, then scrubbed her fists across her eyes. Surely it would clear the images from her head, because how could they possibly be real? She opened her eyes again.

"Where am I?" she asked aloud, though there appeared to be no one around to answer.

Plush white carpeting covered the expanse of the room, with cozy-looking wicker chairs near the window, which rose from floor to ceiling.

Was she in the fantasy chamber? Never had she been in it before, but the Council had often spoken of the room that created an alternate reality. A favorite of the Council had been programming in the code for Hawaii, the mythical islands of paradise that were rumored to have once existed on Earth.

There must be a programming remote around here somewhere. Perhaps the Council had placed her here to recover after the time with Alan Worthington. . . .

But his name wasn't Alan. Had he really told her that? Visions flashed through her head. Her dress being ripped from her body, his hands all over her and inside of her, the surprising pleasure . . . and then nothing.

Something heavy settled in her gut and it became hard to swallow.

"Turn off this stupid fantasy," she muttered and swung her leg out of bed to run toward the door. "Oooh!"

Her scream of pain filled the room as she fell to the floor in a heap. Oh gods. Her foot, why did it hurt so? She lifted the hem of her dress—wait, this wasn't her dress. Ignoring that fact for a moment, she studied her ankle. And the white bandage that surrounded it.

Something was wrong. Terribly wrong. She looked around the chamber again. This was no fantasy room.

The heaviness in her gut increased and nausea rolled in her stomach. Though the room was not overly warm, a sheen of sweat broke out on the back of her neck.

There were a series of beeps from the door and then it swung open.

"No." She shook her head. He was supposed to be gone. Two hours of her time was all the Council had allotted him.

Alan walked slowly into the room, until he towered above her where she had fallen on the floor.

"Good morning, Talia. Did you sleep well?"

"What is happening?" she demanded huskily. "Where am I?"

"You mean you don't remember?" He lifted an eyebrow questioningly.

"Of course I do not remember! Whatever you injected—" Her eyes widened in horror. She remembered. "You drugged me."

"Yes, princess, I did."

"You can't get away with this. The Council—"

"Is doubtless up in arms over the fact that you chose to run off with an oil tycoon."

"Run off . . ." The blood drained from her face. "They'll never believe it."

"Won't they? Even after they find the note you left?"

The room tilted. The Council may very well execute her for this, shortage of women be damned. Her lips trembled. "W-What have you done?"

"I have done what needed to be done." His smile was humorless. "My name is Ryder Jacobs. I am a colonel in the planetary army of Belton. And you, Talia, are my prisoner."

Ryder's jaw clenched as he stared down at her. *She's guilty.* It was the way she'd blanched when he'd stated who he was. Then she'd quickly dropped her head and stared at the floor.

There was information behind that pretty head of hers, and she would give it to him. No matter what means he had to use.

"Stand up."

She didn't move, just sat stubbornly on the floor and avoided looking at him.

"I told you to stand up." He grasped under her arms and

46

jerked her to her feet. Her sharp cry of pain almost distracted him from the softness of her breast against his thumb.

"Please," she begged, leaning her weight on one leg. "My foot is in pain."

"Ah . . . yes, so it would be." He slid one arm under the back of her knees and the other around her waist. Lifting her up, he carried her to the bed.

He set her down gently on the down comforter. "Let me check your wound. Lift your dress."

She hesitated and he lifted his gaze to meet hers. She must've seen the intent in his, or remembered that last time he'd requested she remove her dress. After a terse nod, she gripped the edge of the dress and pulled it up to her calves.

His breathing hitched. He clenched his fists to avoid pushing the dress higher, to follow the trail of her pale smooth skin to the curve of her thigh.

He turned his focus to the white bandage and took a deep breath. *Here's your focus.* Reaching out, he began to unwrap the bandage to see the injury.

"What did you do to me?" Her question was feather light as the bandage pulled away to expose the wound. "Oooh." She closed her eyes and weaved a little.

She was afraid of a little cut? His brows drew together.

"Lie back on the bed and do not watch me if this uneases you."

She flopped back so fast he could not hold back a quiet laugh.

"I removed the tracking device that was implanted in your heel."

She was silent for a moment. "Tracking device? You can't be serious."

"I am." Ryder turned his attention back to the wound. The flesh around the cut had faded to a healthy pink. It would heal fine; her foot would likely be smooth and flawless again within twenty-four hours. "You were not aware that you had one?"

"I would have known," she protested.

"It was likely implanted when you were an infant. Is it still tender?" He drew his thumb across the wound and she made a little moan of protest.

"A bit."

"I'll send for a numbing leaf that we may wrap around it." He stood up and made the mistake of looking away from her foot and up her body.

She leaned back on her elbows, the thin fabric of the pale dress drawn taut over her breasts. Her areolae hinted at a slight berry shade, her nipples just a bit lighter.

His blood flowed heavier and his cock stirred beneath his pants. Gods, he wanted her. Her tongue darted across pink lips before she drew the bottom one between her teeth.

"Ryder?" She said his name hesitantly. "Where have you taken me?"

"You mean you do not know?" He quirked an eyebrow and walked slowly toward the head of the bed. He sat down on the edge, noting the way she eyed him warily. "I have brought you to my home on Belton."

"Belton? But I cannot be here!" The horror on her face pounded another nail into her coffin of guilt.

"Well, princess, I could hardly hold you prisoner on your own planet." He shrugged and reached out to touch the throbbing pulse in her neck. "Why do you look so afraid, Talia? Our planets are allies, are they not?"

She slapped his hand away and turned her head to look at the other wall. "If so, then why do you hold me prisoner? There is nothing you can want from me."

Her rejection of his touch stung more than he cared to

admit. His jaw clenched. "You think not? There are many things I want from you, Talia. And I intend to have them all."

He returned his hand to the pulse on her neck, felt the blood pounding furiously.

"I have many questions. Questions that you will answer." Slowly he trailed his fingers down to her collarbone and then just barely on to the top swell of her breast.

"What makes you think I have the answers?" Her breasts lifted as she took an unsteady breath.

"Because, princess." He leaned over her and strummed his thumb over her nipple. It tightened eagerly and she let out a tiny moan. "You have information about the Council's plans that I need."

He lowered his head and licked the tip of her breast through the dress. The thin cotton, now damp, clung to her pink nipple. He closed his lips around the tip and drew it into his mouth, tasting her sweet flesh even through the fabric.

Her fingers laced into his hair, her breathing grew more ragged. "W-what makes you think I can answer your questions?"

"Because you are their whore, princess."

Her sharp indrawn breath echoed in the room. "And now you intend to make me yours?"

His mouth twitched. "If I do, I promise that you will enjoy it."

"Never."

The fingers in his hair now tried to push him away, but he had no intention of letting her go just yet. He gripped her arms, pinning her to the bed and met her glare.

"You sit within their chambers day in and day out." He pointed out, looking into her eyes, which nearly spit fire. "There is no one else on your planet, save for the Council itself, who would have access to that kind of information."

"Really? Let me just save us both some time. What I do know will stay firmly in my head," she snapped. "I owe you nothing—certainly not the betrayal of my home planet to a callous imbecile such as yourself."

"You think not?" He lowered his head again, paying heed to the opposite nipple. He drew it between his teeth, smoothing his tongue over the now-hard tip. He lifted his head again and used his fingers to toy with the peak. "You will tell me all, Talia. You may give the token protest—I would respect you less if you hadn't—but we both know you will tell me everything."

Her cheeks flooded with color. "And you mean to use seduction as a means to make me talk?" she scoffed, but there was fear in her eyes. "Sex means nothing to me. As you pointed out more than once, I am nothing but a whore."

He was silent for a moment, then reluctantly released the breast he cupped. A warm confidence spread through him, knowing that he'd gotten to her. Had begun to pierce through that thick shell she retreated behind when a man touched her.

He ran the pad of his thumb over her lips. "No, Talia, I think not. When you are in my bed, you will be willing and eager—be damn near begging me to take you. You will not be playing the role of Rosabelle."

He stood up, noting how pale she'd become. "I will send food and the numbing leaf in shortly. Tonight we will begin the first line of questioning."

At the door he turned and gave her a slight smile. "Until then, princess."

# 4

Talia watched the door shut behind him and then threw a pillow toward it. It fell short by at least a few feet, but it did relieve some of her frustration.

The one time she was away from her planet and still she was a prisoner.

She fell back against the pillows, brushing tears out of the corners of her eyes. *Crying solves nothing.* If she had learned one thing being a Rosabelle that would be it.

How was she going to escape? Surely there had to be a way to notify the Council, inform them she'd been abducted.

The tracker. Her throat went tight and she lifted her foot into the air to view the bandage again. She'd truly had a tracker planted inside her foot? As if she were some purebred dog?

*And are you really so different? Bought and groomed to become the perfect pet for a pampered Council?*

A Council that was probably quite upset right now. Would they take it out on her when she returned? If she returned. Damn Ryder Jacobs for doing this to her.

More beeping noises came from the door and she reached

for the small lamp on the table next to the bed. She scowled and glared at the door. This time when Ryder walked into the room he'd better be prepared to duck.

The door swung open, and she lifted her arm to throw it.

"Please, don't!"

Talia lowered the lamp, her hand shaking as she stared in amazement at the doorway. It was not Ryder who stood there, but a young woman, half hiding behind the door, having seen the lamp in Talia's hand.

"I mean you no harm, Talia." The woman hesitated and then stepped into the room. "In fact, I have come to help. I have brought food and a numbing leaf."

Talia's jaw went slack as the woman crossed the floor. Her steps were light, her glossy brown curls bouncing while dark brown eyes glittered with excitement. But it was what she was wearing that truly had Talia shocked: a band of purple fabric that wrapped around her small breasts, leaving her shoulders and navel bare, and then a flowing white skirt that ended above her knees.

"Surely no Rosabelle is allowed to dress in such a manner?" Talia sputtered.

"Rosabelle?" She lifted an eyebrow questioningly; the gesture seeming somewhat familiar. "You must have me confused with someone. My name is Krystal, not Rosabelle."

Did this woman have no idea what a Rosabelle was? Perhaps women were referred to with a different term on Belton.

"Where is your assistant, Krystal?"

"Assistant?" Krystal set the tray on the bed. "Do you mean my chaperone?"

"Yes. Chaperone." They must call their assistants something different as well.

"I look that young, do I?" Krystal grimaced and poured

some tea into the cup on the tray. "I turned eighteen years two months ago, so the chaperone has been reassigned. Thank the gods! Though my brother is not pleased. If he had the powers, I'm sure he'd have it fixed that I remain his kid sister for eternity."

Talia frowned, confusion swirling in her head. The girl had her chaperone *removed* at eighteen? But that made no sense. Eighteen was the age when the few women of Zortou were *given* chaperones. It was then when they were sold and their faithfulness to their owner must be instilled.

"Are you not hungry?"

Talia looked down at the tray with the various fruits, breads, and some form of meat upon it, and her stomach growled. When was the last time she'd eaten? Her stomach clenched for a different reason. How long had she even been away from Zortou? Her sense of time was completely off balance.

"Yes, I am hungry. Thank you, Krystal." She lifted a piece of meat and brought it to her mouth. The spiced meat dribbled juice down her lips as she bit into it. Heaven. She closed her eyes. Whatever it was, they had none like it at home.

"Ah, you like it. Wonderful. Well, you go ahead and eat up, while I place the leaf upon your foot."

Talia nearly choked on the food and she grew lightheaded. "Now? Please, could you wait? I do not . . . do well with my own wounds."

Krystal's gaze stated her obvious amusement. "Of course, if that is what you wish."

"Thank you, Krystal." Talia lifted the tea and took a small sip. "I don't mean to pry, but you seem so . . . happy. You must have the most wonderful owner."

"Owner?" Krystal gave a musical burst of laughter. "Whatever do you mean? Who has owners?—well, save for pets."

Talia set the tea back on the tray, her brows drawn together. Was it possible? Did such a place exist where women weren't forced to live as slaves to men?

Krystal must have seen the disbelief on her face, her smile faded. "Or maybe some people do elsewhere."

*Like me.* Talia's cheeks heated and she chewed her bottom lip.

Krystal's expression softened in understanding. "I've really gone and said the wrong thing now, haven't I? I'm sorry . . ."

"No. Don't be sorry." Talia shook her head, lowering her gaze. "I'm just as surprised, but for the opposite reasons. I did not know there were planets where women are not owned."

Talia didn't need to look up to know what Krystal's silence meant. The woman was obviously shocked.

Not wanting to draw out the silence any longer, she finally murmured, "Thank you for bringing me food. I did not realize how hungry I'd become."

"Of course, Talia." Krystal's shaky voice was a clear indication she was still disturbed by their discussion. "We are not complete barbarians."

No? Perhaps Krystal wasn't. Actually, the younger woman was quite likeable. Now Ryder . . . Talia's brows drew together in a scowl. He was exactly the barbarian she described, though she was hesitant to admit that to Krystal just yet.

She ate about half the plate of food, but with her initial hunger sated the reality of her circumstances once again set in; she pushed the tray aside.

"You are finished?" Krystal took the tray and set it on the table. "I will apply the numbing leaf now. That way you will be free to . . ." She lowered her gaze, obviously remembering Talia was a prisoner. "Free to move around the room at least."

"Thank you, Krystal." She leaned back, closing her eyes to avoid seeing the wound as the bandage was removed.

"I will speak with my brother," Krystal murmured as she unwrapped the bandage. "Perhaps I might be able to convince him to allow you some liberties."

A tiny spark of hope caught in her heart. Krystal's brother was in some form of a powerful position?

"I would not want you to do anything you are not comfortable with, Krystal."

"I don't mind. My brother adores me. I have quite a bit of sway with him," she replied with confidence.

Talia's foot tingled as the cool, crisp leaf was tucked over her wound. She closed her eyes and sighed as the topical numbing leaf did its magic.

Krystal began to bandage her foot again. "I can offer no promises, Talia, but I will certainly try. For I am certain you could not be so guilty to warrant being locked up as a prisoner."

Guilty by association. "Thank you."

"You're welcome. I have left you a few books in case you become restless." Krystal stood and reached for the tray. "I will probably not be back to visit you until tomorrow. I"—she glanced out the window, a mischievous smile playing around her mouth—"have things to do this evening. But until then, try to just relax and think of this as a holiday."

Talia grimaced. "Yes. A holiday where I'm not allowed to leave my room."

Krystal hesitated at the door and glanced back. "Yes, but in a way . . . you're free, are you not?"

A few minutes after the door had shut behind Krystal, Talia still thought about her words. In a completely backward way, Krystal was right. Though she was locked in a room with very few pleasures, for the first time in the past four years her entire day did not revolve around pleasing the Governing Council.

Free indeed. A half smile curled her lips and she grabbed a book and leaned back against the pillows.

Krystal dabbed her favorite scented oil between her breasts and then looked in the mirror. Sighing, she cupped her small breasts and lifted them. Why couldn't she have been born with a big chest? Some women just had all the luck and got blessed with curves. Like that sweet prisoner Talia.

*Hmm. Speaking of.* She needed to make time to converse with her brother.

She glanced at the clock and nibbled on her lip. Though, she was running late as it was. Trevon would be waiting for her out in the aliaberry orchard.

Heat flushed to her cheeks and she brushed her thumbs over the tips of her nipples. He liked it when they were hard, had been unable to take his eyes off them last time. Her blood pounded with excitement, her eyes glittered in the mirror.

At first she hadn't been sure he was the one. For so long she had only allowed long kisses. But now ... perhaps she was ready for more.

What would it feel like to have a man's hands on her breasts? To have his mouth sucking on her nipple? She closed her eyes and tried to imagine, her thumb rubbing harder over the peaks.

So many times she'd pleased herself, brought herself to orgasm, but what would it be like to have a man do it for her?

She slipped one hand beneath her dress and into the slick lips of her pussy, rubbing her clitoris in slow strokes.

*No. You are going to see Trevon. He can do this for you if you decide to allow him.*

She sighed and let her skirt fall back down. Looking in the mirror again, she smiled. At least now her cheeks were pink and her nipples were tight against the bandeau.

*Time to go have some fun.* She slipped out of her room and hurried down the halls of the living quarters.

Hopefully she would not run into her brother, for certainly he would not be pleased if he were to learn whom she was meeting.

She neared the end of the hall, her heart pounding as she spotted the glass exit. Would he kiss her right away? Or perhaps—

"Krystal?"

Her toes caught on the thin rug in the hallway and she stumbled. Damn it! She'd been so close to getting out without being caught. And she knew that voice all too well. Had grown up tagging along behind its owner. If anyone was going to slow her down, she didn't mind so much that it was him. Turning, she offered him a dimpled grin.

"Hello, Dillon. How are you this afternoon?"

He stood a few feet behind her, tall and intimidating in his uniform. Though the intimidation had never worked with her. To her he'd always be that lanky boy with the red hair who was best friends with her brother. She nibbled her lip. Well, the lanky part not so much anymore. Being in the army had really built up those muscles.

"I'm fine." His gaze narrowed with suspicion as he closed the distance between them. "Where are you off to, Krys?"

The blush hit her cheeks before she could will it away. *Oh gods.* She brightened her smile.

"I was going to pick a bushel of aliaberries to make a cobbler with in the morning." She laughed and pushed her hair off her shoulder and behind her back. "Why? Am I in trouble?"

His gaze moved over her, lingering on her chest area and his mouth tightened. "You're picking berries dressed like that?"

"Yes, Dillon." Suddenly self-conscious, she folded her arms across her breasts. "Why?"

His gaze moved on to the bare skin between her bandeau top and waist of her skirt. "There are thorns in the bushes. You have so much skin bared you will certainly scratch yourself."

She rolled her eyes. "I am careful, silly. What is this questioning about? I am hardly one of your prisoners."

"No, you are not." He tilted his head. "But that reminds me. Are you not supposed to be checking in on the female prisoner?"

"I finished about an hour ago." She glanced toward the front door. Surely Trevon would be waiting for her now. "Was there anything else, Dillon?"

He seemed to hesitate and then shook his head.

"No?" Her shoulders relaxed and she sighed. "When you see my brother, please tell him I'd like to have a word with him later."

"I will."

"Thank you, Dillon." She leaned on her tiptoes and kissed him on the cheek, a habit since they were kids, and as had begun to happen more often in the past few months, his body went rigid.

She lowered herself back to her feet, her smile dimming some in confusion. Perhaps he now thought they were too old for such affection.

"Be careful out there," Dillon warned, his voice sounding more strained.

"Of course." She ran her tongue over her lips, imagining Trevon and how he'd react if she allowed him to remove her top. She had to get outside. Now. "Have a nice day."

She turned and hurried out the glass doors, running all the way to the aliaberry orchard. It was near empty, but she spotted Trevon right away.

He lounged beneath a tree, sipping on a flask as he stared up

58

into the sky. His blond hair was longer than most men's, falling over his eye and giving him a disheveled yet sexy boyish look.

Her sandaled feet caught the mud in the orchard, but she didn't bother to wipe it clean, just hurried to the man who consumed her thoughts. The man whose cock would be the first to break her virgin barrier. *Oh, how wicked.*

"Trevon," she breathed, falling at his feet. "I've—"

"Do you have any idea how long I've been waiting?" He sulked and lifted a flask to his lips. "Sitting in a fucking orchard?"

Her mouth parted and her excitement dwindled some. "I'm sorry. I was delayed in the hall."

He reached out and handed her the flask, lifting an eyebrow. Rarely did she drink, but she took it after a moment's hesitation and took a small sip.

"Come on, you can do better than that." He pushed the flask back to her lips, forcing a good amount of the fiery liquid down her throat.

She coughed, pushing the flask away as her eyes burned.

"There you go, baby." He reached out and ran a hand over her bare shoulder, licking his lips. "Your nipples are hard. I like that."

Her pulse sped up and heat spread through her body. "I kind of thought you might."

"Yeah. Aren't you going to kiss me?"

He wanted her to kiss him? She bit her lip and then leaned forward, pressing her mouth to his.

"Fuck. You need to open your mouth." He grabbed the back of her head as his tongue shoved past her lips. He tasted like alcohol, and her stomach rolled for a moment.

*Relax. It gets better. Misty told you some men get like this.* Krystal took a calming breath and let her tongue rub against his.

He groaned and lifted his head. "Yeah, that's better. So, baby . . ." He slid his hand from her shoulder down to the top of her breast.

Her breath hitched. He'd never touched her breasts before. Would he now? A hint of moisture gathered between her legs.

"So . . . are you going to let me see those titties?"

Her brows drew together. Not exactly the most romantic proposition. But then . . . she thought of his lips on her breasts, sucking on her nipples, and suddenly it didn't matter. She wanted to try it.

"I've been thinking all day about it, Trevon. And yes. I want you to be my—"

"About time." He jerked the bandeau top to below her breasts, and then she was naked from the waist up.

The cool air tingled against her erect nipples, heightening their sensitivity. Oh gods. And soon his mouth would be on them. A man would be pleasing her.

"Damn. You don't have a lot to work with, baby, but I'll try."

Humiliation hit hard and she jerked backward, her eyes wide. He may as well have called her flat-chested. Oh gods, how embarrassing. She should just leave now, before this got any worse.

"Ah, don't get so defensive. I didn't mean it like that." He smiled that charming smile that had first made her stomach flip a few months ago. "If we get married I'll use some of dad's money to have larger breasts installed on you. But for now, I can still suck on them."

New breasts installed? She opened her mouth to argue, but he had already pulled her forward and now leaned over her. His lips wrapped around the tip of one nipple and he began to suck.

It felt nice . . . but nothing too exciting. She tried to get into it, closing her eyes and moaning as he made loud, wet sucking sounds. *This was what Misty had raved on and on about?* Ugh. She'd rather stick to her clitabrator.

He lifted his head. "Will you suck on my dick, baby?"

Suck his dick? Her heart pounded, but not because she was excited. She'd never seen a penis and the thought of suddenly having his out in the open . . . Her stomach turned. The idea of sucking on it made her even queasier.

This was too much. Too soon. And she wasn't even sure she wanted to see Trevon's erection right about now anyway.

"I cannot stay. I'm sorry." She jerked the bandeau top up over her breasts again. "We will have to meet later."

"But you just got here!" he whined, brushing a strand of hair out of his eyes.

"I know. Yes, and I am sorry. We have a new prisoner, and I forgot that I am needed." She stood, and before he could protest again, ran back to the living quarters.

# 5

He shouldn't have let her walk out those doors. Dillon did a spinning side kick and took out the collapsible mannequin, then waited—for the tenth time—for it to spring back up.

*Going aliaberry picking, my ass.* The exercise mannequin sprang back into place and he kicked it back down with a roar. Where had her basket been? And who wore perfumed oil to pick berries?

For two years he'd waited for Krystal to come of age. Waited quietly and patiently to make his claim on her. From the moment their relationship dynamics had changed that one summer day two years ago.

They'd been swimming down at the Olasee River and she'd come out of the water half-naked, water dripping off the small curves of her pert breasts. She'd dragged him back in for a water fight, a young woman trying her legs at flirting and having fun. He'd not only lost the water fight that day, but his heart as well.

*Two years.* He did a front kick to the head of the mannequin. And he'd wager his next money installment that today she'd been off meeting some other man.

The mannequin popped back up, but he ignored it this time. He ground his teeth together and headed for the showers. Krystal belonged to him. Now he just had to find out who this asshole was moving in on his territory and set him straight.

Dillon took a quick shower and then headed back to his quarters, but was interrupted when his communication mobile rang.

"Yes."

"Dillon, it's Ryder. Can you drop by my office?"

"I'll be there in two minutes."

He altered his route to swing by Ryder's office, giving a sharp rap on the door before entering.

Ryder stood gazing out the window, unusually stoic.

"What's going on?" Dillon asked, standing in the doorway.

Ryder turned from the window. "I need a favor. I would request that you allow me to handle the entire interrogation process of the prisoner."

Hand over complete control? Dillon's brows drew together. Never in the ten years they'd worked together had Ryder ever made such a request.

"I see." He considered the request. Ryder wouldn't ask if he didn't have a good reason. "All right. I'm available should you need backup, though."

"I know. And I thank you for that." Ryder's jaw clenched. "If you could follow up on those leads about the attack, in the off chance she doesn't talk."

"Will do."

Ryder nodded again. "Thank you, Dillon. For not asking too many questions."

"You'd do the same for me." He already was doing the same.

He guessed Ryder suspected his feelings for Krystal, but had never brought it up.

He turned to leave and then remembered Krystal's request. "By the way, your sister wants to have a word with you later."

Ryder waited until his friend had left the room and then jerked a hand through his hair.

Talia was the key to preventing the attack on Belton. She likely had all the information inside that pretty head, of when and how the attack was to take place.

How he'd get her to talk was the question of the hour. She'd made it clear that she wouldn't tell him, and torture was outlawed on the planet. Not that he'd torture a woman. Hell, even the thought of using it on a man made him uncomfortable.

If she didn't respond to his questioning he would move on to other means. Means he'd find quite enjoyable. He was well aware of her response to his touch, though she continued to fight it and him.

But damn it, they didn't have long. Word on the street was the attack on Belton was planned sometime in the next few weeks.

One thing he couldn't afford was to lose control tonight. He went to the door and pressed in the code to lock it.

Walking back through his office, he headed straight toward the small shower. Turning on the spray, he stripped out of his clothes, dusty from the escape from the Council's building, and stepped under the water.

He would send for Talia in an hour to begin the questioning, and he would need a clear head.

Closing his eyes, he wrapped his fingers around his cock and visualized the scene in her bedding unit in her home early this morning.

Her breasts had been large and crowned with fat pouting nipples. His mouth watered as he recalled the sweet taste of her through the cotton. Oh gods. He stroked the length of his cock, thrusting his hips forward.

Then there was her pussy. Smooth and soft, with perfectly formed labia lips that protected a responsive little clit.

The urge to suck on it made his dick grow even harder. He groaned and moved his hand faster. In his head she thrashed on the bed, calling out his name as he sucked her clit, fucking her sweet cunt with two fingers.

Then the vision changed. She now kneeled at his feet, her lips wrapped around the head of his cock. Deeper she brought him, and harder she sucked on him. He pressed his free hand against the wall of the shower and pumped his cock faster.

"Fuck." His sac tightened and a second later sticky cum shot out under the stream of the shower. Again and again, until he was spent and his erection began to subside.

*Now he had a clear head.*

He reached for the shampoo and washed his hair, then ran a bar of soap over his body. After ensuring he was thoroughly clean, he turned off the shower and stepped out.

He walked straight to the intercom and pressed a button.

"Yes, Colonel?"

"Please prepare the prisoner in the clothes I've instructed, and have her brought to my office."

"Yes, Colonel."

He released the button on the intercom and went back into his office to find some extra clothes.

The knock on the door jerked her out of a deep sleep. Talia sat up, her heart thudding as she blinked in confusion. Oh yes. She was a prisoner. How could she have forgotten?

The door swung open and another unfamiliar woman came

inside. Unlike Krystal, she was more severe in appearance. Brown hair hung down her back in a braid and she wore the same military uniform Ryder had been wearing earlier.

"Get out of bed," the woman snapped. "Your presence is requested by Colonel Jacobs."

Talia covered her mouth to hide a yawn and swung her legs out of bed.

"Colonel Jacobs?"

The woman's smile was condescending, as if she were talking to a toddler. "Yes, the man who brought you here."

"Oh, you mean Ryder."

The smile disappeared, her eyes flashed. "You should not address him so informally."

"Well, perhaps he should not have abducted me." She looked around. Where were her shoes?

"You'll need to change."

Talia glanced back up. "Excuse me?"

The woman's mouth tightened, and her gaze held something. . . . Resentment?

"He wants you to wear this."

Talia lowered her gaze to the small red fabric in the woman's hands.

"What is it?"

The woman's face reddened and she suddenly looked more annoyed.

"You cannot be serious. You need me to explain what it is?" She shook out the fabric revealing just a short tube of fabric. "It is a dress. A night dress, to be exact."

"You wear such things to bed?" Talia's eyes widened, the horror in her voice apparent.

"You really are from another planet, aren't you?" The woman rolled her eyes. "Night dresses like these are worn not for practical reasons, but when one is going to have sex."

Talia's jaw clenched. "I am not having sex with him."

The woman's mouth twisted into a scowl. "Well, apparently he feels differently. Put it on." She tossed the dress at her and it slapped across Talia's cheek before sliding to the floor.

Talia bit back a groan of frustration and leaned over to pick up the dress. There would be no avoiding it. She looked back at the other woman.

"Will you at least give me the privacy to change?"

The woman's mouth pursed. "No. I am to watch you the entire time I am here."

"Surely not while I change?"

The woman just stared at her and made no move to even look away. *What a bizarre person.*

Talia sighed and pulled the cotton dress she'd been issued over her head. The cool air hardened her nipples and she gratefully tugged on the thin red fabric. When she looked down at herself, she groaned.

Nothing was hidden. The dress only began just above her nipples, which could be seen clearly through the fabric, and then ended just below her sex. The cleft of her cunt was just a shadow. Should she bend over, the dress would be above her ass cheeks. As it was, the fabric only came down just below the curve of her buttocks.

"All right. I am dressed. Somewhat." She grimaced and looked up at the other woman. "What else . . ."

The blatant hatred on the other woman's face took the rest of the words from her mouth.

"Follow me. I'll take you to him." The woman turned on her heel and walked through the door.

Talia paled. She had to walk through the halls in this dress? Taking a deep breath, she followed her through the door and into the hall. She kept her head high, her gaze straight ahead.

They passed a few people in the walk to his office, and she

knew her face was burning with humiliation. Never before had her body been on such obvious display in public. The Council had always kept her covered unless she was in the chamber with them.

The woman paused outside a door near the end of the hall and gave a sharp rap.

"You may enter."

A tremble moved through Talia's body at the sound of his voice beyond the door.

The woman opened the door and walked in, not bothering to look back to ensure Talia followed.

Talia hesitated and then stepped inside after the woman.

Ryder stood silhouetted against the window. He turned as they entered the room. His gaze honed in on her, hot and intimate even across the thirty feet or so that still separated them.

Her heart pounded harder in her chest. She wanted to lower her gaze, or look away, but it was impossible. Her throat went dry and her nipples tightened under the thin fabric.

"Here is the prisoner, sir. Would you like me to get you something to drink?"

The other woman's voice had taken on a much more sexual tone, adding fuel to Talia's suspicion that she had feelings for Ryder.

"No." His gaze never left Talia. "We need nothing else at this time."

"All right. . . . Well, you just let me know if you would like me to arrange to have food sent—"

"Leave us, Ines."

The woman went quiet and then she nodded. "Of course, sir. Thank you."

She turned and headed for the door, her gaze sending hateful darts at Talia.

The door clicked shut behind her and Talia licked her lips, her heart beating at a furious pace now.

"I suspect that woman doesn't like me."

"Ines?" He quirked an eyebrow and crossed the floor toward her. "Why do you care?"

Her pulse quickened at the intent she saw in his gaze. "I don't, I suppose."

"Do you like the dress that I had sent to you?"

He stood just inches away from her now. His woodsy scent swirled in her head, making her dizzy.

She closed her eyes. "To call it a dress is a mockery."

"Perhaps." His hands settled on her waist, his thumbs smoothing up and down the fabric. "Your body hides no secrets in that dress. I like it."

Flames licked through her body at his touch and she opened her eyes, meeting his gaze again. "Did you also like having me paraded down the hall so everyone passing might see all *my secrets?*"

His mouth curled into a half smile and his hand slid up her stomach to cover one of her breasts possessively. Her nipples tightened further, pressing into his palm as liquid heat filled her pussy.

"Am I not just showing off my spoils of war?"

"Bastard." Her cheeks warmed and she grabbed his wrist, attempting to pull his hand away from her breast. "Leave me be."

"Princess, we're just getting started." He released her and then reached up to touch the knot on her head. "This will not do."

He had the knot freed before she could attempt to stop him. Her hair spilled heavily down her back and his fingers threaded through it, tightening around the strands.

"Beautiful. So beautiful, Talia." He tugged, jerking her head back. His lips nuzzled the pulse on the curve of her neck. "From now on you will always leave your hair down when you are in my presence."

She closed her eyes as her knees weakened and cream gathered between the folds of her cunt. Was this the part where he seduced her? Convinced her to tell him everything about the Council? And if she did, then what?

*He may kill you.* The thought sent a new stream of terror through her, dousing her desire for him. Perhaps she was just being paranoid, but what reason would he have to keep her around? There was certainly no shortage of women on this planet. And from all she'd heard about Belton from the Council, the humans on this planet were uncivilized heathens. There would be no reason not to terminate her life.

"You may as well kill me now," she ground out, tears pricking behind her eyelids. "As I have said before, I refuse to tell you anything."

"Kill you, Talia?" He laughed, and the cold sound sent chills through her. His hand tightened in her hair. "What gives you the idea that I want to kill you? That would bring me very little . . . pleasure."

He stepped away from her and she opened her eyes, watching as he moved back into the room. He went to the cabinet behind his desk and brought out a bottle of wine, followed by two glasses.

"How long have you been the Council's little sex slave, Natalia?"

Her teeth snapped together. He'd called her Natalia. Only the Council had called her by that name. Obviously he was trying to put her back in the mind-set of her Rosabelle status.

"Answer me." His voice sharpened.

"Four years. Since I turned eighteen."

"Hmm." His gaze narrowed. "You are younger than I originally thought."

She looked away and outside, to where people—women as well—walked freely through a courtyard.

"Come, sit beside me on the couch."

Her throat tightened and she glanced toward the door. She could always try to escape, but she'd be lucky to reach the hall.

"It was not a request, Natalia."

She closed her eyes and then nodded, crossing the room to sit next to him. He handed her the glass of wine and she took a hesitant sip.

"That's better." He touched a strand of hair and held her gaze. "When was the first time you heard them discuss attacking Belton?"

She glanced away. "I don't recall them ever speaking of such things."

He twisted a strand of hair around his finger and tugged. "You're lying, Talia."

Of course she was. They both knew it. "Perhaps. But how can you know for sure?"

"I don't understand. Why do you protect them?"

Irritation sparked in her blood. "I am loyal by nature. If you knew me well enough, you would know this line of questioning is pointless."

"They treated you like shit. Worse than shit. And yet you cover up for them." He took her glass of wine and set it on the table next to his, then grabbed her chin and forced her to look at him. His gaze sparked fire. "Did you fancy that they loved you, Natalia? That they loved their Rosabelle? Or perhaps that you were in love with them?"

Images flitted through her head. Of all the times she'd been forced to tolerate their touch, forced to pleasure them. How brutal they'd been the first time they'd taken her when she'd been a terrified virgin.

No. Love was not an emotion that came to mind when she thought of the Council. She clenched her teeth, refusing to answer Ryder. Her heart pounded heavy beneath her breast.

Something else flickered in his gaze. Something hard. "Or maybe you got off on it. Three men taking turns fucking you."

Her stomach churned, bile rose in her throat. "Stop. You know nothing about my life."

He gripped her shoulders and leaned over her, heat and anger in his eyes now. "Did you like it, Talia?"

"Why are you asking me these questions? You have no right," she ground out and shoved her hands against his chest to try and push him away.

"I have every right. Answer me. Did you enjoy being their personal whore?"

She freed her hand and brought it hard across his cheek. "No! I hated it. You fucking bastard, I hated it!"

Relief flashed in his eyes, before his mouth crushed down on hers. He grabbed her wrists, pinning them behind her back in one of his hands.

She groaned, tried to turn her head but his mouth followed. His tongue slid past her lips and beyond her emotional defenses. Everything inside her melted. Nothing mattered but his touch and the resulting fire that raged inside her body.

# 6

He leaned her back on the couch, transferring her wrists above her head. Using his free hand, he jerked the thin nylon dress off of her breasts. His mouth covered one rigid nipple and he sucked hard. Pleasure arrowed from her breasts to her pussy, and the ache between her thighs built.

His teeth caught the nipple and he bit just enough to make her cry out. He soothed his tongue over the tip and then began to suck again.

A moan tore from her throat and she arched her back, pressing her breast farther into his mouth.

"Talia." He turned his attention to the other nipple, blowing a stream of warm air against the pink tip before wrapping his lips around it and suckling.

He released her hands and pushed the dress over her hips until the fabric just covered her stomach. His massive hands closed over her thighs, spreading them wide as his thumb honed in on her swollen clit.

She dug her fingers into his hair, clutching the short strands, and pressed herself against his hand.

He dipped his thumb into her cunt, coating it in her own slippery juices before moving it back to rub over the sensitive ball of nerves.

"I want to taste you, Talia." He slid down between her thighs and she could feel his hot breath against her pussy. "Have wanted to the moment I first saw you in the corridor yesterday."

"Please."

"That's right, princess. Beg me." He moved his thumb up and down the slit of her cunt. "You're going to beg me to eat your pussy and then beg me to fuck it."

"Ryder . . ." She squirmed against him, her thighs wet with her own arousal.

"Say it. Say you want me to fuck you."

She groaned. "I want you to fuck me. *Please.*"

His tongue thrust into her slit and she gasped. He moved it in and out of her cunt, before sweeping it up and around her clit.

Her hips lifted up and he pressed them back down, pushing two fingers inside her. The sounds of her wetness filled the room as he started to fuck her with the digits.

His tongue flicked faster against her clitoris, circling and pressing, before he finally drew it into his mouth and sucked.

Her stomach clenched and she closed her eyes, throwing back her head. The pleasure built, spiraling higher and harder, and then exploded in her head. Her thighs clenched around Ryder's head, her hands held his mouth to her cunt as he kept licking and sucking on her.

The shaking of her body finally eased and he moved off her. Flipping her onto her stomach, he then lifted her onto her knees.

"Who am I?" He grabbed her hair and tugged, jerking her head back.

She pressed her ass back against him and groaned. "Ryder."

"And you're going to let me fuck your hot little pussy? Aren't you, princess?" His hand moved between her legs, rubbing her wet cunt.

"Yes. Oh gods yes." She gasped when he pinched her clit.

"Beg me."

"Please, Ryder!"

His hands gripped her hips, and then she felt his erection probe the folds of her cunt. The thick head of his cock moved oh so slow into her.

Oh gods he was big. She closed her eyes, the air hissing from her lungs. He stretched her to the point of near pain, pushing deeper and deeper still. Gods, he was long and thick.

He made one hard thrust and embedded himself to the hilt. The walls of her cunt stretched to accommodate his girth and she groaned.

"Talia. You feel so fucking good." His fingers bit into the flesh on her hips and then he started to move.

He pulled out, bringing the head of his cock to her entrance and then thrust hard back in. Again and again he repeated the process. Each long pull of his cock against her vaginal walls dragged a shudder through her.

His thrusts became faster and harder. Her knees grew weak against the leather couch. She fell forward and her ass lifted higher into the air. He pressed a hand against the back of her shoulders, holding her down while slamming his cock deeper into her.

"Talia." He pressed deep and then she could feel his cum thick and warm inside her.

He stayed inside her for a few seconds, didn't move. Her heart raced and she rubbed her ass against him, their bodies both slick with sweat.

When he pulled out of her, she knew immediately he was

upset. She hesitated before standing up and glancing over at him.

His jaw was tight as he pulled his clothes back on. He was not angry with her. Instinctively she knew it. He was angry with himself.

Once dressed he turned and approached her. He reached out a hand and grasped her jaw, the fingers on her skin soft yet controlling.

"Talia . . . In general I don't mix business with pleasure, but with you I'm making an exception." He dropped a hard kiss on her mouth, his tongue thrusting deep and showing just who was in control.

When he lifted his head again there was no emotion in his eyes. "I'll have Ines escort you back to your room. We'll continue the questioning tomorrow."

The shock on her face still lingered in Ryder's head an hour after Talia had left. Gods, why had he treated her like that? Said such harsh words when it was all the woman had ever known?

He was no better than the fucking Council who had spent four years tearing her down physically and emotionally.

He thrust a hand through his hair and shook his head. Fuck, he'd even gotten himself off in the shower so he wouldn't lose control. And look where it had gotten him. Balls deep in the sweetest cunt on the planet.

"Fuck." He crossed the room and stared out the window. Tonight had been a complete failure on his part. He hadn't gotten her to confess anything . . . except that she hated her life as a Rosabelle.

Some of the tension eased from his shoulders. He needed to stop being hostile toward her. If anything she was just a victim in this whole mess. She didn't deserve that life. If she would confess what she knew about the suspected attack, then maybe he could help her.

He'd been naïve to think she'd just confess everything. She didn't trust him. What reason had he given her to?

There was a knock on the door and he glanced toward it wearily. Surely it wouldn't be Talia. He'd sent her back to her room with instructions that she be guarded until further notice.

He took a deep breath and went to open the door.

Krystal grinned at him from the hallway and then walked past him into his office. That's right. Dillon had mentioned she'd wanted to speak with him.

"Hello, big brother. How are things?"

*Things are shit. I just fucked the prisoner and am no closer to preventing a planned attack on our planet.*

He gave a brief smile. "Fine, kid. Everything is fine. What are you up to?"

"Oh, not much. This and that." She wandered around the room, picking up books off his desk and glancing at them before setting them back down. "I had the opportunity to spend some time with Talia today. She's quite nice."

"Is she?" he answered ambiguously.

He'd forgotten that Krystal had been assigned to check in on her. Perhaps that hadn't been the wisest idea. Krystal was soft, tended to only see the good in people.

"She really is, Ry." She folded her arms across her chest and, even though she was a good foot shorter than he was, managed to stare him down. "And I'd like to know why you've condemned her to being treated like a dangerous prisoner."

So Talia had managed to charm his sister as well? Shit. He didn't need this. Krystal might have just turned eighteen, but she had never been afraid to voice her disagreement with him.

Their parents had died in a pod accident some years back,

and Ryder had taken the responsibility of raising her. She adored him and had made it her goal to wrap her big brother around her little finger. She was spoiled and always had been. He didn't mind indulging her, though he could see the error in his ways now. It made her stubborn and determined. And now here she was again, trying to get him to back off Talia.

"Krystal, this is business you know nothing about." And she didn't. She had no idea their lives were in danger. That any moment a supposed allied planet could attack them.

"Yes, but I think I know when someone is being treated in a manner that they don't warrant."

"This is ridiculous," he finally shouted. "She is not locked in some dark dungeon, being forced to only eat bread and water."

"No, of course not, brother. If she had been I would have ordered someone to have you beaten within an inch of your life, not come in here to try and reason with you." She glared at him. "You have a vulnerable woman locked in a room with no company, no access to the outside, and nothing but the fear in her head to occupy her thoughts."

He closed his eyes. Except for when he'd had her dragged in here and then had damn near forced himself on her.

"All right. You may escort her outside the building for one hour, twice a day." He opened his eyes again and gave his sister's shoulder an affectionate squeeze. "And you may have the teletron installed and show her how to use it."

"Oh thank you, Ry!" She squealed and leaned on her tiptoes to kiss his cheek. "You're the best. I will ensure she stays out of trouble."

"Do that."

There was a knock at the door, saving him from adding onto the warning.

"You may enter."

The door beeped as the code was being dialed, and then

opened. Dillon strode in, his steps faltering as he spotted Kry
tal.

"Hey, Dillon." She turned her grin on him.

"Hello, Krystal." His gaze lingered on her just a little too
long before he cleared his throat.

Ryder fought the urge to shake his head. Any time he forgot
how fast Krystal was blooming into womanhood, he just had
to watch Dillon when he came near her. The man was besotted
at best. Which suited Ryder fine. If his sister had to grow up
and run off with some man, then he'd prefer to know who the
lucky bastard was and keep an eye on him.

"I came to check on how the questioning went with the prisoner. I saw Ines escorting her back to the room."

Krystal gave a heavy sigh and poked her finger into Dillon's
chest. "She has a name, you know. It's Talia. And like I just got
done telling my brother, you better start being a little nicer to
her."

Dillon's brows drew together. "Excuse me? What would you
have us do? Have flowers delivered and send in a masseuse?"

"Your sarcasm is unbecoming, Dillon," she chided. "Really,
my brother was so much more reasonable. Anyhow . . . I must
be off. Have a good night, gentlemen."

Krystal sauntered out of the room without a second glance.

"Tell me she's lying." Dillon finally jerked his gaze from the
door she'd exited. "Did you agree to better conditions for the
prisoner?"

Damn, he should've expected this from Dillon. Hell, he deserved it. Everyone on the planet knew Krystal had her big
brother in the palm of her hand.

"I may have agreed to a few allowances."

"You spoil her." Dillon's jaw clenched. "If anyone else had
made the request, you would have turned them down. Natalia

t a guest on our planet. She's the only key to

...,  ryder snarled. Fuck. Krystal hadn't been the entire reason he'd agreed. He still felt like shit for the way he'd treated Talia earlier in the evening. Sisterly pleading had only gone so far; the guilt had sealed the deal.

"I don't understand you, Ryder." Dillon shook his head. "You haven't become involved with her, have you?"

Ryder didn't answer. He'd never lied to Dillon and saw no point in starting now.

"Son of a bitch, Ryder." Dillon strode across the room and looked out the window. "You should let me take over the questioning."

"I'll deal with it."

"How? At least I can promise to keep my dick in my trousers."

"Yeah? And how do I know that? She's beautiful, educated, sexually trained—"

"I have no feelings of lust or attraction to our prisoner," Dillon interrupted quietly. "I think we both know that I am only interested in one woman."

The tension eased from Ryder's shoulders. His friend sure picked a hell of a time to have the talk about Krystal. "I was wondering when you would make mention of it. Though of course I knew."

"You knew?" Dillon turned from the window, his gaze searching. "Does this mean I have your blessing?"

Ryder gave a brief nod. "Of course you do. There is no other man I would trust more to be with my sister." His mouth twisted in amusement. "However, I must ask if Krystal returns your feelings."

Dillon hesitated. "I do not think she considers me anything but a friend, nor is she aware of my feelings for her. But I believe that she will come to love me in time."

Ryder laughed and raised an eyebrow at his friend. "As you have known Krystal since she was in nappies, you do realize she will not appreciate having her future decided for her."

"I have . . . considered that. And I just ask that I be granted the right to woo her by the means I see fit."

Ryder narrowed his gaze. "That's quite a bit of trust you ask of me."

"Yes, it is. And yet you will not give it if you do not think I warrant that trust."

This is why he approved of Dillon. The man was smart, respectful, and would never willingly hurt Krystal. The fact that he had approached Ryder for approval only compounded the fact.

"You have my blessing."

Relief swept across Dillon's face and then a small smile appeared. "Thank you. I should warn you, it may not be as easy as I'd hoped."

Ryder gave a quiet harrumph. "It never is with women."

"No, it isn't. But it appears your sister has become involved with Trevon Andrews."

Ryder's pulse sped up and his jaw clenched. Surely his sister was not such a fool. "Andrews? As in that lazy-ass rich boy who thinks it amusing to seduce virgins?"

"One and the same." Dillon gave a cold laugh. "I suspected something was amiss this afternoon with Krystal, and upon looking into the matter further, realized she imagines herself half in love with the boy."

"Stop her. I don't want her becoming a tally on that man's weaponry belt."

"You can rest assured they will not become lovers. She is my future wife and I intend that she remains untouched by any man save for me."

Ryder's lips twitched, but he wasn't amused. The poor man was delusional. Once Krystal set her mind to something, it wasn't so easily swayed. And if she fancied herself in love with Trevon Andrews, then likely she had already experimented with him, if not already been to bed with him.

He closed his eyes and bit back a groan. By gods, hopefully she wouldn't be such a fool.

"Gods, this is giving me an ulcer. The sooner you wed my sister, the better."

"Worry no more. It shall be done." Dillon hesitated. "And what of the prisoner? Are you certain you do not wish me to assist in the questioning?"

Ryder clenched his fists. He'd lost control this evening. It wouldn't happen again. "I am certain. I will handle this and not allow it to become personal. You have my word."

Dillon held his gaze for several beats, before giving a short nod. "All right. And I will speak with Krystal this evening."

Ryder waited until Dillon had left, before crossing the room and pounding his fist against the wall. Gods. Maybe he should have allowed Dillon to take over the questioning of Talia. How could he possibly trust himself to not touch her again?

His eyes narrowed and the blood in his veins flowed faster just thinking about it. The image of Dillon being the one to question Talia, getting close enough and using intimidation to make her confess.

Perhaps that would be the best solution. Before the thought could even settle, he shook his head. Just imagining it made his gut burn with jealousy. No other man would be allowed to get so close to her.

He closed his eyes and the memory of her lying on his couch

assaulted him. How she'd stared up at him with eyes drugged with pleasure, the way her heavy breasts had felt in his hands.

"Damn. This has to stop," he muttered to himself. "I'm a fucking professional. I will act like it and just get the information from her."

His jaw tight, he headed to the gym to clear his head with a run on the virtual mile device.


Talia curled up on the bed and took deep breaths, inhaling the slight floral scent of her room. She stared out the window and fought against the tears that filled her eyes.

Thank the gods Ines had not lingered after escorting her back last night, had just left her alone in the room, a smug smile on her face as she'd walked out the door. She wouldn't be surprised if Ines had known exactly what had occurred between her and Ryder back in his office.

Her cheeks heated and she closed her eyes with a pained whimper. Never in her four years with the Council had she ever felt so hurt, so humiliated . . . so damn used as she did right now.

Ryder had used her body for his own pleasure and then dismissed her like the whore he believed her to be. But the worst part was that she had wanted him to make love to her, had enjoyed that moment in time with him.

He might not have loved her, but all of the Council put together didn't have an ounce of the passion that Ryder did.

"I'm a fool." She shook her head and rolled onto her back, pressing the back of a hand against her forehead.

The beeping of the door signaled someone was about to enter. Too despondent to even glance up, she waited for them to announce their presence.

"Talia, do you sleep?"

# 7

Krystal's sweet high-pitched voice had Talia sitting upright on the bed.

"You have returned." Her voice cracked with relief at seeing the girl.

"Of course, as I had promised you I would." Krystal winked and walked into the room. "And I come bearing a surprise."

"You do?" Hope sparked in her heart with realization. "You have spoken to your brother?"

"Yes, I have." She grinned. "And I have been given permission to install a teletron."

Talia's hope hissed out on her disappointed sigh. "A teletron?"

"Yes . . ." Krystal hesitated, a frown marring her delicate face. "You are disappointed. I'm so sorry, Talia. You were not hoping I could secure your release, were you?"

Yes. That's exactly what she'd been hoping. Talia closed her eyes. Krystal's brother had been her last hope that she'd be set free.

"I'm so sorry, Talia. Though he adores me, no amount of

begging or harassing him would convince Ryder to release you."

Talia choked and snapped her eyes open. "Ryder is your brother?"

"Yes," Krystal gave her a searching look. "You did not know?"

Talia ran her gaze over Krystal's features. Oh gods. How had she missed it? There were so many similarities: the dark eyes and hair. She was a softer, petite version of Ryder.

Her emotions warred, trying to merge the idea that the only friend she had met on this planet was also Ryder's sister.

"How?" she rasped, her stomach clenching. "You are nothing like him."

"Oh, Talia." Krystal sank down on the bed, a heavy sigh. "I know how it must seem. As of now you've only seen the harsh, military side of my brother. A man who is in the planetary army and does his job all too well." She grasped Talia's hand. "But if you would have met him under other circumstances, where he was not assigned the role as your interrogator, truly you'd realize the man is as soft as a galactic-bred poodle."

A bark of laughter exploded from Talia's throat. Watching Krystal's eyes widen in shock, she fell into a fit of giggles. The bizarre sensation made her stomach hurt and she shook her head.

"What is so funny?"

"Forgive me, but your reference to your brother as a poodle amused me." She wiped a tear from her eye.

"Oh . . ." Krystal pressed a hand to her mouth and hid a smile. "I suppose that did come out a bit silly."

"Yes. Many animals come to mind when I think of your brother, but a poodle is not one of them."

"No. I suppose a poodle was a poor comparison." Krystal let out her own giggle, until they were both laughing outright.

A few moments passed and again they were both calm.

Talia glanced down at her hands. "This will sound absurd—it is absurd—but I am in high spirits right now."

Krystal tilted her head. "Why is that absurd?"

"Why?" Her laugh this time was more despondent. "Because I'm being held here against my will. Because I'm a prisoner on a strange planet." *Because I don't understand the complexity of my feelings for your brother.* She closed her mouth before she could add the last bit.

Krystal's gaze turned somber. "I'm so sorry, Talia. But all will be well in the end."

Would it? Suddenly she needed to know. Needed the reassurance that Ryder would not order the termination of her life in the end.

"Will I truly be safe, Krystal? Can you assure me of that? What will become of me?"

Krystal hesitated. "I cannot answer what will become of you for certain. But I assure you that you will not be harmed while you are here. I trust my brother not to hurt you, Talia. All prisoners are treated humanely—"

"Humanely? Seducing prisoners is considered humane on your planet? Is this common practice for your brother?" The words fled her mouth before she could stop them. What a fool she was! Heat crept up her neck and into her cheeks.

The stunned look on Krystal's face had her stomach clenching. She should not have revealed such details.

"Krystal—"

"Say no more, Talia. I will deal with this." The other woman stood up, her mouth drawn tight. "I will send someone to install the teletron shortly."

"But—"

"I must speak with Ryder." Krystal disappeared before she could get another word in.

Oh gods. Why hadn't she held her tongue? For certain she'd

just driven a wedge between brother and sister. Ryder would be angrier with her now than he had been earlier.

The door shut behind Krystal and the instant loneliness weighed heavy on her heart. For a few moments things had been different. Her guard had slipped with Krystal. When was the last time she had laughed? Gods, had she ever? Perhaps as a child, but even that was frowned upon.

She lay down on the bed and grabbed a pillow, pulling it against her chest. It was better this way. Developing a friendship with Ryder's sister was just trouble waiting to happen.

She closed her eyes tight and bit her lip. She would not cry again. She wouldn't.

*How could he?* Krystal strode through the hall, her fists balled at her side. He had gone too far this time. Never had he ever done something so foolish. Or if he had in the past, she wasn't aware of it.

Up ahead, Dillon rounded a corner and headed her way. Oh, she did not want to make small talk with him now. She increased her pace until she was right outside her brother's office.

"Krystal," Dillon called out. "I must speak with you."

"It is not a good time," she said dismissively and raised her fist to knock upon Ryder's door.

Strong fingers wrapped around her wrist, dragging her hand away from the door.

"What are you—"

"I told you we must speak."

"And I told you it is not a good time. I must address my brother." Her temper flared and she tugged at her hand. "Release me, Dillon."

Instead of loosening, his grip on her wrist tightened. "We will speak outside."

He began walking and she had no choice but to follow. Her blood boiled and she glared at his back.

"I don't appreciate you treating me in such a manner, Dillon. You are completely out of line."

He ignored her, punching in the code to open the glass door that led to the outside. The warm spring breeze caressed her face as he led her out onto a walking trail.

"What is so pressing that you could not wait to speak with me?" she demanded.

He stopped once they'd moved a few yards into the trees and turned around to face her. His expression was hard, his usual easygoing nature surprisingly absent.

"You will answer me truthfully, Krystal. Are you involved with Trevon Andrews?"

She felt a blush burn her cheeks, but she lifted her chin and gave a slight laugh.

"I don't see how that's any concern of yours, Dillon."

His nostrils flared slightly and his jaw clenched. "I'm sorry, Krystal, but from this moment forth you are to have no contact with that man—"

"What?" She inhaled sharply. "Surely you are kidding."

"If it is found that you are continuing your relationship with Mr. Andrews, then you will be placed under a chaperoned house arrest."

"Dillon . . ." She shook her head, her brows drawing together. "Why are you behaving as such? You can't tell me which man I can or cannot get involved with."

He reached out, his hands grasping her elbows and jerking her close. He dipped his head down toward her.

His breath feathered hot across her cheek, sending funny little sensations through her body.

"I need you to tell me that you understand the warning you have been issued."

She jerked at her arms, but his hands were like vices. "I understand you can take your warning and shove it up your—"

"Krystal, *enough*. Answer the question."

Krystal stared at him, fury and confusion flowing through her body. Her lips trembled. How could he do this to her? Forbid her from seeing Trevon?

"You have no authority over me, Dillon," she called his bluff.

His eyes narrowed and his hands moved from her elbow to her upper arms. "The order comes directly from your brother, but make no mistake, I will be the one to enforce it."

A slow shiver moved through her body, from anger or . . . something else, she was not certain.

"Oh really. My brother?" Her lips curled downward. "I would hesitate to trust his judgment at this time. How do you follow orders of a man who fucks a prisoner?"

"Watch your mouth." His expression turned weary. "Swearing does not become you."

There was no surprise in his reaction to her confrontation in regard to Ryder. She shook her head in disbelief. "You knew. You knew he forced himself upon Talia?"

"Ryder would never force himself on a woman, Krys. You and I both know that." His tone gentled as his thumb swirled circles against the bare flesh of her arm. Another warm tremble ran through her.

"It matters not. He had sex with a prisoner! Surely there is some form of law against that." She tried to focus on the conversation instead of the odd sensations flowing throughout her body that his touch created. "Why do you defend him, Dillon?"

"Your brother knows what he is doing." He sighed and his expression softened some. "But you do not. You know not what type of man Trevon is, likely know nothing of his reputation. You've only just come of age—"

"Do not call me a child." The hot anger returned, giving her the strength to jerk out of his grasp. She stumbled backward. "I will continue to see whomever I choose, you and your orders be damned."

"Krystal—"

"And you can pass that message on to my brother as well." She gave him one last defiant glare, before turning and fleeing back to the building.

Talia woke to the sound of the door opening. She rubbed the back of her hand across her eyes and looked toward the window. Gods, it was dark out now; she must have fallen asleep. What time was it?

She sat up just as Ines strode into the room. Her heart sank and she gnawed on her lip. Oh, why did she have to see this woman right now?

"I've come to install the teletron." Ines didn't even glance at her, just crossed the room and began to install a small box low on the wall.

"Thank you."

The silence was heavy, the resentment from the other woman nearly palpable.

Talia cleared her throat and attempted to make small talk. "I'm surprised Ryder would agree to give me such a luxury."

Ines's jaw clenched. "I'm not. You've given him the luxury of your body. Consider it payment."

Talia blanched, her fingers curling into the sheets on the bed. The hatred and jealousy in Ines's voice were blatant.

"You need not feel threatened by me, Ines. I have no interest in Ryder. Whatever ideas he has now about him and me shall pass." She spoke the words easily, but her stomach clenched and her throat grew tight.

She did not have feelings for Ryder. That would be impossible.

"No, I do not feel threatened by you, Natalia. Not in the least. I know where I stand with Ryder, and I can hardly blame him for making use of the whore that has been taken prisoner."

Talia flinched, the turbulence in her belly turning acidic. How dare the woman?

"I'd like you to leave now." Talia's voice shook, but she straightened her spine and held the other woman's gaze. "I have no need for a teletron or your insults."

"A little too late for both." Ines tossed the teletron control device on the bed and headed back toward the door. "Just remember what I've said, Natalia. You'll never be more than a traitorous slut in his eyes."

Ines's words rang in her ears long after the other woman had gone.

Talia squeezed her eyes shut, suddenly nauseous. Sleep. Just go back to sleep. At least while she slept she was free, even if just in her dreams.

She drifted in and out of slumber the rest of the night. Sleep was elusive.

When Krystal arrived at her door she'd already been awake for a couple of hours. Ines's words still lay heavy in her heart.

Talia watched as Krystal crossed her room, carrying a tray and with a hesitant smile on her face.

"Good morning," Talia murmured.

"Good morning. Did you sleep okay?" Krystal set the tray down on the bed and then sat down on the mattress.

"Not very well, unfortunately. But it is to be expected." Talia offered a brief smile and picked up some sort of biscuit and nibbled on it.

She watched Krystal with open curiosity. Had she spoken with Ryder last night? There were circles under her eyes this morning, and her smile seemed strained.

"I did not sleep well, either," Krystal confessed and took an unsteady breath.

"No?" Talia tilted her head. Perhaps she had argued with Ryder. "Is there a reason why?"

Krystal's cheeks turned a pretty shade of pink as she shoved a few curls back behind her ear.

"Yes. I . . . I'm in love."

"You're in love?" Talia set down the biscuit, staring at the younger woman in surprise. "But that is a wonderful thing, is it not?"

"It would be." Krystal sighed. "If my foolish brother and his friend weren't so determined to keep me apart from the man I love."

"Oh, Krystal, I'm so sorry. Why do they object?"

Krystal shook her head and shrugged. "They would have me believe that Trevon is some licentious rich boy and that I'm just a silly child who knows nothing."

Talia hesitated. As much as she hated to side with Ryder, he might be right. The girl was young and quite possibly easily misled.

"How long have you known this man . . . Trevon, is it?"

"Yes. Trevon. I've known him for a few months now." Krystal lowered her gaze and lifted a grape from the tray and popped it into her mouth. "And before you ask, no, we have not made love."

Talia could not stop the relieved sigh as she took a bite of some fluffy yellow thing on her plate.

"But I want to." Krystal giggled and pressed a hand against her breast. "Oh gods, how I want to. I have only known the pleasure of my own hand and a clitabrator."

Talia coughed, nearly choking on the eggs. "You have . . ." She could feel her cheeks heating up. "You have touched yourself?"

Krystal burst into laughter. "But of course I have. Everyone has. It's not like it is a crime to do so."

"It is on my planet."

"You jest! Surely you do!" Krystal's eyes widened and she leaned forward. "Do you honestly tell me you have never pleasured yourself?"

"Never. To do so would mean being given the most severe punishment." She looked away. What would it be like to bring herself to climax? With a sad smile she admitted, "I'm not sure I would even know how to do it."

"Oh, trust me, you would catch on quickly." Krystal gave her a side glance as she reached for another grape. "I have to apologize, Talia. For my brother's behavior. I intended to speak with him last night regarding it, but was waylaid by Dillon."

"Dillon?"

"Yes. He's my brother's best friend. And he's made it clear he will ensure that I never see Trevon again." Her mouth tightened. "Ridiculous is what it is. I intend to fully ignore both his and Ryder's orders. I shall just have to be a little more . . . discreet with my meetings with Trevon. So that they never know."

Talia frowned, somewhat uneasy by Krystal's determination. "Oh, but you must promise to be careful."

"Careful? There's nothing to be careful about. I am the sister of a high-ranking military official. I am never in danger."

"But your virtue may be . . ." Talia murmured before she could stop herself.

Krystal rolled her eyes. "Virtue is nothing more than a word, and truth be told I'd be happy to do away with it."

Talia gave a small smile. Truly she envied the younger woman.

To have such a lighthearted outlook on life and to have such freedoms.

"How do you know you love him, Krystal?" she asked on a sigh. "I don't ask to reprimand you, but out of curiosity. How does one know when they are in love?"

"Hmm." Krystal bit her lip, seeming to think about it, and then grinned. "Well, I just know. He's so handsome, and when he smiles at me I giggle a lot."

"Giggle?"

"Just feel really feminine."

"Oh." Giggle and feminine? Talia lowered her gaze. She had never had that reaction when she was near Ryder. But there was one thing. "When he . . . when he kisses you do you feel flutters in your stomach?"

There was a longer pause this time. "Well, I know there will be eventually. We've only kissed but a few times, so it is still a bit awkward."

Talia glanced again at Krystal, but the woman was staring out the window. "I have been given permission to take you outside twice a day. Perhaps later you would like to go?"

"Oh . . . yes." Tears flooded her eyes, and she cursed herself for the show of weakness. But the idea of being outside, able to breathe in the atmosphere of the planet, took her breath away.

Krystal gave a small smile. "I will confess. I may use our time outside to meet up quickly with Trevon."

"All right." Talia would have agreed to anything to go outside. Though she did worry a bit about Krystal's impulsiveness.

"Well, finish up with your breakfast and get dressed." Krystal patted her hand. "I shall return in about an hour."

Talia waited until the other woman left and then dug into the food with new enthusiasm. Gods, she was going to go outside! Outside! With a squeal of excitement, she set down her teacup and went to inspect the clothes that had been left for her in the closet.

She swallowed hard and ran her fingers over the fabric of what appeared to be a dress. Truly the state of dress on this planet was much more relaxed than back home. She finally lifted a cerulean blue silk dress that appeared to at least go almost to her knees.

She sighed and then tugged the dress off the hook to get changed.

# 8

Ryder exited the training facility, showered and on a mission. He would see Talia this morning. Would make her understand how valuable the information she held was. And he'd realized the most obvious way to gain her cooperation was to show her the world outside. Let her see the people of his planet.

He neared her chamber and spotted Krystal dialing in the code.

"Good morning, little sister. What are your intentions with the prisoner this morning?"

Krystal spun around, guilt flittering across her face before she turned on her usual big smile. She was attired in a dress that displayed more flesh than what was covered, and her perfume lingered heavy in the air.

"Hello, Ryder. I was going to take Talia out for a walk. You did give her permission to leave the building escorted twice a day."

"Hmm. So I did." Krystal was up to something, likely would be attempting to see Trevon Andrews. He narrowed his eyes. "Tell you what. Why don't you let me escort her on this walk?"

Her eyes widened, and then annoyance flickered in her gaze. "Oh, but I already—"

"Actually, if you wouldn't mind, I'd like you to assist Dillon in loading one of the cargo crafts for its upcoming departure. He's over in sector ten."

Krystal's mouth tightened; her displeasure was obvious. "If that is what you wish."

"Thank you, kid." Ryder dropped a kiss on her forehead and then patted her shoulder, sending her on her way.

He took a deep breath and closed his eyes. *Control.* He needed to be in absolute control when he walked into Talia's room. He opened his eyes and typed in the code that would open the door.

The computer beeped its appreciation and then the door swung open. He stepped inside, glancing around the room. His blood began to pound when he didn't immediately see her.

"Give me one moment, Krystal." Her voice rang out from the bathing chamber. "I am attempting to comb my hair."

The image of the red silky strands of hair had him crossing the room to the bathing chamber. He stepped into the doorway.

"Though it sounds absurd, I have never combed my own hair—" Her gaze lifted and caught his in the mirror. The brush in her hand fell with a loud thud to the counter, and the muscles in her throat worked as she swallowed hard. "I thought . . . Krystal was to escort me outside for a brief period."

He took a deep breath, his chest feeling strangely tight. Gods, she was beautiful. Her hair was a long wave of fire against creamy skin. Her shoulders were bare and the top of her breasts swelled above the silky fabric of her dress. His gaze moved lower, to where the dress hugged a small waist before flaring over her hips and ending just above her knees. Shapely calves ended in a pair of laced leather sandals.

"Plans have changed." His words came out hoarse. His jaw clenched as he stepped completely into the bathing chamber. *So much for control.*

Her eyes widened when he came right up behind her, closing in until there were just a few inches separating them.

He reached out and lifted a silken strand, rubbing its softness between two fingers. Pulling her hair off her neck, he settled it over one shoulder, baring the graceful curve of her neck to him.

Leaning down he pressed his lips against her nape, inhaling the smell of soap and woman. Her body trembled beneath his lips, and he watched as her hands gripped the edge of the counter.

Biting back a groan, he reached past her and picked up the brush off the counter.

"Why have you never combed your own hair?" He brought the brush to her scalp and pulled it through the strands.

"I was never allowed to. I had an assistant who did that for me." She curled her fingers around his wrist and he met her gaze in the mirror again. "There is no need to do this for me, Ryder. I'm sure the process is quite simple."

"It is not a chore but a pleasure for me," he murmured, watching as each stroke made her hair more sleek and shiny.

She released his wrist, though obviously reluctantly, and allowed him to finish the task.

He continued to move the brush through her hair, waiting until the tension had eased from her body before asking, "Why will you not confess what you know about the Governing Council, Talia?"

Her shoulders slumped a bit and her gaze lowered. "Because your planet is full of barbaric heathens. You would attack us and would bring nothing but pain and misery to a planet that already suffers."

Ryder frowned. How misguided she was, perhaps brainwashed from years of being under the Council's influence. He set the brush onto the counter once more and gripped her shoulders, turning her to face him.

"You truly believe that?"

Her eyes flashed with defiance, and yet maybe also uncertainty. "Of course. I have heard the stories—"

"From whom, the Council?" He reached out to trace the throbbing pulse in her throat.

"Yes." Another visible tremble traveled through her body and her next breath was ragged. "Please, Ryder. No . . ."

"No?" He cupped her cheek, running his thumb over the mouth that tantalized him.

"Do not take my body for your own pleasure again," she whispered.

He ran his gaze over her once more. Her body had awakened in the past few minutes, her nipples were hard and outlined against the blue fabric of the dress.

"For my pleasure, princess?" He slid his thumb between her lips, until it became moist in her mouth. "Can you honestly say that you experienced no pleasure last night?"

He knew she'd been pleasured, even if she would deny it now. Their eyes locked, and he recognized the exact moment her expression changed from wariness to desire. She closed her eyes. Her only response was the tip of her tongue stroking against the pad of his thumb.

His cock hardened and a groan traveled up his throat. He had plans for her this morning. Plans to make her confess while keeping his desire for her under control. Perhaps there was a way to do both. Relax her and gain her trust.

"Seeing as you believe yourself not to have been pleasured last night . . ." His hands moved to her waist and he lifted her, ignoring her startled gasp as he set her on the counter. "I will remedy that this morning."

He pushed her knees apart and stepped between her thighs, sliding his hand under her dress to stroke her cunt. She was smooth, hot, and already drenched with cream.

He slid two fingers between her labia, scissoring his fingers and opening her to him. The musky smell of her desire filled the room as her slick juices coated his fingers.

She gave a loud moan, but pressed her palms against his chest, her gaze searching his. "Ryder, this does not solve anything."

"Does it not?" He licked his middle finger on his other hand and then brought it between her legs to rub against her clit.

"Oh . . ." Her eyes closed and her hips lifted off the counter.

"Do you want me to stop?" He rotated his finger against the kernel of swollen flesh.

She moaned again. Her hands ceased in pushing him away and instead clutched his shirt. "I hate you for this," she choked out. "But I'll hate you more if you stop."

His blood pounded in triumph and he smiled, pushing two fingers into her humid cunt. Gods, she was so hot and wet. His cock pressed against the fastening of his trousers and he gritted his teeth. *For her, this is for her.*

He kept one finger on her clit, rubbing steadily while he began to slowly finger fuck her.

She leaned into him, wrapping her legs around his waist as he moved his fingers in and out of her hot cunt. He curled his fingers, rubbing against the sensitive spot inside her.

"Ryder." She gasped and jerked his shirt, pulling his head down to hers.

He answered her plea and closed his mouth over her parted lips, thrusting his tongue into the sweet moist cavern. Her tongue moved against his almost hesitantly, as if kissing was a novelty for her.

He moved his fingers faster, deeper into her, mimicking the thrusting of his tongue in her mouth. Encouraged by her husky groans, he added pressure to her clit.

Her thighs tightened around him and she pulled her mouth from his to cry out. Cream surrounded his fingers as she climaxed and her nails nearly pierced his shirt as they clawed at his chest.

She closed her eyes, her breasts rising and falling with each rapid breath she took.

He pulled his fingers out of her channel and cupped her pussy, smoothing his thumb over the silky lips of her cunt.

"Are you ready to go for that walk?"

Her eyes opened and she blinked in confusion. "Walk? You don't need to . . . ?" Her gaze lowered to the crotch of his pants.

"You need not worry about me now." He pulled her dress back down over her hips and then lifted her off the counter.

Her legs buckled and he slipped an arm around her waist to steady her.

"But I don't understand. Do you not want—"

He brushed his mouth against hers, cutting off her prattle. She clutched his shoulders and made the sweetest little moan. He ran his tongue over her bottom lip, before slipping it inside her mouth to rub against hers. His arms tightened around her, and he pulled her flush against him. Her full breasts crushed against his chest and his erection pressed into the softness of her belly.

He brushed his mouth over hers one more time, before he lifted his head.

"Yes, Talia, I *want*. However, the plan for the morning was to take you for a walk, and I have enough control that I will honor that."

Her expression was a mixture of confusion and surprise, and his heart twisted a bit. Gods, the way she must have been treated on Zortou.

He smoothed her hair down her back and murmured, "Let us go outside and we will talk further."

Talia stared at him, unsure what to make of this change in his behavior. It made no sense. He was a different man this morning. Realizing he was waiting for her to respond, she nodded. "Thank you."

He held out his hand and she glanced down at it, before placing her palm in his. His long fingers curled around her hand and he turned, leading her toward the door.

They moved into the hallway and immediately encountered another man in uniform.

"Good morning, Daniels." Ryder paused in his stride. "How is the baby today? Feeling any better?"

The man paused in his brisk stride, his mouth curving into a broad smile.

"Oh, she is good. Marie telemessaged me an hour ago and told me she was eating again. Thank you, sir."

"I'm glad to hear it." Ryder nodded. "Have a good day and say hello to Marie."

"Thank you, sir."

Talia glanced up at Ryder. He had such familiarity with a soldier of lesser rank. Such kindness. Was it all a ruse?

They approached a series of glass doors, and he began to punch in the code. She stared outside at the strange trees and flowers—some form of a garden—and her chest tightened.

There was a series of beeps and then the doors swung open. Warm air brushed against her face and she gasped in the outside air, gripping Ryder's hand tighter.

He glanced over at her, his brows drawn together as he led her the few steps that took her outside the building.

Her legs shook with each step they made. Oh gods. She was outside. Tears welled in her eyes and the bizarre urge to laugh caught in her throat.

She lifted her gaze to the sky. It was blue with fat white clouds in it. Her head shook as she glanced around. So different, so vastly different from Zortou.

"You appear overwhelmed, Talia. You have only been imprisoned for less than two days."

Ryder's words put everything into perspective. She lowered her gaze to the path they walked upon.

"I have been imprisoned since the day I was born." She shouldn't have said the words, but they'd been unstoppable on her tongue.

At his questioning glance, she continued. "I was allowed outside the Council's headquarters once . . . when I was eight years of age." She breathed in the fresh air, her diaphragm expanding as air filled her lungs. The smell of flowers was rich all around them. "And it was nothing like your planet."

His grip on her hand tightened. "You were not allowed outside the building?"

"No."

"Never?"

"Only that one time." She hesitated. "The air was . . . not safe to breathe for long periods of time. When you looked up, the sky was not blue as it is here. It was dark, nearly black, and thick with pollution. They were not willing to risk any contamination to my body."

"Yes. I'm aware of the environment your planet existed in. It was brought on by the current Council."

"Yes." She lowered her gaze.

"So you understand why they would want to attack Belton?" he asked. "To take over our home?"

Guilt clawed in her gut and she bit her lip. "But you are—"

"Barbaric heathens? So you've said, Talia." He stopped and turned her to face him, cupping her chin and tilting her head until she met his gaze. "Are you so sure?"

The intensity of his gaze rendered her speechless. No, she wasn't sure. She didn't know what was real and what wasn't anymore.

"Do not answer that yet." He released her and again took her hand. "Come, let us walk."

They continued along the path. It wound through green hills that were covered with flowers and trees of all varieties. She could not stop breathing in appreciative gasps of the crisp air.

Soon they moved down a hill that led into a small park. Talia stumbled, her mouth parting in surprise.

Children rode a good fifty feet in the air on some kind of flying bicycle, while their mothers watched from the ground and chatted with each other.

"There are children here," Talia murmured in disbelief, her eyes wide as she drank in the sight. "I have not seen a child since . . . My generation was the last of the children on Zortou. There will be no more."

Ryder glanced down at her, his expression dark and unreadable. "You are not able to have children?"

She gave a small shrug, though her stomach rolled. "I am able, I suppose, but a Rosabelle is kept on a strict injection schedule that would prevent us from being impregnated."

His eyes narrowed. "And why is that?"

"When they realized that women had ceased birthing girl babies, it became a problem. Already there were just a handful of women and numerous men." Her throat tightened.

She'd known for quite some time she would never be a mother, had eventually buried the heartache deep within her. Her glance locked again on the mothers at the play area and her lips trembled. To see what could have been made that wall around the pain crack just a bit.

Her voice wavered. "They began giving the injections to ward off pregnancies until they discover why men have stopped generating the X chromosome."

"Interesting."

His tone was so curt she glanced at him again and found his mouth drawn tight, his chest expanding slowly as he took deep breaths.

He did not seem pleased by her words. Uncertainty flicked through her. "Have I angered you?"

"No. You have not. Your words are disturbing, but you just relay the truth. A truth you hold no responsibility over."

She nodded. He blamed the Council. But then who else could he blame? They were after all the ones who had created and enforced the law.

"Come, there is more I'd like to show you." He switched topics and started them walking on the trail again.

The sound of water reached her ears and she looked around, her pulse increasing. Were they near a river? Or a lake?

They rounded a corner and a vast sea of sparkling blue water lay upon the horizon.

"Oh . . ." She sighed and pressed a hand to her heart. "It is beautiful."

Her gaze moved over the people who appeared to be literally walking over the water. Her brows drew together and she glanced up at Ryder who was watching her.

"How do they—"

"There is a raised foot path that is invisible to the naked eye. It hovers just under the water, so when crossing the lake a person is advised to remove any covering on their feet." He smiled. "Would you like to try it?"

Sweat gathered on the back of her neck as she stared at the lake. Could she do it? She'd never been on a body of water—not in a boat, and definitely not walking across it like she was some higher deity.

"Yes, you'd like to," he encouraged, then sank down at her feet and began to unfasten her sandals.

His touch on her foot was gentle, sending heat licking up from her ankles to her womb. He stood up, the straps of her sandals slung over one finger.

"Come, you will enjoy it, I promise."

Excitement pulsed through her blood and she followed him the last few steps to the lake. He toed off his own shoes and held them in his free hand.

He stepped into the lake and then glanced back to make sure she followed. The path was only wide enough for them to go one at a time.

She offered a brief smile and then stepped into the water. The platform beneath her feet had a gel, plastic-type feel that dipped under the water level with her weight.

The water was borderline cold as it sluiced up and around her ankles. Her pulse jumped as she took another hesitant step and the path moved a bit lower. Surely the path would sink under the water.

Ryder called over his shoulder. "How are you doing?"

The lake water was refreshing against her skin, the rush from doing something so new, exhilarating. "I'm wonderful. I'm terrified." She laughed and took another step. "I cannot believe I'm doing this."

His laughter was loud and amused. "It will not sink. I promise you, princess. Just make sure you do not step off the path, because you may not fare as well."

They had to be thirty feet out into the lake now and she lifted her gaze to glance around. There were other paths that crossed through the lake that people strolled upon.

Off the path there were couples that sat in antique-looking wooden boats. One boat held an elderly couple who sat next to each other, holding hands as another man rowed.

The man leaned over and kissed the woman, and Talia's heart twisted with bittersweet longing. What kind of love endured through so many years?

"Watch the corner."

His words reached her a little too late. She jerked her gaze back to the path just after she missed the curve. She lost her footing, her right foot overshooting the path and sinking into the lake.

She waved her arms, trying to regain her balance, but already had tumbled off the path.

"Ryd—"

Her words cut off into a gurgle as she went under. She flailed her limbs, trying to reach the surface as the cool lake sucked at her.

Strong hands gripped her arm, dragging her to the surface and out of the lake.

Ryder's worried glance came into focus. "Gods, Talia, what part of 'watch the corner' didn't you understand?"

Her lips shook and she clung to him as he lifted her into his arms. Surely he wouldn't try and carry her. Would he not drop her?

"I apologize." She coughed more water out of her lungs and pulled at her saturated dress. "I allowed myself to become distracted and lost my footing."

"So it would appear. You worried me, princess. Are you all right?"

He adjusted her in his arms, and his hand slid up her rib

cage, brushing the side of her breast. Her nipple, already hard from the cold water, tightened further.

"Yes. Just . . . cold." Her lips trembled. "I am a fool."

"You're not a fool, you're clumsy," he teased with a laugh and veered off on a new path. The new path led them toward the opposite shore of the lake where a heavy thicket of trees lay.

They moved out of the lake and moved deeper into the brush; she glanced around trying to figure out where they were, seeing as they were not at the original starting point.

He moved them deeper into the woods and then set her down on her feet. He reached for the hem of her dress and she swatted at his hand in dismay.

"What are you doing?"

"You need to remove the dress, Talia. It's soaked through to your skin and the weather is growing cooler."

"Yes, but I will be naked."

"And your point would be?" He lifted an eyebrow and pulled the dress up and over her body. His gaze dropped to her breasts and he issued a strangled groan. "You can wear my overcoat on the way back when we leave within the hour."

Her eyes widened. "Within the hour? What are we doing before then? I am near shaking I'm so cold."

He gave a husky laugh. "Worry not, Talia, I will warm you."

# 9

His lips came down hard on hers, his tongue thrusting deep. She gasped in surprise, reaching out to clutch his shoulders. True to his word, his kiss began the slow spread of fire through her blood.

"I have no control when I am near you," he confessed huskily, and slid a hand down her belly and between her legs.

He slid a finger into her cunt and she lost all ability to stand.

"Gods, you are soaking already." He moved his finger, wet with her juices, up to her clit and began a slow rub over her eager flesh.

"Ryder."

Her body had been ready for him since he'd brought her to climax back in her room. She'd wanted to touch him, to explore him with her hands and mouth, had almost been disappointed when he'd rushed them out.

She pulled away and took a step back.

"Talia?" His brows drew together, his breathing heavy.

"Please. Is it not my turn to pleasure you?" She sank to her knees in the grass, reaching for the fastening on his pants. Once she had it free, she pushed his trousers down to his knees and his erection sprang thick into her hands.

"Oh gods, princess," he hissed and reached down to stroke her hair.

She wrapped her fingers around him, feeling his girth and trailing a fingernail over the swollen red head.

Placing her hands on his thighs, she flicked her tongue over his length. His guttural groan encouraged her, made her bolder. Reaching down, she massaged his sac as her tongue moved over the length of his cock.

He tightened his hands in her hair and pressed his hips forward so that his erection slid past her lips.

She opened her mouth, licking the salty pre-cum off the tip before he slid farther in to touch the back of her throat.

"You are incredible." He groaned again and began timing his hip movements so that he was fucking her mouth as she sucked on him.

She increased the pressure of her fingers as she massaged his sac and was rewarded as it clenched beneath her hand.

"I need to be inside you." He gently pushed her mouth off him and then lifted her to her feet.

He grabbed her ass, lifting her, and she wrapped her legs around his waist while he walked them backward. The smooth trunk of a tree connected with her back, and she was trapped between it and his hard chest.

He lifted her even higher and then dipped his head to her breasts. His teeth caught one of her stiff nipples and teased the sensitive flesh.

She gasped and tried to lower herself onto his thick cock, but he held her immobile while he toyed with and sucked on her breasts.

"*Now.* Please, Ryder."

He released her nipple and wrapped his massive hands around her waist, impaling her downward onto his cock.

His erection pressed thick and deep up inside her. A tremble rocked her body as the air hissed from her throat and her eyes nearly rolled to the back of her head.

"Gods," Ryder gasped, staying deep in her. "You've got the sweetest cunt in the universe, Talia."

A slow laugh worked its way up through her throat. "I would hope that you have not bedded every woman in the universe."

"I have not. Nor would I want to after having been with you." His mouth covered hers again and he slowly moved his cock in and out of her.

Each pull of his cock against the swollen flesh of her vaginal walls sent hot licks of pleasure through her.

His tongue swept the interior of her mouth and he pressed her harder against the tree, his fingers digging into her ass cheeks. She cried out, moving her body the small amount she could against his thrusts.

He thrust harder, faster, and her back rubbed against the trunk of the tree. She buried her face into his shoulder, her tongue snaking out to lick his salty skin.

He angled her body so that her clit got stimulated, and she cried out as she came. Her cunt muscles clenched as trembles racked her body.

"Talia." He squeezed her ass and then she felt him explode inside her. "Oh gods."

He stayed buried inside her, not moving as their shallow breathing filled the air. He lifted his head and sighed.

"Ah, princess . . . what you do to me."

Wrapping her arms around his neck, she clung to him as he walked them away from the tree.

He set her down on the ground and sighed. "We should get you back to your room."

Her heart sank and she glanced out at the lake, biting down on her lip. The idea of going back inside, being locked back in that room, sucked away all her elation.

"Talia. Look at me." His fingers gripped her chin, his touch gentle as he turned her face back to him. "I'm not proud of the way I've treated you the past couple of days, and I won't ask you to forgive my behavior. But I want to say I'm sorry."

The sincerity in his gaze ripped at her heart. She didn't want to humanize him—to see this side of him. The wall around her heart crumbled and emotions slammed into her at once. Sadness, pain, hope, and . . . gods, it could not be love.

Her body began to shake. How could she have allowed herself to become so vulnerable? To willingly allow him into her body and so damn close to her heart? Four years with the Council she'd managed to keep a protective shell around her emotions; guarded her heart from ever feeling anything—be it pain or love. Two days with Ryder and she was putty in his hands.

"You're cold. I should not have kept you out here so long after your fall into the water." He grimaced and slipped out of his military jacket. "Here, let's place this on you. It will ease the chill."

If there was a chill she didn't feel it. A bit numb, she lifted her arms, letting him slide the jacket onto her. The rough material abraded her nipples and fell well past her thighs.

"Come, we will walk back to the housing building." He took her hand and gave it a gentle squeeze.

They did not walk the lake this time, but through the woods on a trail. She made no effort to make conversation or reply to his apology; she just needed the time and silence to analyze her heart and emotions.

Outside her room, he dialed in the code and the door opened. He escorted her a few feet inside and then stopped.

She turned to face him. Would he come in? Would he press her again for the information?

"Talia . . ." He brushed the back of his knuckles across her cheek. "I only ask that you consider what you've seen this afternoon. Ask yourself if you truly believe the people of my planet to be barbaric heathens. To be deserving of the kind of attack Zortou has planned."

She swallowed hard. Already the answer lay in her heart.

"I will send for you in a few hours and we will dine together." He dipped his head and brushed his mouth across hers. "Until then."

He turned and left, the door closing shut behind him.

She lifted her hands, thrusting her fingers through her hair and groaned. Oh gods. What was she going to do?

Krystal stormed through the halls, anger brimming in her blood and her fists clenched. How dare he assign her a silly duty with Dillon? She would see Trevon today, no matter what her brother said.

He had no right. Ryder did not know Trevon as she did. Most women on the planet would give their left eye to be the center of Trevon's attention. He was handsome, fun, exciting, not to mention rich and influential.

Her thoughts turned to yesterday's encounter in the aliaberry orchard, when she'd allowed him to kiss her and touch her breasts. Her stomach twisted a bit. Doubt pricked at her, and she shook her head. *No, stop this.*

Trevon had apologized, explained that he had been drunk and selfish in her first experience with letting a man touch her. He'd begged her for another moment alone, another chance. And if she could arrange it, she'd give him that moment.

Her eyes narrowed and she increased her pace. It would serve Ryder and Dillon right for trying to take control of her romantic life.

Her feet began to throb and she scowled. She wasn't dressed for this long walk to the sector; she'd dressed to meet Trevon. Stepping off the path, she made her way to the nearest sky taxi center to hail a pod.

"To sector ten, please," she commanded the computer and then sat back in her seat as the pod rose into the air.

Resting her head against the neck rest, she toyed with a curly strand of hair. Perhaps if she could gain Dillon's support in her relationship with Trevon, then he would convince her brother to allow her to see him.

*Hmm.* She frowned and glanced down at the canopy of trees they flew over. Dillon had seemed a bit anti-Trevon as well, though.

She plucked at the short hem of her dress and smiled. Well. She would just have to convince him. As with Ryder, Dillon had always been easy enough to twist around her finger. She'd just have to turn on the charms a little bit heavier this time around.

"Arrival at sector ten."

The pod lowered the hundred feet to the hangar, and she tugged her dress down in an attempt to look more modest before climbing out of the pod when the door slid up.

Her heels clicked across the concrete as she made her way to the entrance of the hangar. A mega-pod was docked in the middle of the building, the cargo unit door in the back wide open.

Where was Dillon? She glanced around, but didn't see anyone.

"Hello?" Her voice resonated off the walls as she walked toward the back of the building. "Dillon?"

The sound of footsteps came from her right, and she turned

her head to see Dillon striding across the room with a box in his hand.

"Hello, Krystal." He offered a slow smile, his gaze locked on her. "What brings you by?"

"My brother." The way he looked at her sent a warmth she didn't understand through her, and she folded her arms across her chest defensively. "He asked that I help you load the cargo ship, but you look like you're doing just fine by yourself."

Dillon's smile widened and he lifted an eyebrow. "Some place you'd rather be?"

*Yes. With Trevon.* She could hardly say it aloud, so she offered a shrug instead.

His gaze became knowing, his mouth suddenly tight. "Well, thank you for coming by. I could use the help."

He strode past her and set the box down in the back of the pod.

*Nice job, Krystal. If you want to convince him that your relationship with Trevon is not a bad thing, then you may want to work on not angering him right away.*

"So what are we loading?" she asked, forcing a smile and following him as he went back to pick up another box.

"Medical supplies that are being shipped out this evening to the city of Glorus." He glanced over his shoulder. "Are you sure you can walk in those shoes?"

She rolled her eyes and grabbed one of the smaller boxes, lifting it high against her chest. "I love my shoes, and I have been walking just fine in them since I turned the age of fifteen."

He lifted a huge box and laughed. "I remember that. When you stopped wearing ragged old athletic shoes and put on those teetering high heels."

She grimaced. "Oh, please, do not remind me of my lack of fashion as a child. I idolized you and Ryder so much that I think at times I fancied myself a boy."

"You could never be a boy." He set the box in the back of the ship next to the other one and shook his head. "Trust me on this."

"Thank you, Dillon. Although some may argue with you about that." She set her box down and went back to grab another.

The room went quiet, and she turned around to make sure Dillon hadn't left her alone. He was still at the loading dock, but now he looked angry.

What had she said? "What's wrong?"

"Who said it?"

"Said what?" She gave a nervous laugh and continued to grab another box.

"That you look like a boy."

She scooped up another box, not answering right away. *You don't have a lot to work with.* Trevon's comments about her breasts had stung. Had made her feel anything but sexy. *Forget what he said, he didn't mean it. He was drunk.*

"No one said it outright, and it does not matter." She shrugged as she walked past him with the box. "I have always been a little self-conscious about my body."

"You have no need to be."

She gave a wry smile. "You're practically under obligation to say that, being that you are my friend."

He caught her elbow and halted her. Where his fingers touched, her bare flesh tingled. She lifted her gaze to meet his and the air locked in her throat. His eyes seemed a darker shade of blue and were intent upon her.

"I do not say that as your friend, Krystal."

Something about the way he said the words made it seem as though he was being more than just supportive.

"You don't?" She ran her tongue over her lips and his gaze

dropped to her mouth. Her pulse quickened and she blinked, trying to force away the sudden haze in her head.

What was happening? Why couldn't she form a straight thought? Wasn't she here to get Dillon on her side about her being allowed to date . . . Her mind came up blank.

Trevon! Oh gods. How could she not even remember his name, when not even an hour ago he consumed her every thought?

"No, Krystal, I do not." He reached up and touched one of her curls. "I say that because—"

"We should finish loading the ship." She cut him off before he could finish. She didn't want to hear the rest. Something deep in her gut knew it would change everything that had ever been simple between them.

Dillon's mouth tightened, but he sighed and released her. "Yes. I suppose we had better. I need to take this shipment out before the next hour."

Krystal's hands trembled as she went to grab another box. What had just passed between them? The undercurrents in the room had changed into something heavy and thick. She lifted the box and closed her eyes. She wanted it back, that light and friendly ambiance they usually maintained.

More minutes of silence passed as they moved boxes, and finally she couldn't take the quiet anymore.

"Do you remember when I was a child and used to spy on you and Ryder?" She brought up an old memory, something amusing to lighten the mood.

Sure enough Dillon's mouth curved upward. "Of course. You always were a naughty little child."

"I was not naughty, I was curious." She grinned. "Naughty would be Ryder when I spotted him throwing gillie fish eggs at his instructor's pod."

Dillon laughed. "Ah, you saw that, did you?"

"Yes. I was quite scandalized." She giggled. "And I remember this one time you had taken a girl to the lookout over Ilescot Crater, and I followed you."

"You did?" He raised an eyebrow, now looking very interested. "And what did you see?"

"What did I see? I saw—" She broke off as the image filled her head. She'd seen him kiss the girl, and then remove her shirt and kiss her breasts. His hand slipped under her dress.

A blush heated her cheeks. At the time she had thought it disgusting and good for a laugh, but now . . . now it did not seem so funny.

"I don't remember," she finished, her voice husky.

His eyes twinkled with amusement and something else she couldn't put her finger on. Her stomach felt a bit fluttery and she pressed her hand against it. Perhaps her lunch did not agree with her?

"Is everything loaded?" she asked to change the subject.

"Yes, I believe that is everything." He kept watching her and her stomach fluttered again.

Was she ill? She should hail a sky taxi and leave before it got much worse. Trevon. Oh gods. She'd completely forgotten to bring up Trevon. How would she ever sway Dillon to her side if she didn't make an effort?

"Dillon?"

He shut the cargo door. "Yes, Krys?"

She hesitated. "You want to see me happy, do you not?"

A beat passed before he answered. "More than anything. You know I do."

Her pulse skipped. Maybe he would help her. She took a deep breath and then plunged on. "Then surely you could not protest my relationship with Trevon. I am in love with him and he with me—"

122

"You haven't figured it out yet, have you, Krystal?" He turned to face her and all traces of amusement were gone, his jaw tight.

"Figured it out yet?" she repeated, frustration clawing in her gut now. "What? That you and my brother do not want me to go anywhere near him? Yes, that's fairly obvious."

"No." He closed the distance between them and slid an arm around her waist, jerking her hard against him. "That you belong to me."

# 10

The shock of his words penetrated, just before his mouth crushed down on hers. His lips were hard and demanding. She gasped and the movement allowed him to press his tongue inside her mouth.

He tasted faintly of mint as his tongue rubbed slowly against hers. The fluttering in her stomach doubled and seemed to burst, sending heat between her thighs.

Confusion warred in her head. The urge came on strong to pull him closer, to find out what would happen with the heat in her body if he kept kissing her.

*This is Dillon. Stop this at once.*

She lifted her hands between them to push him away. Her palms met solid muscle under the linen of his shirt and everything went hazy again. Why had she never noticed how solid his chest was?

His kiss gentled and his tongue curled around hers and he began to suck rhythmically. She groaned, feeling a familiar dampness between the folds of her pussy. Never had she grown this wet unless she was using her clitabrator, and yet here he was evoking the same response.

He backed her up until her ass bumped into the wall and then his hands moved down to her hips, squeezing them. His knee thrust between her legs and his thigh moved snug against her cunt.

He tore his mouth from hers and kissed the curve of her neck.

The room spun and she clung to his shirt to remain upright.

"I do not feel well." She gasped as his tongue flicked over a sensitive spot.

"How do you feel?" His lips closed over her skin and she gasped.

"Dizzy. Oh . . ." She closed her eyes. "Hot. Flushed."

"Do you, now?" His laugh was deep and husky, sending shivers through her body. "That is a good thing, kitten."

She arched against him and whispered, "How could it possibly be a good thing?"

His thigh rubbed hard against her sex and she gasped.

"You are wet for me." His voice was confident.

She struggled to focus again. There was something she should be remembering.

"For me, Krystal, not that rich-ass boy you fancy yourself in love with." His knee rubbed in circles against her. "You will end whatever you have with Trevon immediately."

*Trevon.* How had he slipped out of her thoughts? She stopped clutching at Dillon and shoved hard against his chest.

"Release me. At once, Dillon, release me." Her voice echoed shrill in the hangar.

His gaze narrowed, but fortunately he stepped away from her.

She pulled her dress back down, ignoring the ache between her thighs and the pounding of her heart.

"Have you lost your mind?" She shook her head. Why were her hands trembling so badly? "You are my friend, Dillon. Nothing more."

Even as the words left her mouth she heard the ring of false-hood in them. *Oh gods, this was wrong, so wrong!*

He was oddly calm as he turned and walked back toward the cargo ship. "We will be married before the month is over."

She gaped, aghast. "Married?"

"Yes. It would be in your best interest to inform Trevon that you no longer—"

"No. How *dare* you? Nobody tells me whom I will marry. *Nobody.* Ryder will probably have your ass strung up for what you have done—"

"Ryder is in agreement with me, kitten," he said quietly. "It has been decided, and it will be done."

Her jaw went slack and she blinked. Ryder knew about this and approved? The slow boil of anger worked its way up from her belly.

"I see." She clenched her teeth. Arranged marriages had never been in fashion on Belton and she would be damned if she became the first casualty. "I will head back to my quarters now."

Dillon stepped in front of her, blocking her path. "You will end things with Trevon. Is that understood?"

She would show them. Dillon and Ryder. But until she could figure out how . . . "Yes. I understand completely."

Surprise and suspicion flickered in his gaze. "I am not so sure I believe you."

*Smart man.* She forced what she hoped was a docile smile. "It is just unexpected, Dillon. Perhaps I need a little time for it to sink in."

He watched her for a moment longer and then gave a brief nod.

"I will be back tomorrow in the morning. Why don't we have lunch? I will come to get you around one."

Her smile felt brittle. "I'll put it on my calendar, Dillon."

He reached out, the pad of his thumb moving along her bottom lip. Another shiver ran through her body and the ache between her thighs increased.

"See that you do, Krystal."

She stepped back and walked around him. Tears of frustration pricked at her eyes. Gods help her, had the entire planet gone mad?

It was madness. Complete madness. Talia stared out the window of her room, a tiny smile curving her lips. She was in love with him.

Wrapping her arms around her waist, she rocked back on her heels and sighed. Denying it was futile at this point. She'd attempted to talk herself out of the fact for the last couple of hours to no avail. The sheer fact was that Ryder affected her in a way that no man before ever had; had touched her on the deepest level.

She dragged in a deep, shuddering breath and walked to the closet to find a dress to wear to dinner.

Tonight she would share all she knew of the Council's plans with Ryder. She should have done so earlier. Belton was not the evil planet that she had been led to believe. It was a wonderful, thriving planet; full of beauty and good people.

She pulled a black dress from the closet and held it against her body. It had no straps, would hug her breasts before falling in soft folds to the floor. Running her hands over the fabric, she sighed. What sort of material was this dress? Soft and slippery, so unlike the starched fabric she'd worn back on Zortou.

Was there time to bathe before Ryder came to see her?

Her door beeped and she glanced up in surprise. Was he early?

Krystal strode into the room, her face blotchy and stained with tears.

"Krystal?" Talia hurried forward, her brows drawn together. "Tell me, what has happened?"

Already she prepared for the worst. That the man Krystal was seeing had forced himself upon her, or maybe they'd already made love and perhaps she was now pregnant—

"I hate him." Krystal heaved an unsteady sigh and dashed her hand across her cheek.

Talia nibbled on her lip before asking, "Hate whom?"

"Dillon. Ryder. Men in general." Krystal flung herself down on the bed and said something else, but with her face buried in the pillow Talia could not understand her.

"I'm sorry, I did not hear you," she said hesitantly and went to sit next to the younger woman on the bed. "What is the matter?"

Krystal lifted her head and her lower lip trembled. She looked so incredibly young and vulnerable that Talia had to remind herself Krystal was just barely a woman.

"Apparently my brother and Dillon have decided that it is in *my* best interest to get married." Her lips curled downward and her eyes flashed. "To Dillon!"

Talia blinked and took a careful breath in. "To . . . Dillon? Are you sure? What makes you certain?"

Krystal snorted a most unladylike sound. "Besides Dillon telling me as much? His assault on my person was a fairly decent clue."

Talia's mouth tightened and a slow burn of anger built in her belly. "He assaulted you? Are you hurt? Did he . . ." *How to ask this delicately?* "Penetrate your barrier?"

"My barrier? Oh. My barrier." She flushed. "No. And I am not hurt. Though I felt sick during the entire episode."

"Sick? How so?" Had he beaten her? Restrained her? If so, she would have words with Ryder. As it was, she intended to.

"I was dizzy and flushed, and my heart was beating as if I'd gone running for hours." Krystal shook her head. "Truth be told it was very odd, Talia. Never before have I experienced such a feeling."

Talia drew her lip between her teeth. What Krystal described was very similar to what she experienced with Ryder. But Talia was not inexperienced enough to mistake that for illness.

She looked more closely at the other woman. She knew Krystal pleasured herself, but was she really so innocent that she did not recognize the physical affects the right man could have on one?

Talia bit her lip and then murmured, "Perhaps this match with Dillon is not such a bad thing?"

"Not such a bad thing?" Krystal's eyes widened. "You are on their side as well! You think Dillon to be a good match for me?"

"I do not know Dillon and could not be a judge of that, but . . ." How to explain Krystal's reaction to Dillon, when she herself was still a bit new to love and desire? "There must be a reason Ryder would have you marry him."

"I could not say. And Dillon is not a bad man; he is actually quite wonderful at times. But I love Trevon and that is the point." Krystal sulked and beat her fist against the pillow. "It is completely ridiculous that they are attempting to control my future."

Talia sighed. Krystal's conviction seemed genuine. It was entirely possible she *was* in love with Trevon. Still, doubt lingered heavy in her gut.

"What do you intend to do?"

Krystal rolled onto her back and stared at the ceiling. "I have not yet decided, but there are ideas in my head."

Talia lowered her gaze and twisted her hands together. "I am sorry, Krystal. And please, if you need to talk, I will always be willing to listen."

"Thank you." There was a small pause. "How are you fairing, Talia? Has my brother improved his treatment of you?"

Talia's body heated and she tucked a strand of hair behind her ear. "Ryder has improved his treatment significantly."

"Hmm." Krystal sat back up, looking unconvinced. "I still find what he's doing to you appalling."

The urge to confess her newly discovered feelings for Ryder came on strong. She bit her tongue to keep from telling Krystal everything. It was just too soon; there was still so much she needed to figure out for herself.

"I should leave. I have a massage scheduled in twenty minutes." Krystal stood up and yawned. "Thank you for listening to me."

"It is no burden." Talia hesitated, and then stood and embraced the girl. She surprised herself by making the gesture. Hugging was not something she'd partaken in . . . ever, really.

"Thank you," Krystal murmured again, and then drew back. "Oh! Talia, I nearly forgot. I came here with a purpose. More than to unload my troubles on you."

"Oh?" Talia watched as Krystal dug into the pouch around her neck and pulled out a small pink bag that fit into the palm of her hand. "Here, take it."

Talia lifted the bag, noting it was light but with some small object inside.

"What is it?" She raised an eyebrow as she pulled the strings to open it. She turned the bag upside down and emptied the contents into her hand. A small clamplike object fell out and then a thin, narrow object.

"It is a clitabrator." Krystal giggled. "I picked up one for you this morning at the Erogenous Zone shop. You did say you have never masturbated."

Talia could feel the blood rush to her cheeks. "Oh. But I—"

" 'But I' nothing. You will use it and enjoy yourself." Krystal pointed to the clamp part. "Fasten that onto your clitoris, and then that thin object is the remote that will control the speed."

"Okay . . ." Talia murmured weakly.

"I will come see you later this evening if I can." Krystal left the room as quickly as she'd arrived.

Talia waited for the door to slide shut, before glancing down at the object in her hand. Hmm. Did she dare to try it? She lifted the clamp and opened it around her pinkie. The pressure was light, not at all painful. She chewed her bottom lip before turning the remote onto the lowest speed.

A soft vibrating massage moved through her finger. *Oh gods.* Heat spread between her legs. What would it feel like upon her clit?

"I do not have time for this," she grumbled, curling her fingers around the object and walking to the bathing chamber. "I need to bathe and a clitabrator likely does not work under water."

She set the pleasure toy on the side of the tub and leaned over the bath. Yesterday she had partaken in the shower. The bathtub was still uncharted territory. After analyzing the various buttons, she pressed the one that she assumed would turn on the water. There was a gurgling sound, before the tub began to rise from the small hole in the middle.

Reaching a hand into the water, she winced. Gods, that was hot. She rocked back on her heels and eyed the tub thoughtfully. There was no reason to bathe in scalding water; the Council was not here to enforce that she do so.

She pressed another button and the sound of the water shifted. Dipping a finger back in, she noted it was growing cooler.

Talia stood and shrugged out of the robe she'd donned after coming back inside. She let it fall to the floor and it hit the tub on the way down, knocking the clitabrator into the water.

"Oh dear." She leaned down to retrieve it. Oh! It still vibrated, even under water.

A flush worked its way through her body and she shivered. *No, Talia, it would be wrong.*

She stepped into the tub and sat down in the lukewarm water, eyeing the pink clamp that rested on the side of the tub again. *No.*

Glancing at the buttons again, she located one that would likely hold the shampoo. When she pressed it, a small spout popped out from the side of the tub, and she placed her hand under it. Thick cream oozed out of the spout and into her hand. She lifted it to her nose and sniffed. Sweet and floral-like. Very pleasant.

She massaged the cream into her hair and over her body, attempting to do what Dane usually did for her. She glanced around for a pitcher, something to rinse her hair, but saw nothing.

With a sigh, she closed her eyes and leaned back in the tub, dipping her head under the water to rinse. She surfaced again and gasped in air, laughing at her own inexperience.

Her gaze landed on the clitabrator again. She had to try it. She just had to. As with the hot water, there was no reason she should not just experiment. She was not at home on Zortou, where she would meet the most severe punishment for pleasuring herself.

Talia lay back in the tub, letting her legs fall open. Her other hand rested on her stomach, and she bit her lip. Would she actually do this? It still seemed so forbidden, the thought of even moving her hand farther south sent cold waves down her spine.

*Do it. They cannot control you now.* She took a deep breath in and slid her hand downward. Slowly. Her fingers encountered the smooth mound of her pussy and her pulse jumped. Swallowing hard, she closed her eyes and moved her hand lower. Her pussy lips were silky and hot. She parted the labia and found her clit, brushing it quickly with her fingers. A hot tremor rocked her body.

Oh gods. To think she'd never been allowed to do this before. She stroked again, her long moan filling the bathroom.

What did the inside of her cunt feel like? During sex, Ryder would tell her how hot and wet she was.

She moved her fingers lower and pushed them inside her opening. Another groan resonated in the room, only this time it did not come from her.

Snapping her eyes open, she choked. "Ryder! I thought you were not arriving until later."

"I could not wait to see you again. Gods, princess, do not stop on my account," he murmured huskily from where he leaned against the doorway.

She bolted upright in the water. "I am so sorry. I should not have . . ." She lowered her gaze, shame burning her cheeks. "Whatever punishment you wish to implement I will accept."

"Punishment?" he asked quizzically, and she could hear his footsteps as he crossed the floor. "There is nothing wrong with pleasuring yourself, Talia."

She lifted her gaze, her fear dissipating. "You are not angry?"

"Not at all." He chuckled and picked up the tiny clamp on the side of the tub. "What do we have here?"

"Oh . . ." Her cheeks burned hotter. "It is . . . Oh gods, this is embarrassing."

"Do not be shy. I'm not unfamiliar with this toy." He grinned and fell to his knees beside the tub. "Here, allow me."

Bringing the clitabrator underwater, he opened it and then parted her pussy lips. His fingers rubbed her swollen flesh before he tugged on her clitoris and then placed the clamp upon it.

Heat speared through her body. The pressure of the clamp made her entire pussy tingle and he had yet to turn it on.

Ryder lifted the remote from the side of the tub and she bit her lip in anticipation. He stared at it for a moment and then stretched out his hand toward her.

"I want to watch you."

# 11

"You want to . . . watch me?" She took the remote from him, felt the weight and knew the power it held.

"Yes, Talia. By pleasuring yourself you will in turn be pleasing me."

"Well, why did you not just say so?" She smiled and turned the remote onto the lowest level.

He laughed at her startled gasp. "How does it feel?"

"Sssh, you cannot expect me to carry on a conversation at a time like this." She groaned and closed her eyes, focusing on the sensual vibrations against her clit. She turned the speed up another level. "It is paradise."

"Talia . . ." Ryder growled. "Use your other hand and touch your breast."

She obediently lifted her hand and cupped her breast.

"Pinch the nipple."

Her fingers closed around the tip and she squeezed, crying out as pleasure shot straight to her cunt.

"How do you feel?"

"Amazing. Oh gods." Her hips lifted in the water, sluicing

liquid over her belly. No matter how she moved her body, the explosive sensations followed. "Oh, I cannot take it."

"You can, love. Turn the remote up higher."

She obeyed, turning the lever to the highest level. The intensity of the vibrations tingled through her clit, making it even more sensitive and swollen.

Without his urging, she lifted her hands and cupped her other breast, kneading the firm flesh and pinching her stiff nipples.

"That's right. Let yourself go, Talia. I want to watch you come."

His thick words were the gentle push over the edge she needed.

"Mmm . . ." She threw her head back as lights exploded in her head. Her cunt clenched and her stomach quivered. She gasped in air, gripping the edge of the tub as the trembles racked her body.

She went limp and slid under the water, an inane smile on her face. Ryder's hands on her rib cage pulled her up and out of the tub.

"That good, hmm?" He unfastened the clamp, set it on the side of the tub, and then wrapped a fluffy robe around her body.

She slipped her arms into the sleeves, murmuring, "That good. And more so. I shall have to thank your sister for the clitabrator."

Ryder winced and shook his head. "I really wish you would not have shared that bit of information."

Talia wrapped her arms around his neck and dropped a kiss on his lips. "She's a grown woman, you know."

"Mmm. Who is?" He leaned down to kiss her again, but she pulled back.

"Krystal. She's not a child anymore."

"I realize that." Ryder's brows drew together and he straightened up. "What has brought this on?"

She sighed and stepped past him to lift the brush off the counter.

"Her unhappiness about being forced into a marriage with a man she does not love."

She could see the clenching of his jaw in the mirror as she brushed through the strands.

"I see. It seems my sister is taken with you enough to make such confessions."

"Perhaps." She met his gaze in the mirror. "Did you never consider her feelings for the other man?"

Ryder's lips curled downward. "Trust me, the other man is a pathetic man who would make her miserable. She is new to the world of men, and Dillon will take care of her well."

"But how do you know that? How do you know it is the right choice for her?"

"Because Dillon is in love with her."

Talia exhaled slowly and set down the brush. "I see. I do not believe she is aware of that."

"Well, he has not yet told her, that I know of. Still, he is a good match and whatever fondness Krystal holds for him will likely grow into love."

"That is quite a big assumption." She raised an eyebrow and walked back into her room. "On the other hand, I am not so sure I trust this other man's intentions."

"You are wise not to." He followed her into the bedchamber. "Are you hungry?"

"I am." She grabbed the dress she'd left on the bed and slipped it on.

Ryder groaned, his gaze sweeping over her. "You are beautiful. If I had not promised you dinner I would toss you onto the bed and make love to you for hours on end."

*Make love.* Never had being intimate been referred to as making love. Perhaps having sex, or even fucking her senseless, but never making love.

Her heart skipped and she took an unsteady breath in. She lowered her gaze, grabbing her sandals off the floor and slipping them on.

"You flatter me." She lifted her head and offered him a shy smile. "Where are we dining?"

"I've arranged an intimate ride on one of the observation pods. That way I can show you the city at night while we eat."

"Truly?" She clasped her hands together and smiled. "It sounds wonderful."

Ryder gave a brief smile, but behind his eyes she could sense the urgency and anticipation. He wanted her to talk tonight.

She stepped forward and placed her hand in his. "I am ready when you are."

He took her hand and led her out of her chamber. They made their way through the hall and to the outside of the building.

She sucked in the air greedily. Never could she imagine growing used to being outside of a building. It was too new, too surreal. The light from the two moons lit up the garden path, the sweet smell of flowers teased her nostrils.

It was absolutely too wonderful. A small giggle escaped her, and Ryder glanced down at her.

"And what are you thinking about, you naughty woman?"

"Just how amazing it is here." She glanced up at him from under her lashes. "You may have taken me against my will from Zortou, but in truth you have set me free."

Ryder halted her on the path and ran a finger down her cheek.

"I apologize again for the way I treated you initially, but I am glad you have found some peace here." His thumb rubbed across her mouth. "Have you considered what I said earlier at the lake?"

Talia's pulse sped up and she pressed her tongue against the back of her teeth. "Yes, I have."

"And?"

She looked up at him, her gaze searching his face, searching for a reason not to trust him. There was nothing but a somberness that made her heart twist.

"And I will tell you everything I know."

He exhaled and his shoulders relaxed. "Talia, you are my goddess."

"I am nothing of the sort," she murmured and wrapped her arms around his waist, laying her head against his chest. "I am a woman who realizes the wrong I have been led to believe. If I can prevent this attack in any way, I will do so."

"Thank you." His hand smoothed down her back and she closed her eyes. "We can discuss this over dinner."

She nodded against his chest and gripped him tighter.

Footsteps sounded along the path, and she drew back from him reluctantly.

"Good evening, sir."

Talia spun around, her stomach clenching as she recognized Ines's voice.

"Good evening," Ryder replied absently.

The woman nodded at them, but did not stop. Simply continued past them. How much had she seen? Heard? The idea that she might have fueled the fire of Ines's jealousy turned Talia's stomach sour.

"Come, the pod is awaiting our arrival."

She nodded and smoothed her dress down, then followed him along the trail.

They took a sky taxi to where the pod was stationed.

Ryder took her hand and helped her inside. It was sleek outside, with a lush interior. There was a half-circle table with a curved velvet bench inside, intimate and romantic.

"This is quite amazing," she breathed. "I have never been in something so striking."

"Not quite true, princess. You have been in a pod before, but it was much smaller. It is how we left Zortou." He offered a lopsided grin as he settled down next to her on the velvet bench.

She rolled her eyes, her pulse kicking up as his thigh rubbed against hers.

"Yes, but I do not remember that trip. I do believe you drugged me?" she teased and lifted an eyebrow.

He gave a low, sexy laugh and then kissed the side of her neck. "Yes, I did. Because you were hardly going to come willingly."

"Mmm. True." She closed her eyes and took a deep breath in. The smell of food tickled her nostrils and her stomach growled.

"Tour the city, please," he commanded and the doors slid shut, the pod lifting into the air. "Hungry?"

"Yes, actually I am."

Her stomach flipped as they kept rising higher into the air, faster every second. Soon they leveled off and began a slow steady movement. She leaned forward to see. The upper half of the pod was transparent, allowing her to view the city below.

She sighed, drinking in the sparkling lights from the buildings. "It is incredible at night."

He lifted a strand of hair and curled it around his finger. "I am glad you enjoy it."

"The way the moons' light reflects off the lake." She turned her gaze away from the view and smiled at him. "Is that the same lake we walked upon earlier?"

"Yes."

"Thank you for bringing me here, Ryder. It is beautiful."

His gaze softened and he leaned forward, his lips rubbing in a soft caress against hers. When he lifted his head, she was a bit lightheaded and it had nothing to do with the altitude they were at.

"I had dinner prepared and sent along for our ride."

He straightened and pressed a button on the panel of the pod. The wall opened and he pulled out a steaming tray with a lid on top and set it on the table before them.

"It smells wonderful."

"It is a wild yard bird sautéed in aliaberry wine, atop mushroom rice." Pressing another button, another panel opened and a bottle of wine sat inside with two glasses.

He pulled them out and then poured Talia and himself each a glass of the red wine.

"I have never had yard bird," she confessed. "We grew low on any form of meat on Zortou."

"Belton dealt with a similar issue at one point."

He lifted the lid from the tray and she eyed the colorful meal. There was enough for both of them to share off the same plate.

"During my last trip to Earth a few years back, I made some trades with a farmer for three dozen birds."

He cut a piece of the bird and lifted it to her lips. She opened her mouth and he slid the meat inside. The tartness of the berries mixed with the flavorful meat.

"Once back on Belton, we were able to breed the birds and had tripled our supply within a year." He used his thumb to trace a bit of sauce off the corner of her mouth.

She chewed the meat and then swallowed, her gaze locked on his.

"The Council stated that you were an oil tycoon from Earth. I am assuming that was not true?"

"Correct. It was an alias I used to gain entry into the Council's inner circle and to get to you."

"I see." She lowered her gaze and wrapped her hands around the glass of wine. "I was your target, then? At all times?"

"Of course you were, princess. You know this. I have admitted to as much."

"I know . . ." He had gone through such deceit and planning simply to get to her. The thought was mind boggling.

She lifted the glass to her lips and took a quick drink. The tart wine slid down her throat, sending warmth through her and into her belly.

"Do you like it?"

"Mmm." She took another sip. "It is wonderful."

Ryder watched her steadily, letting her enjoy the meal and her time in the pod. He wished this evening were only about giving her pleasure, showing her more of his planet and letting her explore. But it wasn't. There was so much more at stake.

His body grew rigid with tension and he glanced out the pod window. At this very moment the Council could be preparing to launch an attack on his home planet.

"Are you not going to eat?" Her sweet voice broke through his thoughts.

"I am not very hungry." Still, he lifted the extra fork and ate a few bites to appease her.

Talia had said that she would tell him everything, but what if she didn't? The doubts pricked deep. He should trust her now, he knew this. Yet still, all his training as a soldier indicated that he not be so free with his faith in others.

Perhaps it truly was her way of pacifying him to gain more time?

"What are you thinking, Ryder?" She set down the fork and took his hand. "Your face does not hide your thoughts well."

"Does it not?" he murmured vaguely. "And what does it say?"

"That you still do not trust me." She squeezed his hand. "And that is all right, I understand. In your eyes I will always be the enemy."

His gut clenched. "Talia—"

"No. Please, I do understand." She lowered her gaze. "I have given you nothing yet to earn that trust, but I swear now I am ready."

He blinked and his blood began to flow faster. "Are you?"

"Yes." She lifted her head and her solemn gaze met his. "Ask me anything you wish and I will answer if I can."

He took a quick breath in, before plunging into the questioning. "Is there an attack planned on Belton?"

She did not even hesitate. "Yes."

The confirmation made him nauseous, but he pressed on. "And when is the planned attack?"

"On the fifteenth of the upcoming month."

The fifteenth? That left them with just a few weeks to prepare.

"How many troops are being sent? What is their plan of action?"

"About eight hundred troops are to be deployed in a surprise attack at night." She took a deep breath. "While at the same time a skilled assassin will infiltrate the emperor's bedchamber."

A slow rage worked through his blood. Assassinate the emperor? He had not anticipated the lengths the Council had intended to go to. Zortou may have been a planet with few resources, but they were ruthless bastards. Fought dirty.

His gaze focused hard on Talia. She'd had this information in her head for the past two days and had originally refused to tell him? Gods. What if he had not uncovered this truth?

"I assume they have just a small amount of weaponry?" The fact that they'd been so desperate for his backing when he'd been posing as Alan Worthington led him to that conclusion.

"Well, not exactly. Though not nearly what they had hoped to obtain, they have more than one would expect. They had dealings with organized crime from the planet Vandri two years back."

He nodded, his mouth tightening. Belton had just spent an obscene amount of money on obtaining some of the best weapons on the market. Still, it would probably be best to relocate the emperor to an undisclosed safe house as soon as possible.

Talia continued to eat the dinner, giving him anxious glances every few seconds.

"What happens now?" she finally asked.

"We attack them before they can strike."

"Oh." Her fork, halfway to her mouth, stilled. "What will become of the people on Zortou?"

"Do not worry, they will be treated humanely." He narrowed his eyes. She had asked about the people of her planet, but was it possible she had meant the Council? Were her loyalties to them truly dispelled?

*She just confessed everything she knows, and still you doubt her.* His conscience protested his own doubts bitterly.

Ryder thrust a hand through his hair and glanced out over the city. He needed time to drink this in, to get the information out and ensure the emperor was kept safe.

Talia's hand moved to his thigh, sending his blood pounding through his veins. She glanced up at him from beneath her lashes, appearing hesitant. "I hope I have pleased you—"

"You have no need to please me, Talia. I am not the Council," he replied more tersely than intended. Her gaze flickered with hurt and he cursed himself for being such an ass. He gentled his tone. "Though I am grateful for the information you have shared with me."

She set down her fork and scooted closer, kissing the side of his neck.

"I would like to share more with you."

*You can't think with a hard-on.* He brushed her hand off his leg and turned away.

"You know that I would love to, princess. But I'm afraid we do not have time right now. Return to the launch pad," he directed the computer that controlled the pod.

"Oh."

Her single word hung in the hair, emphasizing her vulnerability and hurt.

"Talia, please understand, your words have added pressure to an already urgent situation."

"No, I quite understand." She looked out the side of the pod, her tone not validating her words. "It was a nice dinner while it lasted."

"I am sorry, princess." He touched her cheek as the pod descended. He'd hurt her again. Damn. But when this was all through he'd make it up to her.

"Say no more, Ryder. I am quite tired in reality. Perhaps tomorrow we could take another ride—"

"I cannot make promises yet, Talia. Things will be in a bit of chaos the next few days as the military prepares. But I will try to see you—"

"Of course. I am being selfish," she interrupted and sighed. "See me when you can. The safety of Belton is your first priority."

The pod landed, jolting them on the couch. Ryder, unable to resist, leaned forward and dropped a hard, thorough kiss on her mouth.

"You are amazing, Talia. Thank you again for what you have done tonight."

She raised her gaze, such trust in her eyes that his heart melted a bit.

"Thank you for tonight. You must do what needs to be done." She smiled. "I will miss you until we see each other again."

"And I you." He took her hand and helped her out of the pod. "I will see you back to your room."

They walked to the living quarters in silence. His thoughts swirled around the future and the danger they were all in. And though he was thankful for the information, part of him resented the fact that she had initially been so unwilling to share.

Hadn't she thought of her own safety while withholding the information? If she had not confessed, and Zortou attacked, she very well could have been killed.

Once outside her door he pressed the code to open it. She stepped inside and then turned around to face him.

"Good night, Ryder. I hope to see you tomorrow."

He knew it was not likely, but forced a brief smile and kissed her cheek.

"May your dreams be sweet, princess."

# 12

Ryder stepped out of the doorway and the doors shut behind him, locking automatically. He turned and strode back down the hall toward his office, typing in the code and then waiting as the door swung open. He headed straight to his desk, where he quickly summoned Dillon.

His friend arrived moments later, seeming unconcerned at the late-growing hour.

"Did you question her again tonight?" the other man asked, his brows drawn together.

"Yes." Ryder nodded his head and sighed. "The attack is planned for the fifteenth of the upcoming month. There will be an assassination attempt on the emperor as well. I need you to take your soldiers and relocate the emperor tonight. Place him in the safe house that was established for this type of scenario."

Dillon gave a quick nod. "Consider it done."

"That is our biggest concern at the moment. I will consider our plan of actions and we can discuss it in the morning."

"Very good." Dillon hesitated. "Are you willing to share the details that Natalia has given?"

*Natalia.* The name reminded him of her life with the Council. To him she would always be Talia. Or princess. His lips twisted with amusement.

He took a deep breath and then relayed the conversation he'd had with her to Dillon. His friend nodded throughout, his expression growing grimmer.

"Thank the gods we learned of this before they could attack."

"Yes." Ryder sighed. "My sentiments exactly."

"Thank you. I will get a team together to relocate the emperor at once. I will send confirmation once it has been done." Dillon nodded and then left the room.

Ryder watched the door slide shut and then went to sit behind his desk. There was another loose end that needed to be tied up, that he'd put off far too long.

"Computer on," he ordered and waited for his planner to come up.

Talia paced her room, her stomach fluttering with nerves. Right now Ryder was probably arranging the attack on her home planet.

The possibility of what would happen to her if Belton did not win and the Council reclaimed her sent a shudder through her.

"We will win," she murmured to herself.

Her mouth twitched. Funny how she now considered herself a citizen of Belton.

The door beeped and she swung around, startled. Had he returned so soon?

Ines walked through the door and Talia's eyes widened, her stomach twisting. Gods. She did not want to deal with this woman right now.

"What do you need, Ines?" she asked warily.

"What do I need?" Ines sneered. "It does not matter what I need. I may visit you at any point I wish; you are the prisoner, need I remind you."

Talia nibbled on her lower lip and folded her arms across her chest. Why not just be direct? Ines had seen the moment between her and Ryder out in the gardens.

"I guess you have realized that things have changed between Ryder and myself."

"Changed?" Ines lifted an eyebrow. "How so? Do you fancy that since you've spread your legs for him he is now in love with you?"

Talia's teeth sank deeper into her bottom lip, until she tasted blood.

"Possibly," she answered, though she knew her tone lacked the conviction the response warranted.

Ines laughed and strolled around the room, picking up objects and then setting them back down.

"For all your experience as a whore, you sure are naïve. If he loves and trusts you, then why are you still locked behind the walls of this room? Why do you not reside in his quarters, in his bed?"

Talia opened her mouth to argue, but no answer came to her. The question was valid. After everything that had passed between them today and all the information she'd given him, still he gave her no freedom.

"You are still the enemy, Talia. A detainee upon our planet. He will never trust you." Ines stared hard at her. "You would be a fool to believe that Ryder holds any emotion besides lust for you. He takes lovers on a regular basis and grows bored with them even quicker."

Talia could feel the blood draining from her face. She knew they were just spiteful words from the other woman, but the possibility they were true cut deep.

"That's right. You'd best realize this now, princess." Ines sneered the nickname Ryder had given her. "For you will not be in his thoughts for long. Just consider yourself a prisoner that he finds amusement in fucking. Once he is through . . ." She shrugged and a malicious smile crept over her face. "Perhaps he will send you on to entertain the soldiers in training."

Talia raised a trembling hand to her mouth, completely incapacitated by Ines's cruel verbal attack. The other woman gave a short laugh and the sound reverberated in her head.

She would not give Ines the pleasure of cowering her. Lifting her head, she forced a smile.

"I feel sorry for you, Ines." She turned away to look out the window, so Ines wouldn't see the trembling in her hands. "You must really love him to come in here and throw such desperate, weightless words at me."

She heard the strangled gasp from the other woman. "You foolish bitch. Just you wait, you'll see."

A beeping sound came from the other woman and Talia listened as she shuffled something.

"Ah, not a surprise, but it is Ryder paging me. Perhaps you left him unfulfilled, Natalia. Have a good night."

Her footsteps echoed in the room and then Talia heard the door open and shut. A moment later it was once again silent. Thank the gods.

Ines's brutal words still rang in Talia's ear. She clutched her stomach, feeling as though she might be sick. Was it possible Ines was right?

Talia thought of the pod ride earlier in the evening, and how Ryder's demeanor toward her had changed the moment she'd disclosed the information about the Council's plans.

*He seduced you to get the information.* Her hands balled into fists, and bile rose into her throat. *You suspected that was his motive from the beginning.*

Oh gods. She closed her eyes as a shudder racked her body. When threatening her had not worked, he'd switched tactics, gaining her trust and weakening her resolve. He'd ensured that not only her loyalty belonged to him, but her heart as well.

She spun around and ran toward the door.

"Be unlocked," she yelled at it. "Damn it, be unlocked!"

Punching at the button to open it, it did not move.

She sank down to her knees, tears spilling down her cheeks. She was still a prisoner and likely always would be. Ryder did not love her—she was a means to an end.

She curled her knees up to her chest and rolled onto her side, allowing the tears to flow down her cheeks, the sobs to rack her body. Years of pain, depression, and frustration emptied out with all the tears.

When she couldn't cry anymore, she gasped in sweet breaths of air to clear her senses. Her stomach burned and her pulse kicked up.

Tired. She was so tired of being used by men for one reason or another. Whether it be for her body or the information in her head. And in Ryder's case, both.

Pulling herself off the floor, she walked to the bed and sank down. There was nothing left to do. Closing her eyes she dragged in an unsteady breath. Nothing more to do except wait to see what the gods had in store for her.

Ryder took a sip of water, hoping it would ease the turbulence in his stomach. This would not be a pleasure. The trick would be to keep the conversation neutral, not allow her to think it was anything personal.

A knock sounded on his door. Finally. He had summoned her nearly half an hour ago. He pressed the button on his desk that would release the lock.

Ines strode in and the unease in his stomach intensified. She was not expecting what he had in store. Not the way she was dressed. The dress revealed all her flesh, her nipples almost vulgar in their blatant showing beneath the thin fabric. He jerked his gaze back up, refusing to drop his gaze lower than her face, knowing he would only be staring at the details of her crotch. And she would get far too much enjoyment out of that.

Ines crossed the room, her smile sultry and her eyes narrowed with arousal.

He cleared his throat. "Ines—"

"I knew you would summon me." Her laugh was husky.

"We must speak." If he did not stop her soon, it would only add to the discomfort.

"Yes. We must. One woman, especially a submissive little whore, could never satisfy you. I know what you—"

"Ines. You are being transferred to a different unit." Heat crept up his neck and his jaw went rigid. Damn. He had meant to make the news sound like a promotion, portray it as a good thing. But the moment she called Talia a whore, he had spat it out in vengeance.

And she knew it. Her eyes widened and her lips parted. She stared at him for a few seconds, and then there was the audible click of her teeth snapping together.

"You're transferring me?" Her voice was low and unsteady.

*Fuck. Try and get this under control.* He drew in a deep breath. "You are being promoted."

"A promotion?" She shook her head, her lips tightened. "How dare you do this to me."

"You will have an increase in salary—"

"I do not need any more fucking money. I want—"

"The position starts immediately." Walking around to his desk he picked up her transfer papers.

She knocked them out of his hand, her body shaking. "Do you transfer every woman after you fuck them?"

"Ines, do not make this harder than it needs to be," he murmured, pushing back his own temper. "This is truly a great opportunity for you."

"Is it?" Her nostrils flared and she spun around and headed for the door. "Well, guess what? I can create my own opportunities, Ryder."

The door slid shut behind her and he sighed, setting the papers on the desk. That had not gone well. Not well at all.

Franklin paced the floor of the Council's chambers, his teeth clenched as he knocked a metal paperweight off the desk.

She'd been gone for three days. Three days they'd tried to track the trail of Alan Worthington, only to find out the man did not exist.

*He did not exist!*

"Franklin, please be seated," Ramirez grumbled, obviously ill at ease. "You are making the situation all that much worse."

For three days they'd all gone without sexual release. Tempers were raw and patience was nonexistent. The fact that they'd all been so easily susceptible to the deceit of the alleged oil tycoon made matters worse.

Franklin moved to the window, pressing the button that lifted the shades. The outside world was as toxic and dismal as ever. The streets were bare with all the citizens required back inside after certain hours of the day.

Gods. After the attack on Belton, he would arrange a discreet termination of Ramirez and Victor—made to look like an accident, of course. Then, the chances of repeating such a ridiculous blunder would be nonexistent. Only idiots made such mistakes. He did not consider himself to be one.

All would be well soon, and if he could somehow locate Natalia, everything would be perfect.

"Are we still planning to attack Belton at that time?" Ramirez asked, breaking the silence.

"We are," Victor agreed. "The plans have been laid; the troops are trained and ready to be deployed."

"And what of—"

The intercom buzzed, cutting off Franklin's response.

Victor crossed the room and pressed the speaker button. "Yes?"

"Thank you, sir." The guard cleared his throat. "Ten minutes ago we apprehended a woman who was attempting to break into headquarters."

Franklin's brows drew together as all glanced at each other.

"A Rosabelle was attempting to break in?"

"She is not a Rosabelle, sir. She is not from Zortou. Shall I bring her in?"

*A woman not from Zortou? Interesting.* Franklin gave his nod of approval at Victor and Ramirez.

"Yes, escort her in." Victor stepped away from the intercom. "This should be interesting."

Franklin's eyes narrowed as he stared at the closed door.

All were aware that other planets did not suffer the same fate of a dwindling supply of women as Zortou did. At one point they'd attempted to abduct women from other planets, and had suffered a terrible retribution for the effort.

It had taken years to recover from the attack and was the main reason their atmosphere was toxic now.

The doors hissed open and the guard strode in, gripping the arm of an unfamiliar woman. She was taller than most women on Zortou, with brown hair and brown eyes. Her breasts were not very large, her hips narrow; overall she was rather unremarkable. Franklin was no fool, though. To all three of the men in this room, she represented the possibility of getting fucked.

Even *his* cock stirred to life as she was brought to the center of the room.

"Identify yourself," Franklin murmured quietly.

The woman said nothing, just ran her gaze brazenly over all three of them.

*Hmm.* Franklin tilted his head and stroked his thumb over his chin. Interesting. Obviously she knew nothing about how women were to behave on Zortou. She would not have dared meet their gaze with such disrespect, but would have kept hers lowered as she showed her submissiveness.

And the way she was dressed? Her dress was far too revealing. It came above her knees and hung from thin straps at her shoulders. The fabric was a pale white and her dark nipples showed through. He lowered his gaze. The shadow of black curls was visible between her thighs.

His mouth curled downward. How barbaric. Women on Zortou were to have hairless cunts.

"You realize you are gaining our hostilities by not answering," Ramirez said sharply. "Identify yourself."

The woman pulled her arm free from the guard and offered a disdainful smile.

"My name is Ines. I am a soldier on the planet of Belton."

Franklin's fists clenched and he took a slow breath in. Very interesting. A woman soldier from the planet they were about to attack, standing here in the Council's headquarters.

Victor and Ramirez stood up from their desk, the apprehension on their faces obvious as they approached her.

"What brings you to our planet, Ines?" Victor rasped.

She sauntered around the room, her hips swinging. Franklin's cock hardened further and his gaze dropped to the curve of her ass.

"It depends, gentlemen. I believe I may have some information that could benefit you."

Did she know about the planned attack? No. That would make little sense. If Belton suspected that their planet was in danger, they would not have sent a woman to make negotiations.

Tired of her vague responses, Franklin crossed the room and gripped her arm.

"And what information is that, madam?"

Her eyebrow lifted and her lips twitched. "You're quite aggressive with a woman who has no obligation to tell you anything."

Franklin gave a soft laugh. "You have yet to see my aggression. And I would be real careful, madam, or you might find out just what kind of obligations women hold on our planet."

"Easy now," Victor broke in. "We are not known for our lack of manners."

Franklin glanced at the other two men. Despite Victor's words of peace, both men leered at Ines as if she were the only food on a planet of starving men.

Ines glanced down at her arm and then back at Franklin.

"You have a strong grip, Mr. Councilman. I do love a powerful man."

Franklin growled and tightened his grip. "Share your information now or you—"

"Relax." She placed her finger against his mouth and smiled. "I will talk."

Some of the tension eased from Franklin's shoulders. "Why are you here?"

"To inform you that at this very moment Belton is making plans for a preemptive strike on Zortou."

"*Fuck!*" Victor's curse echoed in the chambers. "How did they find out?"

Franklin watched the amusement flicker across the woman's face. She was enjoying this. The power she wielded over them at this moment. Would she be so amused when they took turns fucking her shortly?

"You really should be careful of whom you let infiltrate the Council's walls," she murmured and looked directly up at Franklin.

"Whom do you refer to?" Though he asked the question, his blood began to pump faster. He knew who it would be before she even answered. It all added up now.

"Did it never occur to you not to trust him? Why would an oil tycoon want to invest an extraordinary amount of money for something that benefits him in no way?"

"Alan Worthington?" Ramirez choked. "Gods. He is not an oil tycoon, is he?"

"No, sir, he is not." She gave Ramirez a look that clearly said she thought him an idiot. "Nor is his name Alan Worthington. It is Ryder Jacobs. He is a colonel in the Belton planetary army."

"It is far worse than we thought," Ramirez muttered.

"Indeed it is." She smirked and glanced away. "Your Rosabelle seems quite fond of Belton, though."

"Natalia?" Ramirez demanded. "She is on Belton?"

*Of course she was.* Franklin's jaw clenched. Already he could see her in his mind; her voluptuous curves, those pale blue eyes that would flicker with fear any time he spent time alone with her.

His cock strained against his trousers, his erection full and aching now.

"Yes, she is on Belton." Her glance turned back to Franklin, as if she knew his weakness for Natalia. "And she is quite enjoying her time in Ryder's bed."

White rage filled his head, made everything hazy. His grip on her arm became crushing, and Ines cried out, falling to the ground.

159

"Gods, Franklin, have you gone mad?" Victor strode across the room and removed Ines from his grasp. "You nearly broke her arm." He stroked her arm, the tips of his fingers brushing her breast.

"And I do not apologize for it," he muttered and strode to the window, staring outside without seeing.

"Are you all right, my dear?" Victor asked, his voice soothing.

Franklin scowled and ignored any response she may have made. Natalia was enjoying another man's touch? The whore would pay. Gods, if it was the last thing he did, he would see to it that she suffered.

"Why have you come here today?" Ramirez rasped. "Freely giving us information that could cost you your life."

Franklin turned to look at her again, curious as well to hear her response. Gods, he hated the bitch. The malicious pleasure in those dull brown eyes.

"I have come here today to form an alliance," she admitted. "Between myself and your planet."

"Why?" Franklin asked sharply. "I trust no one anymore, especially a woman from Belton. You will likely not leave this planet alive."

"I will leave alive." Her confidence was bold. "And you will freely let me go."

"We shall see about that."

"The reason I have brought this information is quite simple." She moved to the couch in the center and sat down. Her dress moved up past her knees, showing a good expanse of her thighs. "I hate Ryder Jacobs. I want him dead."

Franklin tilted his head. The woman might hate him now, but it was quite obvious she had at one time loved him. Could it be so simple? Was she simply a woman scorned bent upon revenge?

160

"There must be more to it. Surely you would not risk your life over the matter of hating someone," Victor murmured, sitting down next to her on the couch and laying a hand on her thigh.

She did not remove Victor's hand, Franklin noted, and pursed his lips. If anything, the woman seemed excited that she was being paid attention to in a sexual manner.

He watched as she parted her legs just slightly. He brought his gaze up to her face and found her watching him.

"You want him dead?" Victor's hand curved between her thighs, sliding up slowly. "We have that in common, my dear. I would prefer to see him die quite painfully for what he has done to us."

"He took your Rosabelle." She leaned farther back on the couch, opening her thighs wider; her mocking eyes still locked on Franklin. "And has been making quick use of her abilities as a whore."

Victor's hand disappeared underneath her dress and from the way Ines inhaled sharply, Franklin had no doubt Victor was rubbing her pussy.

"Is that why you have come here today?" Franklin stepped toward the middle of the room. His cock throbbed beneath his pants. "To offer yourself as our replacement whore?"

# 13

Ines held his gaze, her breathing grew heavier. "I am no whore, but if this proves my newfound loyalty to you, then so be it."

"It certainly could not hurt to prove your loyalty." Victor's voice grew hoarse as he leaned forward, his fingers disappearing deep between her legs. "You certainly are quite wet, dear."

"Take off her dress." Ramirez's voice drifted from the corner, where he stood stroking himself through his trousers. "I want to see her naked and submissive."

Franklin closed the last few steps between them and gripped the neckline of her dress between two hands. With a grunt, he ripped the fabric straight down the middle. The dress fell to the sides, exposing her breasts and the mass of curls between her legs.

"I think I shall enjoy breaking you in, Ines." Victor groaned and leaned down to fasten his mouth around her nipple. Her moan echoed in the room.

Breaking her in? Franklin's mouth twisted with disdain. Just breaking her would be fun. He unfastened the fly of his pants and pulled his cock free.

Her eyes, glazed with pleasure, widened. He leaned over her, and before she could protest, grabbed her by the hair and pulled her mouth down onto his cock.

"Suck me," he ordered, thrusting deep into her mouth and touching the back of her throat.

She made a small shocked sound, but he ignored it and focused on the sweetness of having a woman's mouth on his cock again. It wasn't Natalia, but if he closed his eyes he could imagine it was. A mouth was a mouth, and a hole was a hole.

He thrust deeper, his fingers tightening in her hair. The woman loved it; her excited little moans proved it.

"Ramirez, you must enjoy our guest," Victor called out as he slid down Ines's body, kneeling on the floor in front of her and pushing her knees apart.

Ramirez approached slowly and sat down on the couch, both hands reaching out to fondle her breasts.

"I am not used to a woman's pelt. We do not allow a Rosabelle to have any hair on her body. But your pelt is soft," Victor murmured, pulling on the curls between Ines's legs. "Let us see how a cunt from Belton tastes, shall we?"

Franklin thrust his cock in and out, fucking Ines's mouth while watching as Victor's tongue lapped at her engorged pussy lips.

"Mmm." Victor made a noise of approval and ground his face into her sex, his tongue disappearing inside her.

Ramirez unfastened his trousers and pulled his cock free. Grabbing her hand, he forced Ines to stroke it.

She did not seem to mind anything that was happening to her. She seemed to respond to Victor's mouth on her cunt, gasping and sighing. Her hand pumped up and down Ramirez's shaft, while she sucked and licked on Franklin's cock.

"Let us all fuck her at once. I am sure she will be accommodating." Franklin suggested, his lips curling, watching her eyes widen.

Victor sighed and stood up. "All right, but I would like to continue with the tasting of her cunt at a later time."

Franklin pulled his cock free from her mouth, gripping it and running it down her cheek.

"Ramirez, you lie down on the couch and have her sit atop you and ride you that way."

Ramirez hurriedly lay down and Ines hesitated briefly before climbing on to his lap. She sank down onto his cock and gasped.

"Ines, place your hands on the arm of the couch and lean forward," Franklin ordered.

She obeyed, gripping the couch and leaning forward so her ass lifted higher into the air.

Franklin knelt behind her on the couch, watching as Ramirez's cock moved in and out of her hole, slick and shiny with her juices.

He glanced at Victor and nodded. "She will take you with her mouth."

Victor moved to stand beside the couch, pulling his cock free. Ines groaned and leaned over a bit, opening her mouth and taking him deep.

"I want her ass," Franklin muttered and ran his hand over one soft cheek. He moved his fingers over the crack and then pushed two fingers inside her.

She whimpered, sounding more afraid this time as her muscles clenched around his digits. He added another finger and smiled, beginning to stroke his cock again. He was going to enjoy this.

The few times he had fucked a woman in the ass, he had always been gentleman enough to use spit as a lubricant. But fucking this bitch dry would be a pleasure—for him at least, not likely for her.

He worked his fingers in and out of her for another minute before removing them. Gripping his cock, he moved it over the tiny hole.

He pressed forward, spurred on by her increased moans. He slid past the first ring in her ass. Without lubrication she was tight and hot.

"Do you like having your ass fucked, whore?" He jerked on her hair and pushed in past the second ring.

She did not answer, just whimpered and kept rocking back and forth on Ramirez's cock.

"Gods," Ramirez sat up a bit to flick his tongue over her nipple. "She must like it. Her cunt has grown wetter."

*Interesting. The woman enjoyed pain. Well, then.* Franklin gripped her hips and plunged to the hilt. Her loud cry was muffled around Victor's cock.

Franklin moved slow at first. He closed his eyes as he imagined it was Natalia he was fucking. Unlike this whore, Natalia hated having her ass fucked. Those pretty blue eyes would fill with tears, even as she would lift her ass toward him in submission.

He picked up the pace, fucking her harder and feeling the pressure of Ramirez's cock through the thin wall.

This was not something they had ever done. Had not thought Natalia emotionally or physically strong enough to handle it.

But Ines was a sturdier woman, thicker and obviously used to an aggressive lover.

His fingers dug into her ass cheeks and he moved harder inside her. She cried out and he glanced up to see her head thrown back, Victor's cock momentarily set free as she appeared to have an orgasm.

Victor made a grunt of protest and grabbed her head, forcing her attention back to his cock.

Ramirez groaned long and loud, then went still, obviously having spent his load himself.

Victor came a moment later with a cry. Franklin watched Ines's throat work as she swallowed his cum.

Grinding his teeth together, his sac tightening, Franklin came a second later inside her. Again and again, until his cock was drained and his mind empty.

He pulled out of her and stood, pulling up his trousers.

"Have I proved that I am loyal?" Ines asked, sprawled out on the couch, a contented smile on her face.

"No." Franklin tucked his cock back inside his pants and fastened them. "You have proved you will let yourself be fucked by three men."

He smiled, enjoying the flash of shock that raced across her face.

"Franklin," Victor warned and cleared his throat. "Though we are more inclined to trust you now, dear. We will arrange a room for you to stay in—"

"I cannot stay." She shook her head and stood up. "It would draw suspicion from the army on Belton. We must decide a course of action tonight and then I will leave."

"What course of action did you have in mind?" Ramirez turned away from the counter where he was pouring himself some water.

"I will give you the details of when they are planning their preemptive attack. I will give you any information you desire about our military and our resources."

"And the emperor?"

"The emperor?" she raised an eyebrow and turned her gaze to each of them. "Do you intend to kill him?"

"Yes." Franklin saw no reason to lie. Besides, he still was not convinced she would leave this building alive tonight.

"I see." She seemed to consider it for a moment and then shrugged. "It does not matter. He was too soft in my opinion anyway."

"And what do you want in return from us?" Victor asked.

Franklin narrowed his eyes. This conversation was reminiscent of the one they'd had with Alan Worthington. But unlike Alan Worthington, his gut was beginning to trust Ines. She was dirty and vengeful, and in a way not so unlike himself.

"I want to be the envy of every woman in the universe. I want to be the lover of the most influential men." She toyed with a strand of hair, moving her gaze around the room again. "The lover to the Governing Council of Zortou."

"We have a Rosabelle, we do not need another," Franklin said harshly.

"You will not want her now. That I can promise you. And I do believe she would rather die than come back to you." Her mouth twisted. "Though, having experienced you three, I think she is a bit of a fool."

Ramirez and Victor laughed, beaming like schoolboys. Franklin shook his head in disgust. *How easily they could be swayed by a woman willing to play their whore.*

Yes. He would agree to her terms, but she would not live long enough to enjoy them. She would be terminated along with the other two men when the time came.

"We will discuss this further tonight." Franklin pursed his lips. "For now, I will escort her to Dane so that he may bathe her."

Victor and Ramirez, obviously relaxed and satisfied with the turn of events, both nodded and went back to their desks.

"Come, Ines. Let us walk together." Franklin led her out the door of the chambers. "How long has Natalia known this colonel from Belton?"

Her gaze turned knowing and her mouth tightened. "So the whore has you enchanted as well, does she?"

"Your lack of respect will gain you painful punishments, Ines," he warned, irritation pricking him again. "Submission is a requirement when you are in our presence."

"Mmm." She gave a small laugh. "I have no problem being submissive, sir. And as you may have noticed, I also enjoy pain." She paused. "Though I would be hesitant to think your Rosabelle did."

"She did not," he muttered. "Though she will receive a fair amount upon our reunion."

Ines stopped and turned to face him. "If I arrange a meeting between you both it will be your last. For me to agree to this deal, I must be the only woman for the Council."

Franklin smiled without amusement. The lie flowed easily from his lips. "Of course. I just wish my face to be the last thing she sees before her death."

Ines watched him a second longer and then nodded. "It will be done."

"Good. Come, we must not linger. I will introduce you to Dane for your bathing."

# 14

Talia rolled over onto her side and groaned. It was no use. Even though it was far past the midnight hour, she could not sleep. She sat up in bed and rubbed a hand across her eyes. They were swollen and stung slightly from the constant state of tears.

Her mind could not let it go, what had happened at dinner with Ryder. How quickly he had changed the moment she'd given him the information.

Restless now, she swung her legs out of bed and went to use the bathroom and rinse her face. When she glanced up into the mirror, her face was pale. Gods, she looked terrible.

*You are still the enemy. He will never trust you.* Ines's vindictive words ran through her head again, refreshing her nausea. *You would be a fool to believe that Ryder holds any emotion besides lust for you.*

Oh gods. How would she last here? There was no way she could survive another moment of Ryder's touch, knowing she was nothing but the prisoner whore in his mind.

A series of beeps signaled someone was entering her chamber. Talia jerked her head toward the door of the bathroom. Who was out there?

She took a steadying breath and stepped back into her room. Krystal stood in the doorway, pale and nervous-looking.

"Krystal? What is the matter? Do you realize what hour it is?"

Krystal crossed the room, pressing a finger to her mouth. "Shhh. Please, you must speak quietly."

"All right." Talia lowered her voice and took her friend's hands. "What is the matter?"

"I am leaving tonight." Krystal's gaze was determined. "I intend to marry Trevon."

"Marry him?" Talia's stomach twisted. Oh gods. Ryder would lose his mind if he were to find out.

"Yes. I am meeting him shortly. We are running away to a nearby county to exchange vows."

"I see." Talia swallowed hard and lowered her gaze, feeling the sting of tears. She would be losing the only friend she had on this planet. "And you have come to say good-bye?"

"No."

Talia looked up, her brows drawing together. "I do not understand—"

"I have come to set you free, Talia," Krystal said firmly and squeezed her hands. "I will not leave you here tonight. I will bring you with me."

Talia's heart skipped a beat and then began a steady thud. "Set me free?"

"Yes. Will you come with me tonight?"

"Krystal . . . I don't know." Talia licked her lips. The thought of leaving Ryder tore at her heart, but the idea of being his prisoner for one more day nearly broke her.

"What don't you know? I cannot condone the way Ryder has treated you, Talia." Krystal shook her head. "It is deplorable. You should never have been brought here as prisoner in the first place."

"No, please. He had his reasons." Talia grimaced. Why did she still defend him? Though part of her knew he'd had no choice. She sighed. "If he had not taken me, your planet would still be ignorant to the attack planned."

"Perhaps, but it does not excuse his treatment of you." Krystal leaned forward. "Come with me, Talia. I will see that you are put on a pod back to Zortou—"

"No." Bile rose in her throat and her knees felt suddenly weak. "I will not return. I would prefer you to send me to another planet . . . somewhere where I can have choices."

"Gods, I am a fool." Krystal winced. "I had forgotten the manner in which you were treated. Of course, I will send you to a neighboring planet for sanctuary."

"Thank you." Talia bit her lip. This was insane, was it not? Did Krystal realize what she was risking? "Are you sure about this? The trouble you would be creating is not worth—"

"Only if we get caught. And I do not intend for that to happen. Come." Krystal stood up and began grabbing articles of clothing from the closet. "You must come with me, Talia. It would not be right for me to leave without you."

Talia didn't reply and stared at her hands. What reason did she have to stay?

"Talia?" Krystal whispered again, more urgently now. "Will you come with me? Please?"

Talia gave a slow nod. If anything, she would go to keep an eye on Krystal. She was not so sure Krystal's faith in Trevon was well placed.

"Yes. I will come with you."

"Good. I knew you would. We are doing the right thing, Talia." Krystal began to stuff Talia's clothes into a bag and then slipped the straps over her shoulders.

"I would advise you to put on your warmest dress and a jacket. There is a chill in the night."

Talia took a deep breath and then slipped off the bed, forcing her feet to move. She dug through the closet until she located a warm dress and pulled it on. After slipping into shoes, she grabbed a heavy jacket and pulled it on over the dress.

"I think that is everything you shall need. Are you ready?" Krystal asked.

Talia bit her lip and glanced around the room one last time. A myriad of emotions swept through her. Regret. Sadness. Resignation.

A bittersweet smile twisted her mouth. She had come to Belton a prisoner; now she was fleeing. Yet her heart would always be Ryder's captive.

She gave a slow nod. "I am ready. Let us go."

"Good. Please, keep as quiet as possible. We will get out of here, I promise, but it may not be easy."

Talia groaned. *Of course she tells me this after I have agreed.*

They left the room and moved quietly down the hall. Each step they took made Talia's heart pound harder. They moved past Ryder's office and she clenched her teeth, barely breathing. Surely he would open the door and spot them immediately.

They passed by without any such incident happening, and some of the tension eased from her muscles.

She waited at the glass door as Krystal typed in the code. A moment later the door slid open and they hurried outside.

Out on the garden path Talia allowed herself to relax, breathing in the crisp night air. She followed alongside Krystal, keeping quiet until they were a good distance from the building.

Where were they going first? "Where are we headed now, Krystal? To the pod or to meet your lover?"

"We must meet up with Trevon first, and then I will ask him to take us to a pod." She paused. "And we are not lovers yet, but I intend to remedy that soon enough."

Talia's stomach twisted and she gave a sharp glance at Krystal. How could she reason with the younger woman when she was so determined? So disillusioned?

She suspected Trevon was an utter louse; it was her gut instinct that had little to do with Ryder's side of the conversation.

"Where do you intend to marry him?" Talia asked, glancing at her. "Will you stay on Belton?"

"I know nothing for sure." Krystal nibbled on her bottom lip. "Trevon has promised that everything is planned for this evening."

"Does he know that I will be joining you?"

"No, I did not have the opportunity to inform him, but it will be no bother. I promise."

The bad feeling in her gut increased and she swallowed. Gods, maybe this hadn't been a good idea. "Are you sure about this, Krystal?"

"Quite sure." Her tone seemed a little too confident, though.

They walked for a while, finally turning onto a path that led toward some kind of orchard.

The light from the moons faded the deeper they moved into the trees. The sounds of the night grew crisper, the loudest being the strange humming noises coming from unseen insects or bugs.

"He should be here," Krystal murmured, twisting her hands. "He promised—"

"There you are, baby."

Talia and Krystal both yelped and spun around.

"Trevon. I was starting to get worried," Krystal's words were rushed. "I began to think you might not come."

175

Trevon laughed. "Not a chance."

Talia's gaze narrowed on the man strolling down the trail, a bottle of what looked like ale in his hand.

He wasn't an overly large man, smaller than Ryder, but definitely taller than her or Krystal. He was almost pretty with white blond hair that fell across one of his eyes, a round face, and wide eyes.

His obvious intoxication and the blatant lust in his gaze sent an uneasy shiver down Talia's spine. His glance shifted and his eyes locked on Talia.

"Did you bring a friend?" His grin widened as he looked her up and down. "Baby, you sure know what I like. We sure are going to have a good time tonight."

Talia felt the blood drain from her face. Would Krystal have done such a thing? Brought her out here for . . . She knew the answer even as the question passed through her head.

No. Besides, Krystal's pinched expression showed she was just as startled by his comments. Annoyance flashed through her and she crossed her arms across her chest, hoping the contempt she felt for him was obvious in her expression.

"Trevon, do not be silly. Talia is not a gift for you." Krystal's tone indicated her irritation. "She is a prisoner I have set free. I was hoping you could direct me to a pod that might—"

"A prisoner?" He laughed and turned his gaze back to Krystal. "All the better then, baby. She has no choice than to do our bidding."

He stepped toward Krystal and pulled her hard against him, his mouth lowering toward her. She turned her head and his lips connected with her cheek.

*Good girl, Krystal.* Talia took a deep breath, her fists clenched at her side.

"You reek of alcohol. You promised you would not drink

again." Krystal's voice shook. "And where is your bag, Trevon? I thought we were to elope tonight."

His lips curled downward in a sneer. Obviously he was not pleased by her rebuff. "Elope? That was just an excuse to get you alone tonight."

Talia sucked in a quick breath, her gaze darting to Krystal. The other woman's jaw went hard and her eyes narrowed.

"So you are a prisoner, my pet?" Trevon turned away from Krystal and directed his attention at Talia.

Talia's eyes narrowed as he circled her. The urge to taunt him was too great. To retaliate for any emotional pain his actions might have caused Krystal.

"This is the man you intended to marry, Krystal?" She forced out a light laugh. "I would encourage you to think twice in the future about the men you date."

Trevon's teeth snapped together. "Why don't you shut that pretty mouth of yours, prisoner. You're much more attractive when you're not speaking." He gave a hard smile and lowered his gaze to her breasts. "And you'll do just fine where Krystal lacks. Gods, look at those tits. Definitely more than a handful."

He reached out to touch them, but Talia was prepared, slapping his hand away with force.

"You go too far," Krystal snapped. She strode forward and grabbed him by the shirt, dragging him away from Talia. "What was I thinking? You are exactly as my brother and Dillon warned me. A pathetic leech."

Her gaze locked on Talia's and Talia nodded. Thank gods the woman had come to her senses.

"Pathetic leech?" he repeated, his voice rising. "They are envious of my money—everyone is."

"Believe what you must, Trevon." Krystal's tone was sarcastic now.

With Trevon's back facing her, Talia waved her hand, encouraging Krystal to come to her.

Krystal gave a quick nod. "It does not matter, we will be leaving now. It was foolish of me to agree to come out tonight, Trevon. You are obviously not the man I thought you were."

She strode past him and Talia felt the tension ease from her shoulders.

"I don't think so, baby." Trevon's arm snaked around Krystal's waist and he jerked her back around.

*Oh gods.* Talia's breath locked in her throat. *Foolish!* They'd been so foolish to come out tonight.

"I have been waiting for months to try out your tight little cunt, you fucking prude. I do not intend to leave here tonight until I have done so."

The force and anger behind his words, and how he squeezed Krystal's breast until she cried out, sparked Talia into action.

"You'll leave now." She came up behind them, her fist balled and arcing toward the side of his head.

Before her hand could connect, he spun and backhanded her, sending her flying backward.

"Oh!" Talia cried out. Her foot caught on a tree root and then her body was in the air.

Her head smashed hard against the side of the tree, and she went blind in an explosion of lights.

"Oh gods! Look what you have done!"

She heard Krystal's hysterical cry and wanted to sit up, but her body felt heavy. The lights faded and a thick darkness started to fill her head.

"She'll live. And when she wakes up we'll include her in the festivities. But for now, baby, why don't you and I get better acquainted?"

Krystal's protests became distorted, the darkness grew.

*Must stay awake.* Talia tried to move her head but nothing happened. *Must help Krystal . . .* Darkness claimed her.

Ryder sat up in bed, unease clawing at his gut. Glancing at the time, he noted there were still a few hours before the dawn. Something was wrong.

He climbed out of bed and pulled on clothes. There would be no sleep for him until he realized what had caused his unease.

The building was quiet, the halls empty, and nothing seemed out of place. His glance moved farther down the hall to Talia's door.

His gut twisted and he sighed. He should have visited her before retiring for the night. He'd intended to, but by the time Dillon had gotten back with confirmation that the emperor was safe, the midnight hour had long since passed.

Perhaps that was why he'd awoken. The guilt at the abruptness in which he'd treated her.

He moved down the hall, not really sure what he intended to do. The light under her door gave him pause. She was awake? At such an hour?

Frowning, he reached her door and typed in the code. The door swung open and he stepped inside. Not seeing her in the bed, his blood pounded harder. He glanced in the bathroom and found it empty, and then strode to the walk-in closet to glance around.

"Son of a bitch." His fist slammed against the wall, his body began to shake.

Half her clothes were missing and she was nowhere in her room. Somehow she had escaped—possibly with someone else's help.

He ran out of the room, his legs eating up the length of the hallway as he moved to Dillon's room. Why had she run? His gut clenched. Had it been out of guilt? Or had he just pushed her too far? Fuck!

His fist pounded on the metal frame, resonating through the hallway.

"Dillon, you must awake!" he shouted.

There was activity inside the room, and then the door swung open. Dillon stood frowning in the doorway in his robe.

"What has happened?"

"Talia, the prisoner," he clarified, "has escaped."

"How is that possible?" Dillon shook his head, his gaze narrowing. "Unless someone has assisted her."

"Those would be my thoughts exactly."

"Shit. Hang on, let me get dressed and we will find her."

Dillon disappeared back inside and the door shut behind him.

Ryder growled in frustration, ignoring several people who'd come out of their rooms to discover the cause of the early morning disturbance.

Who could have freed her? There was only one person he could think of, and to imagine his sister capable of such an act of treason made him ill.

The door opened and Dillon came out, fully dressed and seeming wide awake now.

"Have you checked your sister's room yet?"

"No." Ryder shook his head grimly. "I already fear what I will find, and I will need your help in locating both of the women."

"Fuck. I should have chained her to me," Dillon growled. "I should have expected her to run."

"Let us not be too hasty until we are certain."

They entered another corridor and Ryder exhaled in an attempt to calm his pulse.

Reaching Krystal's door, he typed in the code he'd recently installed. The door slid open and they both filed inside.

The room was empty. Her closet and drawers had been ransacked; shoes were strewn across the floor.

"Damn. Well, I've learned my lesson." Dillon's jaw went tight. "Your sister or not, she will be residing in my quarters from this point forward."

Ryder didn't protest, as he intended to enforce the same plan with Talia. If they retrieved her. His scowl deepened. No, they would retrieve her. And once she was back, he intended to teach her a bit of a lesson. No prisoner escaped from him, damn it. Especially not one that he was half in love with.

"Do you have any idea where they may be headed?"

"I suspect she has run off to meet Trevon this evening." Dillon's harsh tone conveyed his anger. "And she freed a prisoner. She cannot be allowed to get away with this, Ryder."

Ryder nodded, not at all pleased with the idea of his sister being punished, but knowing she must be. Anyone else would receive a severe lashing and days in the confinement brig.

"I know, and I will let you handle her. Just promise me that when we find them . . ."

"I will not be overly harsh," Dillon assured him.

"Thank you." Ryder shook his head as they made their way back through the building. "Let us check the grounds within close proximity of the building first off. If there is still no sign of them, then we shall have to notify the general."

"Do you think Talia is fleeing back to the Council?"

"No," Ryder answered immediately. There was no way he could know for certain, but his gut had a pretty decent instinct that she would not return to them.

"Are you sure you are not speaking what your heart would like to believe?"

"Don't try to analyze me," Ryder snapped. "I am not in the fucking mood."

"Gods, you are right. I apologize. I am on edge as well." Dillon was silent for a moment. "Wait a minute. That's it. I have a feeling I know where they are."

"Where?"

"The aliaberry orchards. Krystal had met Trevon there once before, if not many times."

"Then let's go. It is all we have to go on right now."

They exited the building, moving quickly through the gardens. The night was lit by the light from the moons and stars, but in the shadows of the trees one could still hide.

"How far to the orchards?" Ryder asked. "I cannot remember the last time I traveled there."

"It is but a few minutes off the path once we reach the turnoff by the lake."

"Good."

*Gods, let them be there.* Ryder's blood pounded harder and he increased his pace, his mouth drawn tight. What if she had left him? What if Krystal had sent her on a pod back to Zortou?

*No. You cannot think that way.* They reached the turnoff by the lake and took the trail that led to the orchards.

"Do you hear that?" Dillon paused, gesturing for him to stop.

Ryder went still and tilted his head. The faint, high-pitched sound of something crying—a bird or a woman—rang through the night.

"Did you bring a weapon?" Ryder asked quietly.

"I did not bring my electro-mace. But I have my fists, and they will serve me well."

"I have a knife in my boot should we need it." Ryder ran his glance over the rows of aliaberry bushes, but could see nothing. "Let's continue forward."

They surged forward with a practiced stealth, moving down one line of bushes. Ryder kept his ears tuned for another cry, but there was nothing.

Ryder cursed under his breath. "Perhaps it was not a woman—"

"You bast—" Another scream ripped through the air, but was immediately cut short.

Dillon issued a low growl and sprinted forward toward the sound. Ryder removed his knife from his boot and then did the same.

That scream had come from Krystal. He'd recognize his sister's voice anywhere.

They rounded another row of bushes, and the form of two people struggling on the ground came to light under the moons.

Dillon launched himself at the pair, jerking Trevon away from Krystal and throwing him back a few feet.

Ryder went forward to help his sister, not bothering to check on Trevon, who was undoubtedly getting the life beaten out of him.

He grasped his sister's arm, pulling her to her feet. Her body trembled and she gripped the edge of her dress, which had been ripped.

"Release me," she hissed. "Dillon, do not kill him!"

Ryder's concern faded into annoyance. "Have you gone mad? He was attempting to—"

"Do *not* kill him," she repeated. "I want to cut off his penis with a dull blade before you do."

Ryder blinked, momentarily thrown by her statement, and then shook his head. "Where is Talia?"

Krystal made a strangled gasp and pointed to a tree at the end of the row of bushes.

"She has not moved, Ryder. I tried to get to her . . ."

His sister's voice grew dim in his head and he sprinted toward Talia's limp form. He fell to his knees, the blood roaring in his ears as he reached to check her pulse.

Relief weakened his muscles and he lowered his head, the air rushing from his lungs. Thank gods. She lived. Her pulse was slower than it ought to be, but still strong.

"Talia." He smoothed the hair back from her forehead. "Can you hear me, princess?"

She groaned and her eyelids fluttered.

"There you go. Open your eyes, Talia."

Her eyelids fluttered again and then opened enough to reveal the blue around the pupil. Her gaze seemed unfocused, and then suddenly became quite alert.

"Oh gods," she whispered. Her face lost more color, if that was possible. "Ryder . . ."

"Do not say anything right now, Talia." His jaw hardened. Her fear of him, knowing she'd tried to run, was evident in the way she stared at him. "I am not in the mood to listen."

He slid his arms under her body and cradled her against his chest. No, when he had her safely in his quarter, then they could discuss just how foolish her decision had been.

"Dillon, I am taking Talia back to my quarters. Deal with Krystal—"

"Deal with *me*?" Krystal shouted back, planting her hands on her hips. "Why do I need dealing with?"

Ryder stared at his sister and attempted a calming breath. Whatever punishment Dillon chose to deal out, she deserved.

"You went too far this time, Krystal." He shook his head and turned to head back to the building.

# 15

Dillon raised his fist and then crashed it back into Trevon's jaw again.

"Dillon, enough!" Krystal cried from behind him.

Her voice, and knowing she might have even been begging for Trevon's release, infuriated him further. He punched him again and heard the rewarding crack of bone. Trevon fell limp against the ground, now out cold.

Satisfied he'd inflicted enough damage for now, Dillon stood up and turned around.

The blood rushed through his body, pounding in his veins. He sucked in a large gasp of air, attempting to regain some of the control he'd lost.

"Do you beg for him, Krystal? Your lover?" He stalked her slowly, his gaze moving over her slender body. The swell of her breasts could be seen through the fabric of her dress that Trevon had ripped.

Her gaze widened as he advanced upon her, and she ran her tongue over her lips.

"I just do not want you to beat him to death, Dill."

"Does he not deserve it? Would you have me believe that you were a willing participant in that little exchange?"

Her cheeks filled with color and fear flickered in her gaze. She took a step backward. "You know I was not."

"Then do not ever defend him." He closed the space between them and grabbed her arm. "Come with me."

"What? Where are we going?"

Her steps could not match his long ones, and she stumbled as she attempted to keep up. He took a deep breath and slowed his steps.

He did not intend to take her back to the living quarters. Not right now. Having Ryder in the same building would simply not do for the intentions he had for Krystal.

"Dillon, wait. You have missed the path back to the living quarters," she protested.

"We are not going back to the living quarters."

Turning them off the trail, he weaved them around the lake to where a small cabin was located.

"Not going . . ." she repeated and then tugged at her hand. "Release me. I am tired and do not wish to deal with this nonsense."

"Nonsense?" His pulse spiked again. "You dare call the stunt you have pulled tonight nonsense?"

"You are overreacting. I did not even marry him as was planned."

She had been on her way to marry him? A chill swept through him. Gods, to think how close he'd been to losing her tonight.

He spotted the cabin up ahead. It was a historical building, one of the few wood structures left on the planet. Generally it was rented out to honeymoon couples for a large chunk of money. Thankfully, tonight it appeared vacant.

"What are we doing here?" She glanced over at him, but he

ignored her and went to work breaking into the old-fashioned lock.

The door swung open, squeaking on its hinges. He stepped inside, tugging her after him, but she dug her heels in.

"Dillon, I am not going in here. It smells like . . . ugh. I do not even know what, but it smells bizarre." She shook her head. "I insist you take me back to my room at once."

Dillon released her hand long enough to turn on the lights. "Get inside, Krys."

She hesitated, her mouth drawn tight, displaying her displeasure. Finally, she sighed and stepped through the doorway.

Pleased with the small success, he shut the door behind her and twisted the lock.

The interior of the cabin was small, with just a bed, dresser, and small bathroom. Krystal walked to the middle of the room and folded her arms across her breasts.

"What is the problem, Dillon? Why have you brought me here?"

Her brown curls spilled over the pale curves of her shoulders. Her brown eyes flashed with defiance. Gods, she was beautiful. Beautiful and ridiculously naïve.

He took a step toward her. "Do you realize what you have done tonight, Krystal?"

She blinked and then shrugged. "It matters not. I had intended to marry Trevon, but as you can see, that is no longer an option I intend to consider."

"You were foolish to sneak out and meet him. If we hadn't come along—"

"I had perfect control of the situation." She tossed her hair over her shoulder and glared at him.

"He would have forced himself upon you."

"I would have gained the upper hand."

"You are a petite woman, I seriously doubt that."

Her nostrils flared. "Did you just refer to me as short? You are an ass."

"And then there is the other matter," he murmured approaching her.

"And what matter would that be?" She lifted an eyebrow, her lips twisting.

He stopped in front of her, leaning down until his face was just inches from hers. "You freed a prisoner."

The next breath she took did not sound as steady, and as she stared at him he could see the dilation of her pupils.

"She was being treated unfairly. If I had had more time I would have sent her on the first sky taxi off the planet."

Dillon's jaw hardened. The woman thought she was invincible, could get away with anything.

"You have gone too far this time, Krystal. You cannot go unpunished."

"Too far?" Her hands planted on her hips and she lifted her chin. "You and my brother have gone too far. Ryder for thinking it is perfectly all right to fuck a prisoner—"

"Watch your mouth."

"And you for thinking you can control me," she continued as she glared at him. "Thinking that I would ever be desperate enough to consider you as a husband."

His blood raged through his veins and he clenched his fists at his side. "You will be my wife."

"The hell I will! Fuck you."

"That is *it*." The anger exploded inside him and he grabbed her arm and dragged her toward the bed.

"Release me! What will you do? Force yourself upon me just as Trevon attempted?" she cried out, pounding his back with her free hand.

"No." He sat down on the bed and dragged her across his

lap, jerking her dress up over her ass and up to her waist. "I am doing what should've been done to you years ago."

He brought his palm down hard on the pale curve of her ass, ignoring her choked scream.

"How dare you!"

"You have brought this upon yourself, Krystal." He tightened his grip on her and brought his hand down again, ignoring her fists that beat against his leg.

"Oh!" She squirmed on his lap, the humiliation in her tone evident. "I hate you, Dillon."

"You want to act like a child, Krystal? Then you shall be treated like one." Smack. The cracking sound amplified in the cabin as her pale flesh grew red.

Smack. He slapped her ass again. His breathing grew heavier as he stared at the contrast of his red handprint against her pale white flesh. How hot her buttocks became from the spanking.

His cock stirred and he took a deep breath. *This is not supposed to turn you on.*

"Would you prefer lashes?" Smack. "Or time in the confinement brig?"

She sobbed again, her stomach grinding into his cock. All thoughts left his head momentarily and he stiffened, his erection stabbing into her belly.

"You would not do that to me . . ." she sobbed and her tears dampened his pant leg.

"I would prefer not to, Krystal. That is why I have taken your punishment into my own hands."

Literally. He let his hand linger after the next slap, molding the soft flesh of her buttock into his palm.

She groaned again. This time it didn't sound like that of a woman in pain. He glanced at her face. Her head was turned and she faced the wall; her eyes were closed.

He inhaled sharply and slid her farther down his lap, so her ass was raised higher and he could see the cleft of her cunt between her legs. The pale pink folds glistened with moisture. *She was aroused.*

He brought his hand down again, less hard this time. Taking time to move his fingers up the crack of her ass, circling the tight little hole he intended to fuck someday. Her breathing grew heavier and she no longer squirmed against him.

"Do you realize the mistakes you have made tonight?" His voice grew hoarse.

He felt her nod against his leg.

He brought his hand down again on her reddened ass cheek, and then slid his palm downward. He used two fingers to run over the slit of her pussy, feeling the hot wetness that gathered on her lips.

She inhaled sharply and her body stiffened

"I think you liked getting spanked, kitten."

"No . . ." she groaned, but her ass lifted against his palm. "Nobody likes getting spanked."

"Really?" He pressed his two fingers together and then slid them between her folds. Hot cream met the tips of his digits and he groaned.

"Oh gods." She gasped and wiggled against him. "Please, Dillon."

He took a deep breath and then thrust the two fingers inside her. Her choked cry gave him pause. Gods, if she was this tight around his fingers, what would she feel like squeezing his cock?

Her muscles clenched around him, and she made the sexiest little moans.

"You like that, kitten?"

"No," she gasped the word, and her nails dug into his thigh. "Yes."

He laughed and pulled his fingers out slightly, before moving them back inside her wet channel, deeper this time.

"I do not understand. Every time you touch me I feel ill."

"That is not ill. That is the effects of your desire for me." He lifted her off his lap and sat her down on the bed. "I will assist you in easing the discomfort."

She did not protest as he pulled the dress from her body. Her breasts were small and firm, with large red nipples that were already hard.

Her waist was tiny and her hips had just enough curve. Between toned thighs, soft brown curls shielded her swollen sex.

"Krystal." His voice cracked. Gods, she was beautiful. How long had he imagined her like this? Imagined touching her and tasting her.

Her breasts lifted with each quick breath she took in. Her gaze locked on his with complete trust.

"Lay back, kitten. Let me help you." He climbed onto the bed and pressed gently on her shoulders, easing her backward until she was supine.

Sliding his hands up her legs, he pushed apart her thighs and kneeled between her legs. Bringing one finger to her sex, he slid into her slick folds again to find her clit.

Her hips bucked when he found it, and he rubbed the thick swollen flesh as he watched her face. Her breathing grew heavier and she closed her eyes.

"Do you like that? And do not lie to me this time."

"Yes," she sighed. "Oh yes, Dillon."

"Good." He slid his finger toward the entrance to her cunt, gathering more cream and bringing it back to lubricate her clit while he rubbed it.

She groaned, the tension in her body visible as her fingers clutched the bedspread.

"Relax, kitten. Take a deep breath and just let yourself enjoy the pleasure."

He used his other hand to hold apart her pussy lips, so he

could observe the hot flesh he massaged. Her pink clit was swollen, nestled between the folds of her cunt and covered with shiny cream.

He wanted to taste her. To watch her lose control when he took her clit in his mouth.

Leaning down, he nuzzled the side of her thigh and breathed in the musky scent of her desire.

"Dillon . . ."

He glanced up at her. Her eyes were wide open again, her gaze hesitant as she stared at him.

"Shh. Close your eyes, Krys, and just enjoy."

He pressed his tongue against the hot button of flesh and her guttural cry filled the room. Gods, she tasted good. Tart and sweet, the purest of feminine juices.

He licked her again, sliding his hands under her ass to lift her cunt snug against his face as he drew her clit into his mouth.

Krystal gasped and her thighs tightened around his head.

Suckling her sensitive clit, he brought his fingers to her entrance and eased them inside. Again he paused when the hot silky walls of her cunt clenched around his fingers.

"Oh gods," she hissed.

"Easy." He moved his fingers in and out, preparing her for when his cock would ultimately be inside her.

He swirled his tongue around her clit as the vision of what was to come filled his head. His cock lengthened another inch. Gods. To be inside her, to be able to stake his claim on her.

Her desperate cries increased, her hips lifted against him as her stomach began to tremble. She was close, he realized. Wanting to push her over the edge, he closed his teeth over her clit and thrust his fingers faster inside her.

"Dillon!" she screamed and her hot cream coated his fingers.

He lowered his mouth to plunge his tongue into her cunt,

lapping up her juices. He stayed with her, drinking her essence and kissing her sex until her body went slack and her shallow breaths filled the air.

"How do you feel now, kitten?" Dillon sat up, still cupping her pussy in his palm.

Her eyes were dazed, her lips parted and damp. "I . . . amazing."

His mouth curled into a smile and he lay down on his side next to her. He drew his finger across her collarbone and then down between her breasts. Her breasts lifted as she took in a deep breath, pressing her distended nipples closer toward him.

He drew his fingers across the swell of the breast closest to him, circling the areole but ignoring the tip.

"You did not mind . . ." she began and then paused, her cheeks turning pink. "Touching me there with your mouth?"

"You tasted exquisite, Krystal." He lowered his mouth to hers, plunging his tongue between her lips to find hers.

She groaned and her tongue rubbed against his, hesitant at first before growing bolder. Dillon circled his fingers around her nipple again, before moving to pinch the tip. He caught her gasp in his mouth and deepened the kiss.

Massaging her nipple, he broke his mouth from hers and kissed her neck, running his tongue against her throbbing pulse, before moving lower. He kissed the slight swell of her breasts, and then continued to the dusky areole. Tracing his tongue around the circle, he finally drew it across the rigid tip.

"Oh." Her hands clutched his hair, holding his head against her breast.

He gave a husky laugh and wrapped his lips around the nipple. Drawing it into his mouth, he suckled the warm tip while continuing to fondle the other one.

When her cries grew desperate, he switched his mouth to the

other one, biting, licking, and suckling the tip until her body writhed beneath him.

He released her nipple slowly, the suctioning pop loud in the cabin. Sitting up he removed his shirt and then reached for the fastener on his pants, keeping his gaze on her face.

Her eyes widened and she watched his movements with an intensity that would have made him laugh had he not been so damn aroused.

He pushed his pants down and off, his cock springing forward hard and thick.

"Krystal, you must trust me," he murmured and laid back down, covering her body with his own.

Nudging her thighs apart, he positioned himself between her legs. He lowered his head, covering her mouth while using his hand to guide his cock between the lips of her cunt.

A tremble racked his body as her fingers traced the hair on his chest. His tongue rubbed against hers and he sank an inch into her wet heat.

She groaned and lifted her hips, her nails brushing against his nipple.

He hissed and pressed inside another inch.

"Dillon, please." She squirmed under him, her head twisting back and forth against the pillow.

He took a deep breath, gripped her hips in each hand, and thrust all the way inside her. His brain registered the thin barrier after he'd already torn through it.

"Dillon." Krystal gasped and her palms pushed against his chest.

Gods. Dillon remained still not moving inside her. "I'm sorry, kitten. The sting will pass shortly."

He glanced down at her face. Her eyes had a sheen of tears and her mouth was tight. He had suspected she was a virgin, but could not be certain until he'd plunged into her tight channel.

His chest tightened with emotion and he tenderly brushed a curl off her face.

"I do not know if it will pass, Dill." She whimpered and the muscles of her cunt clenched around him.

"Trust me." He lowered his mouth again and initiated a slow, thorough kiss.

After a moment she stopped pushing him away, and her body relaxed under him. He felt more warm cream surround his cock and tentatively made a shallow thrust inside her.

Her moan was one of pleasure this time. He growled in approval and made a few more shallow thrusts until she was lifting her hips to meet his penetrations.

Placing one hand on the bed, he braced his weight above her and increased the pace. The silky, hot sheath of her cunt squeezed his cock and the air hissed from his lungs.

"Krystal, by gods you are amazing." He moved his free hand between their bodies and found her swollen clit.

She gasped and her cunt contracted around him again.

"You're so hot, kitten. So perfect."

He thrust deeper and rubbed her clit faster.

"Dillon . . ." Her head shook back and forth on the pillow. "Oh gods, Dillon, what are you doing to me?"

"Loving you." He pressed hard against her clit and she screamed, her body shuddering beneath him. "I love you, Krystal."

His sac clenched and he groaned, just as he came hard inside her. Each thrust back into her he emptied a little bit more of himself, of his soul.

Krystal lay still beneath him, but he could feel her fingers drawing circles upon his chest.

He gave a ragged sigh, before rolling off of her and pulling her into his arms. She flowed with him, until he was on his back and she lay on top of him, her head nestled under his chin.

His heart pounded a mile a minute and he stroked his fingers through her hair. She was his. Now and forever.

"That thing you just said . . ." Her lips moved against his neck and he bit back another groan as the blood in his cock stirred again.

"What thing?"

"You said you loved me." Her tongue flicked his pulse. "Did you mean it?"

"Yes. I meant it."

Her cheeks turned pink and a tiny smile curled her lips. He slid his hands down to rub over her ass. If he looked at it, would his handprints still be on the hot cheeks?

"I've loved you for two years, kitten."

Her lips parted and her eyes widened. "For two years?"

"Yes. For two years I have watched you and waited."

"Waited for what?"

He slid a finger into her cunt and then brought it back to the rosebud between her ass cheeks. "Everything."

He heard her breath hitch. "Everything?"

"Everything, kitten." He wiggled his finger into the smaller hole, loving the little cry of surprise she made. "And one day soon, this as well."

"Oh. That sounds kind of different." She moaned and then yawned. "Oh gods, I'm sorry. What time is it?"

"Mmm. I don't even want to know." He glanced out the window where the faintest hint of daylight glanced through the curtains. "I wish you would have picked a time other than the middle of the night to run away."

"You would have caught me if I had left in the afternoon."

"I caught you anyway, kitten," he reminded her with a light tap on her ass.

"Ah yes, I suppose you did." She snuggled against him, her arms tightened around his waist. "And I have to say, I am glad you did."

He was damn glad, too. His brows drew together. What if he hadn't arrived in time? What if Trevon had . . . *Don't go there.*

"Why did you want to marry him? Trevon?"

She was silent for a moment. "I'm not sure. But in the end he did not want to marry me. He just wanted . . ."

"To bed you?" His mouth tightened and his blood pounded harder through his veins. "Were you really in love with him?"

"No, I don't think so." She kissed his neck again. "I think I was in love with the idea of being in love."

He took a deep breath in. "I must know. Will you think about him after tonight? Try to see him again?"

"No, Dillon." She lifted her head and gave him the sweetest smile. "You have opened my eyes. Compared to you, Trevon is but a pathetic, spoiled boy. You are . . ." She drew a fingernail down his chest. "A hard, virile man who knows exactly how to please a woman."

His chest swelled with pride and his grip on her ass cheeks tightened. "I pleased you?"

"Yes. You know you did." Her hand moved farther down his abdomen until it reached his penis, which grew harder by the second.

"Krystal," he groaned, thrusting against her hand.

"Yes, my love?"

*My love.* He jerked his gaze to her face. Had she realized what she'd just said? Her gaze was confident and honest. She knew.

"Nothing. Just don't stop." He groaned and pulled her head down for another kiss.

# 16

Ryder adjusted his grip on Talia and carried her through the door to his bedding chambers. He brought her straight to the bed, thinking briefly how strange it was. No woman had ever stepped foot in his private chambers. It was his sanctuary.

Laying her on the bed, he pulled off her jacket and brushed a strand of hair off her face. Gods, she was too pale. At least she had responded out in the aliaberry orchard, if even briefly.

"Talia," he patted her cheek again. "Please, open your eyes, princess."

She made a small noise but did not open her eyes.

His pulse jumped and he grabbed her hand and gave it a light squeeze. "Good girl. Now, can you open your eyes?"

"I would rather not," she said, her voice faint, but it sent relief through him. "I have the worst ache in my head."

"Gods, princess, you had me so worried. It looks like you hit your head pretty hard."

"It felt pretty hard," she muttered.

"Let me get you some water." He jumped to his feet and strode to the refrigeration unit built into the wall.

After pressing one of the buttons, a cup dropped onto the shelf below and began to fill with water. Once it had filled, he took it and strode back to the bed where she continued to lay still.

He sat down on the bed next to her. "I'm going to hold a cup of water to your lips. Can you tilt your head up a bit?"

She grunted, but obligingly lifted her head a little. He pressed the cup to her mouth and she parted her lips, drinking a few sips.

After a moment, she pushed it aside and lay back against the pillows.

"Are you angry with me?"

Her voice wavered. With fear? Regret? He couldn't be sure. His jaw tightened as he continued to stare down at her.

Her eyes were still closed against her pale face, silken strands of red hair spread out on the pillow. He ran his gaze over her.

"Am I wrong to assume that you were planning to leave Belton?"

She was silent for a moment and then a quiet, "No. You are not wrong."

"Why?" The question ripped raw from his throat. "Gods, why, Talia? After last night—"

"After you gained all the information you needed from me, you mean? After I became of little use to you?" Her words were weak, but the accusation behind them strong.

Ryder took a deep breath. Would they never get past this? This lack of trust they seemed to have for one another?

"Is that what you truly believe?"

She sighed. "It matters not." The hint of tears at the corner of her eyes undermined her words.

"It does, Talia." He leaned down and trailed the back of his hand across her cheek.

Her eyes opened, the uncertainty in her gaze obvious. "Why?"

*Good question.* "Because it does."

Her smile was weak. "That is not a good enough answer."

"Well, it will have to do."

"Am I to be punished?"

"No." He placed the palm of his hand over her forehead and then smoothed back her hair. "Though any prisoner would be locked up in a maximum security cell after an escape attempt."

"And when will I be placed there?" Her tongue ran over her lips and he bit back a groan.

"You won't. I have decided you will stay in my chambers until we decide what is to be done with you."

Heat flared in her eyes and he heard the shift in her breathing. Was she pleased that she would be staying with him?

"What do you mean when you say done with me?"

"We cannot keep you as a prisoner forever," he murmured. "But we cannot free you until the situation with Zortou is under control."

"I see." She sighed and turned her head, so that she looked at the wall.

"How are you feeling?"

"A bit dizzy, and my head throbs." She raised her hand to touch the back of her hand. "You were right about Trevon, he is a vile—" Her words cut off on a gasp. "Oh gods. I nearly forgot. How is Krystal? Was she hurt? The last thing I remember . . . oh no."

"She was well when I left her." How concerned she sounded. Perhaps the bond between his sister and Talia was greater than he had realized.

"When you left her?" She struggled to sit upright and then fell back to the pillow with a groan. "Where is she now?"

"With Dillon, who is likely carrying out her punishment as we speak."

"Krystal is being punished?"

He watched as the color faded from her face and gave a brief nod. "Of course."

"She is your sister." Her tone sharpened.

"And she not only freed a prisoner, but disobeyed strict orders to cease any contact with Trevon." He pulled the blanket up to her chest and then stood and walked toward the door.

"She is young and determined," Talia argued. "Will he hurt her?"

"I have ensured that she not be hurt, but I have left the punishment up to Dillon's discretion."

Her expression grew pinched and she closed her eyes. "The poor girl, she has already been through enough."

"By the fault of her own choices." He typed in the code to open the door. "I will send someone in with medicine. Rest for now."

He stepped out and the door swung shut behind him.

Talia lay in bed, staring at the flecks of color in the black ceiling.

Was it possible that he cared for her? Could Ines's words have held more jealousy than truth?

She had prepared herself for the worst. For a whipping that would likely leave scars. Or, as Ines had threatened, to be handed over to Ryder's soldiers as a plaything. How could he not be furious? She had attempted to escape!

And yet the only reprimand she was to receive was being forced to stay with Ryder. Which, in truth, was no punishment at all. More a pleasure . . .

There had been no anger in his gaze when she'd awoken. Only a desperation and concern.

Where was she anyway? She turned her head, ignoring the ache as she glanced around. It was a luxuriant room, the bed she was upon more extravagant than one she'd ever laid in. The mattress nearly molded to her body, the pillows sweetly scented and soft as air.

There were chairs in the middle of the room, a sink and refrigeration unit on the side, and a large-looking bathing chamber near the door.

The room wavered and she laid her head back against the pillow to ease dizziness. The medicinal woman had come into the room shortly after Ryder had left and given her some form of medication.

It appeared to be taking effect. She closed her eyes, tightened the blanket around her, and let the medicine take her away.

Two hours passed and still she slept. Ryder checked in on her numerous times, but whatever medicine she'd been given for the pain had put her into a deep slumber.

He placed a call to Dillon's communication mobile and when there was no answer disconnected the line.

Likely Dillon was struggling to persuade Krystal of his feelings of love at this moment. Or else beating the stubbornness out of her.

His lips twitched as he walked back to his office. The door at the end of the hall opened, and he saw the silhouette of a woman.

"Good morning, sir."

*Ines.* He sighed and gave her a brief nod. "Good morning."

He watched her approach, already prepared for her to make some form of a sexual advance, but she gave him a funny little smile and then kept walking.

A bit relieved, he turned and watched as she continued down the hall. Perhaps he had been hasty in his decision to have her relocated, though she certainly appeared to be taking it well enough. Perhaps she had come to realize what a great opportunity it truly was.

He narrowed his eyes and then opened the door to his office. It mattered not. There were more important issues at hand. Such as checking on the status of the emperor.

Krystal opened her eyes, having been awakened by the sunlight that slipped through the curtain of the cabin.

She smiled and shifted backward, closer to the hardness of Dillon's body. His cock pressed snug against her ass and his arm draped heavy around her waist.

A small giddy sigh escaped her throat and she shifted her legs. There was a bit of soreness between her thighs, but it was a delicious and wicked feeling.

Never would she have considered Dillon to be a possible lover. Even after that day in the hangar, she'd been convinced that she'd only had a momentary lapse in sanity.

*I should have known.* For years they'd had a close friendship, had spent many hours together, and still she'd missed the signs. The signs that Dillon had been viewing their relationship in a different light.

Too bad she had not learned of it earlier. Last night had been wonderful. Her nipples tightened and liquid pooled between her thighs.

She closed her eyes and stifled a groan. If Dillon had not spent half the night punishing her and then making love to her; she would have awakened him and initiated another session. But he was a soldier who needed his sleep.

Moist, hot air caressed the back of her neck. "Are you awake?"

Or maybe he considered sleep to be overrated.

"Very much so."

His lips moved against her nape and a tremor shot through her body.

"How do you feel this morning? Are you sore?"

"Only just a bit." She gave a breathless laugh. "I am more . . . aroused, so to speak?"

"Mmm. Is that so?" His husky laugh brought more cream between her legs.

"Yes."

The arm around her waist shifted and then made a slow descent to the curls between her legs.

"Very wet." He dipped a finger between the folds of her sex and she gasped. "Did you dream of me, kitten?"

"I do not recall."

"I would like to be the only man you dream of from now on." He slid the finger up to her clit and began to tap it, until she squirmed against him. "And I would like you to come for me."

"Dillon . . ." She groaned and parted her legs. Gods, she wanted his fingers inside her. She wanted his cock inside her. *"Please."*

"I will not take you so soon with my cock." The regret in his voice was evident. "Your body is still recovering. But I will take you with my mouth."

He rolled her over onto her back, and then slid down her body. He wasted no time, and when his lips fastened around her clit she nearly leapt off the bed.

Gods, he was so good at this part! She thrust her fingers into his hair, clutching the soft strands as his tongue circled the hidden sensitive nub.

She lifted her hips with a whimper, the walls of her cunt clenching and unclenching with the need for something to fill it.

As if hearing her silent request, he slipped a finger inside her and began to move it in and out slowly.

The pleasure spread through her body, the heat taking over. He suckled her clit harder, curling his finger inside her cunt and pushing her over the edge.

Her toes curled and she cried out, riding through the explosion of bright lights in her head and the racing of her heart.

She gasped and opened her eyes, pulling him away from her and urging him up to kiss him. Gods, how fast he could bring her to orgasm.

His mouth covered hers and she tasted herself, rubbing her tongue against his. He gave a murmur of approval and slowed the kiss, before lifting his head.

"I like that you no longer fight us."

"How can I?" she murmured. "We are a perfect fit. And speaking of which, please . . . I must have you inside me again. The mouth was wonderful," she smiled and bit her bottom lip, reaching her hand between them to touch his cock. "But it is this that I am craving."

"All right, love, but I will need to be extra gentle." He tapped her nose and sat up. "Before that, however, my communication mobile is blinking. Give me a moment to check it and then I will be back. We have all morning to enjoy one another."

She watched as he climbed out of bed and went to the dresser. He had the most beautiful backside. Pressing a hand to her mouth to hold back another giggle, she swung her legs out of bed and walked toward the porch.

The cabin they were in resided on a lake, and she could not resist peeking at the view.

Opening the door, she stepped outside and inhaled the fresh air. It mattered not that she was naked; the cabin was isolated with no one to see.

She yawned and braced her arms on the railing of the cabin, watching the sparkle of sunlight on the lake. A reflection in the sky caught her eye and she lifted her gaze.

"Odd. My communications mobile has become unresponsive." Dillon stepped outside and came up behind her. "What are you looking at?"

"I'm not quite sure."

He lifted his gaze and then went still. "Go back in the cabin."

The urgency of his words and the sudden rigidity in his body sent a chill through her blood. "Dillon? What is happen—"

"Get in the cabin, now!"

She turned on her heel and rushed back inside, the air locked in her lungs. Her body trembled and she glanced in the mirror above the dresser at her pale face.

Oh gods. It was bad. Whatever it was, it was bad.

"Krystal . . ."

She turned as he came back into the cabin. The grave expression on his face had her gripping the wood frame on the bed.

"What is it?" she whispered, her stomach in knots.

He took a deep breath. "The planet is under attack."

"No." Her knees went weak, but she held her ground. "Oh gods. Dillon . . ."

"It appears the electronic and communication field has been jammed and that is why I cannot call out." He stepped forward and cupped her face, dropping a kiss on her lips. "I need you to stay here."

"Alone?" Fear clotted in her throat.

"The pods have only just entered the hemisphere. It is quite possible no one has spotted them as of yet."

"Do you not have a way to track them? Wouldn't the planetary army be aware—"

"Not with our electronic field jammed, and these pods are stealth." He gripped her hands. "I must go and send out the alarms as soon as possible."

"Take me with you."

"If something happens to me—"

"Then let it happen to me, too," she interrupted harshly. "I will not leave you. If you do not take me then I will follow after you leave."

"You are stubborn."

"You have known me since I was a child. Do not pretend to be surprised."

Dillon sighed and shook his head, but did not reply as he pulled on his clothes.

Krystal hurried to follow suit, pulling on her dress from last night.

"We must hurry in our trek back to the city, Krystal." He turned to her again, his gaze intense. "I know they will not hesitate to kill me and I do not want to imagine what they would do to you."

"I love you, Dillon. And I refuse to leave you. We will get through this; we have to." She took a deep breath. "I am ready."

Dillon groaned and took her lips in a quick, hard kiss. "I love you, kitten. Let us go."

The scream came from inside his room. Despite his intentions to meet with his superiors, Ryder backtracked and typed in the code at his door, his heart pounding with sudden fear.

The door slid open and he lurched inside, prepared for the worst.

Talia lay in the bed alone, though she thrashed beneath the blankets.

He rushed to her side and sat down on the bed, the mattress dipping beneath his weight. Touching her forehead, he checked to see if she was feverish. She was warm, but not overtly so.

She groaned and jerked her head away, her hands raised as if to strike him.

He caught her wrists and pinned them to her side.

"Talia, open your eyes."

She continued to struggle beneath him, gasping and making little cries.

"It is Ryder. Relax, princess."

Her brows drew together and she went limp beneath him, before her lids opened. Her gaze was confused and took a moment to focus on him.

"A nightmare?" He stroked his thumb over the furious pulse on her wrist.

"I . . . I am not sure." She blinked and a shudder racked her body. "Yes."

"What about?" he asked, while he kept up the soothing strokes over her wrist.

"It does not matter." Her eyes closed, but the anguish in them had been real enough. "Do you plan to send me back to Zortou?"

Her question threw him and for a moment he could not even answer.

"I see." Her voice cracked and she jerked her hands away, rolling onto her side and drawing her knees up to her chest.

"Talia—"

"Please, touch me no more," she cried. "I am a whore in your eyes. A prisoner whose body you find fulfillment in, I understand that. But I beg of you, do not touch me again."

Ryder shook his head, his gut twisting at the pain in her voice.

"That is not true and we both know it."

"How do I know it? *How*, Ryder?" She made a choked sound and then gasped in a shaky breath. "I do not ask, I beg you. Please leave me be. For you know not how close you are to breaking me."

"Breaking you?" he whispered and placed his hand on her shoulder, pulling her onto her back so she had to look at him. "If anything you have broken me, Talia. What kind of soldier gives his heart to a prisoner?"

Her eyes widened, a sheen of tears reflected in them. Her mouth parted and her tongue darted over her lower lip; it was his undoing.

"Gods, how can you doubt me?" he rasped and lowered his head, crushing her mouth with his own.

Her moan mingled with his as her hands gripped his head, holding herself against him.

He slid on top of her, pressing his knee between her thighs and against the heat of her sex. His tongue slipped into the moist cavern of her mouth, tasting her sweet passion and circling her tongue.

Her hands slid out of his hair and moved to his shoulders as she ground herself against his knee.

He lifted his head, his hand already moving down to cup the weight of one of her breasts.

"I should be in a meeting soon."

"Please do not leave me," she pleaded, her hands sliding lower to unfasten his pants. "Not yet. Please, Ryder."

"Talia . . ."

"Please, Ryder. I need you."

*Fuck the meeting.* Ryder jerked off his shirt and eased his pants off. He could be late. He slid the straps of Talia's dress off her shoulders and kissed the curve of her neck.

Pulling the fabric down her body, he exposed her breasts and the hard pink nipples. Pulling the dress farther, he paused to kiss the crater of her navel before drawing the dress over her hips and down her legs.

"Beautiful," he murmured, burying his face between her

breasts and then turning his head to flick his tongue over her nipple. "You are so beautiful, princess."

She sighed and dug her nails into his shoulders. "Make love to me, Ryder."

With a groan, he opened his mouth and drew one stiff nipple inside. He flicked his tongue over the ridges and dents of the areole, then sucked on the tip until she cried out.

He switched to the other breast, repeating the process with the other nipple until his cock was rigid with need.

"Inside me." Her hand wrapped around his erection again, her fingers rubbing the drop of pre-cum over his flesh. "I can wait no longer, Ryder."

He grasped her wrists and pinned them above her head in one of his hands, and then used the other to guide his cock between the moist folds of her cunt.

Lifting his gaze, he looked down into her eyes and saw the heat and trust there. With their gazes locked on each other, he thrust into her hot center.

Her eyelids fluttered shut and the air hissed from between her lips.

"Oh gods, Ryder . . ."

"Mmm. Yes, princess?"

The walls of her vagina squeezed around his cock with such pressure that he groaned, glancing down at where they were joined.

"I think I am in love with you," she blurted.

He lifted his head and met her gaze, expecting to see humor, but her expression was raw with honesty.

He lowered his mouth to hers, hoping to convey his emotions in the kiss as he started to move slowly inside her.

Her flesh hugged him as he pulled out to her entrance before sinking back inside her. He slid his hands up from her wrists to intertwine his fingers with hers.

He increased the pace of his thrusts, moving in and out of her, feeling her heart pounding beneath him nearly in time with his.

His fingers tightened around hers and she lifted her lips, gasping. The walls of her cunt clenched around his cock as she orgasmed.

His sac tightened and then he was exploding inside her. There was a roaring in his ears and his throat locked with emotion as he emptied himself again and again.

Dimly, he heard a sound, a small beep, but it was out of his head before he could analyze it.

The slick walls of her sex massaged him through his orgasm. He dragged in a harsh breath and his muscles relaxed, his weight falling heavy on her.

Touching her lips, his lips curved slightly. Gods, he loved her. He could no longer deny it. To himself or to her.

Her eyes widened. "*No.*"

"Talia, I—"

"Ryder!"

Stinging pain exploded in his buttock and then radiated down his thigh. *Fuck.* He reached back to remove the dart, but knew the damage was done.

"Well done, Natalia." The male voice came from behind him. "Although I am not sure you needed to fuck the bastard to show your loyalty to Zortou."

Already Ryder could feel the dart's poisoned tip taking effect. He stared down at Talia, seeing the horror and fear in her eyes as he struggled to pull himself off her.

*Please do not leave me.* Her words from earlier echoed in his head. *Not yet, Ryder.*

212

"Oh gods, Ryder." Her words were hoarse as her nails dug into his shoulders. "I am so sorry."

His eyelids grew heavy, her face and words distorted. One thought filled his head before all went black: whom had she really betrayed?

# 17

Ryder's body became a dead weight atop her and his eyes drifted shut. Terror clotted in Talia's throat as her gaze shifted to Franklin.

"Did you miss me, baby?" He stepped forward and grabbed Ryder by the hair, jerking him off of her and throwing him to the floor.

What was happening? Had the Council instigated the attack early? Or were they here because they'd realized where she was, and had come to return her? *Never.*

Her heart beat faster and she glanced around for anything that might work as a weapon. *You are not the same person as you once were. You do not have to go back to that life.*

Talia grabbed the lamp off the bedside table, but Franklin swung around and knocked it aside with a roar.

She jerked back against the pillows, her eyes wide, her pulse pounding.

"I am sure each day we have been apart has been *agony* for you, Natalia." He sneered and lurched forward, grabbing her arm and dragging her forcefully from the bed. His gaze raked over her naked body. "You little bitch. You will regret the day that you whored yourself to him. And he will not live long enough to regret the poor choices he made."

He planned on killing Ryder? Oh gods. What had been on the dart Franklin had shot Ryder with? Her gut clenched and bile rose in her throat. She gripped his jacket, tears burning her eyes.

"Franklin, what—"

The sound of weapons fire came from the hall, drowning out her desperate plea.

Franklin cursed and glanced down at Ryder before tightening his grip around her arm.

"Attire yourself. Now." He released her and strode to the door, going to speak to someone in the hallway.

Without a thought, Talia rushed to Ryder and knelt down. She pressed her fingers against the pulse in his throat and the air hissed out from her clenched teeth. Tears of relief spilled down her cheeks. He was still alive. But for how long?

She grabbed her dress off the ground and tugged it on. If Franklin came back and she had not obeyed his orders, she would not live long enough to get Ryder the help he needed.

"Come. We are leaving." Franklin reentered the room with a strip of fabric in his hand.

He grabbed her wrists and jerked them behind her back, binding them with the fabric.

"Will he die?" she asked, her words shaking.

Franklin stepped in front of her, and the cold malice she saw in his gaze sent a chill through her blood. "It is almost certain."

His words barely had time to sink in before he dragged her out of the room. Her chest constricted with agony and tears blinded her vision.

Ryder could not die. She would find someone to help him.

The world outside was unrecognizable. Smoke and fire burned

in every direction. Women and children screamed as they tried to find safety and avoid the combating soldiers from both worlds.

It was truly a field of war. Her feet stumbled, the blood left her head, and she grew lightheaded.

"Keep moving," Franklin ordered and nudged her in the back.

A familiar face surged through the chaos and Talia lurched away from Franklin and crossed the grounds.

"Ines!" she cried. "You must help Ryder. He is in his bedding chamber—"

Franklin's hand bit into her shoulder with enough force that her knees buckled and she fell to the ground with a cry of pain.

She glanced up with a whimper, hopeful that Ines would be running toward the building. Talia's brows drew together and she took in a deep breath. Ines had not moved, but instead looked at Franklin with blatant irritation.

"What treachery is this?" Ines demanded. "You promised that she would be disposed of."

Talia blinked, unable to draw in a breath. Whatever response Franklin made, she did not hear it. There was a roaring in her ears and everything spun.

*Ines had betrayed them.* Ines was the reason Ryder was near death, why the people of Belton were running for their lives.

"Get up." Franklin pulled her to her feet again.

Talia's gaze landed on Ines's again. The now-familiar hatred was once again in the other woman's eyes.

"Just follow orders, Ines." Franklin dragged Talia away from the other woman and farther across the grounds.

This was it. There was no more hope. For her or for Ryder. Oh gods. *Ryder.* Tears burned against her eyes again. Why did it have to end this way? If Ines had not betrayed them, then Belton would have gone ahead with the preemptive attack as planned and all would have been well.

"What are you giving her to betray her home planet?" Talia demanded.

"She came to us, if you must know. And as to what we are giving her . . . it is of no concern to you." He glanced down at her. "I do not care for this belligerent side you have acquired. You were much preferable when you only opened your mouth to accept a cock inside it."

*Bastard.* Hot anger swept through her. "Where are you taking me?"

"A place where we won't be disturbed."

Every part of her went numb; the blood left her face. Yet she grew strangely calm. He would kill her. She was almost certain. But only after he'd raped her until she wished for death.

Her bare feet grew sore from walking across the terrain; her arms ached from being tied behind her back.

Death. For years she had wished for it on Zortou, saw it as her only escape from her hellish life as a Rosabelle. And then came the irony of finding safety and love as a prisoner on Belton.

Her stomach twisted and she blinked away any remaining tears. Perhaps death would be the preferable option again if Ryder assumed she had betrayed him. That is, if he lived to assume anything.

Franklin's grip on her shoulder tightened. "Keep moving."

Live or die. The decision was out of her hands.

They entered another building, one she had not yet been in. He opened the door to a room and then thrust her inside.

Talia fell to the floor, her shoulder hitting the hard surface first and sending sparks of pain through her body. She could not stop the sharp cry that escaped.

Franklin smirked, obviously pleased that he'd hurt her.

He stepped into the room and then knelt down beside her, untying the strap that bound her wrists behind her back.

Talia let out a ragged breath. Tingles spread through her body, and the blood began to circulate again.

"He is dead by now," Franklin taunted. "You realize that. Do you not, Natalia?"

The sheer agony his statement evoked sent a shudder through her body, but she clenched her teeth. She would show him no reaction. He wanted her anger and ultimately her submissiveness. He would not get it. Never again.

"Where did he first fuck you, baby?" He stroked the back of his hand across her cheek, a tight smile on his face. "Was it in your bedchamber before he stole you from us?"

Her skin crawled at his touch and she slapped his hand away. His palm came back twice as fast to glance across her cheek. Tears of shock flooded her eyes, even though the slap had not hurt much.

"How quickly you have forgotten your place," Franklin chided with a rough laugh as he stood up. "But I will enjoy reminding you."

All of a sudden she didn't want to die. She wanted to kill him. Kill this man who had taken away any hope she'd had. Talia ran her tongue over her lips and glanced around the room. There was a stove and countertops full of cooking utensils. They appeared to be in some oversized kitchen.

"Why are you not out fighting with the soldiers of Zortou?" she asked, with the hope of diverting him.

"Fight?" He lifted an eyebrow and then went to pour himself a glass of water. "Me? I am a Council member, Natalia. We govern, not fight."

And where *were* the other Council members? She had yet to spot Ramirez or Victor.

Her glance landed on the knives on the other side of the room, suspended above the counter near the sink. If she could somehow get over there and retrieve one, then perhaps she would have a chance. As he had said himself, Franklin was not trained to fight.

"What are you doing?"

Talia jerked her gaze away from the knives. He stared at her and then looked at the knives.

"What are you thinking, baby?" Franklin crossed the room and gripped her arm, jerking her to her feet. "That you would take one of the knives and use it on me?"

*Yes.* She didn't answer, just lifted her chin and met his gaze stoically.

"You little bitch. I would have broken your wrist before you could get within an inch of me." His grip on her arm tightened and she winced. Would he break her arm anyway?

"Gods, it is true." A voice called from the doorway at the other side of the room. "You have recovered our precious Rosabelle."

Without looking, her gaze still locked on Franklin's, Talia knew Ramirez and Victor would be in the doorway.

Franklin's gaze lit up with what looked like excitement and he released her, turning toward the door.

"Gentlemen, you made it. Where is Ines?" His tone sharpened on the last question.

"I have no idea, quite honestly." Ramirez offered a small shrug. "She said she would return in a bit."

"I see." Franklin did not sound pleased, and Talia looked over to see his jaw was tight.

"Natalia, my darling. Gods, how we have missed you." Victor crossed the room toward her.

*No. No. No.* Talia took a step backward, her pulse jumped and her stomach knotted. Gods, she could not handle their attentions any longer.

"Your state of dress is completely inappropriate, though as always you are beautiful." Victor seemed to not notice her distress. He closed the distance between them and reached out to touch her hair.

"*No!*" The word exploded from her and she jerked away. "Do not touch me. Any of you!"

Ramirez froze and Victor's gaze jerked to her, his eyes widened in surprise. Only Franklin gave a soft laugh of amusement.

"Natalia, you are confused." Victor's voice soothed as if he spoke to a child as he approached her. "All will be well shortly. All too soon we will take control of Belton and relocate our headquarters—"

His words ended in a gasp as Franklin's arm slid around his neck. The flash of a knife was a blur, but the line of crimson that appeared at Victor's neck was all too real.

Talia lurched back with a scream, blinking in horror, as Victor fell limp to the ground at her feet.

"Actually, Victor, there's been a change of plans." Franklin muttered and then spun around and leapt after Ramirez, who had run toward the door.

The older man did not stand a chance against Franklin, and his scream was cut short as Franklin slit the man's throat.

He'd gone mad! Nausea swept through Talia. She groaned and ran toward the knives, determined to defend herself before she took her last breath.

She reached the knives, lifted out her hand to grab one, and was pushed harshly to the floor. Franklin straddled her and pinned her wrists above her head.

She flinched and then let out a long whimper, making a poor attempt to prepare herself for death.

"You have nothing to fear, Natalia." His breath was hot on her neck. "I had to kill them. There was no reason to keep them any longer."

*Had to kill them.* He had just killed two men without provocation!

"Don't you see, baby?" His gaze softened and he drew the flat side of the knife across her cheek. "It will be just you and me now."

*You and me?* A shudder ripped through her body. Oh gods. His obsession with her had taken a sick turn. All his violent tendencies toward her and obsessive behavior made sense now.

"Once this war is over—and it will not be long before the troops are successful—then you will sit beside me as my empress."

He believed himself to be the future emperor of Belton? Gods, he was beyond mad.

"Franklin, you must cease now," she pleaded. "Please, you will not succeed. Ryder has—"

"Do *not* mention that man's name again. *Ever*, Natalia." His jaw clenched and he rolled the knife on her cheek, the movement light enough that she only felt pressure, but not the sting of a cut. "You will soon forget him. I know that you love me, baby. I know—"

"How foolish do you take me to be?" A calm female voice said above them.

Talia jerked her gaze up and saw the moment Ines brought the clublike weapon down onto Franklin's back. His head reared back as he gasped in pain.

Talia whimpered and thrust him off her, rolling to the side.

Franklin's body began to spasm and he fell onto his back. His head rolled to the side and his gaze locked on hers. Disbelief and pain was clear in his eyes, and then they went flat and his body stilled.

"You killed him," Talia muttered, disbelief freezing her limbs.

Talia closed her eyes and let out a ragged breath. The Council members were dead—all three of them.

"Thank you," she whispered and pressed her hand to her chest.

"Now why would you be so silly as to thank me before I take your life, Natalia?"

Talia opened her eyes to find Ines staring down at her, gripping the club in front of her in both hands.

Ice invaded her veins and Talia realized the stupidity of her assumption. Ines had not rescued her; she was obviously a woman intent on her own vengeance.

Would pleading for her own life gain her any ground? Not likely. Talia licked her lips as her brain raced to form a plan.

Ines took a step toward her and Talia acted on instinct. She kicked out her leg, knocking the club from Ines's hands. The club dropped to the ground with a loud bang and then rolled jaggedly across the floor.

Ines gave a shriek of fury and dove after it. Unwilling to let the other woman gain the upper hand, Talia jumped on her back and grabbed a handful of hair.

They rolled on the cold marble floor of the kitchen. Talia drew blood as her nails dragged down Ines's cheek.

"Cease at once!"

The shouts rang out as men charged into the room. Talia raised her head and saw the soldiers of Belton rushing into the kitchen.

She went limp and rolled off of Ines. Thank gods they had arrived just in time.

Ines leapt to her feet, blood dripping down her cheek while chunks of hair lay on the ground. She glanced at Talia and then at the soldiers.

"This woman is an escaped prisoner," Ines yelled, pointing a trembling finger at her. "She has been on a rampage killing three men, and just now tried to kill me. Lock her up at once."

"No!" Talia gasped, her eyes widening, her heart pounding. "She is a traitor, she—"

"This prisoner was one of the people behind the plot to assassinate the emperor," Ines cut her off. Grabbing her arm, she thrust her to a soldier who immediately restrained her.

"No! She is lying." Talia shook her head. Gods, this looked terrible. Ines wore the uniform of her planet, and yet only Talia—a prisoner!—knew that she had turned traitor. Of course they would not believe her.

Ines seemed to realize she had won. The tension in her body visibly eased and her lips almost curled into a smile as she stepped forward. "Arrange for her immediate execution."

Talia froze, the breath in her throat locking.

The soldier holding her hesitated. "Are you quite sure, ma'am? That seems—"

"Her *immediate* execution," Ines interrupted. "By the orders of Colonel Jacobs just before he died by her hand."

The room went quiet, save for Talia's choked sob. Her heart nearly ripped from her chest and tears sprang to her eyes. Ryder was dead. Oh gods. She had known it was a possibility, yet in her heart she had held out hope.

There was a roar in her ears and the room began to spin. Dead. The man she loved, the man who had given her reason to live was now dead himself.

Every muscle in her body seemed to go lax at once and then the nausea took over, closing her into a sea of blackness.

# 18

There were voices talking above him. Ryder tried to open his eyes but the movement was impossible. He opened his mouth to speak and only a groan came out.

"Ryder?" His sister's voice rang clear in his ears. "Dillon! I think he is awakening!"

Hurried footsteps sounded, and then a strong hand grasped his shoulder.

"Ryder, can you hear me?"

Ryder groaned again.

"I have administered the first shot in a series of three for the anecdote to the poison you were given," Dillon told him just as Ryder felt the pinch of the needle go into his arm. "And there was your second. Give it a few minutes and you will gain some strength back."

Ryder lay still. Gods, his head felt as if it were in the midst of a whirlpool. Gradually it eased and he attempted to open his eyes again, this time with less difficulty.

He glanced around the room. He was not in his chambers. It

was cold and dark, the smell of soil heavy. Krystal and Dillon hovered nearby, watching him with obvious concern.

"Where am I?"

"We moved you to a bunker thirty feet beneath the earth." Dillon loaded up another injection. "We saw the troops from Zortou preparing to attack and came back to warn everyone. It was only then did we find you near death."

"Have the troops been activated?"

"Yes." Dillon plunged the third shot into Ryder's arm. "The planet is under attack and has been for nearly an hour. The troops are rallied and doing what they can."

The third shot eased away whatever ill effects remained. Ryder stood, a bit unsteady on his feet, and blinked. Taking a deep breath, he crossed the room to pour himself some water.

He downed the cup, struggling to place the memory of what had happened. He'd been in his room, making love to Talia . . . and then . . . *No.*

He tossed the cup back into the sink. "Where is she?"

"She?" Krystal repeated, biting her lip.

"Talia. Do not be dim. You know whom I refer to."

"Have more respect for your sister," Dillon said harshly. "And why you would care where that traitorous prisoner is makes little sense to me."

"She is not—"

"Likely she is on a pod back to Zortou after she stuck a poisoned dart in your ass," Dillon finished with a roar. "Fleeing with her lover as the attack on the planet got under way."

*With her lover?* No. "Talia would not have done that. She hated her life on Zortou."

"I saw them, Ryder," Krystal blurted and then shook her head and looked away, the devastation on her face blatant. "They were running through the grounds together, obviously fleeing."

"No . . ." Ryder clenched his teeth and took a ragged breath in. Something wasn't right.

"You cannot be serious." Dillon slapped his fist against the wall. "The planned attack was not scheduled until the fifteenth. Nearly two weeks from this date, my friend," He pointed out harshly. "She has been gaining your trust under false pretenses."

"No . . ."

"I hate to believe it as well, Ryder." Krystal's voice wavered. "But it appears Dillon is right. We were all fooled by the illusion she—"

"How can you say these things, Krystal?" Ryder demanded, pacing the room. "You were the lone one out of all of us who believed in her goodness. Long before I did." He shook his head, remembering the horrified look on Talia's face before he'd succumbed to the poison. "I cannot believe she was a part of this. I won't."

He would fight and then he would find Talia. Gods. The danger she could be in right now. Was she even alive? His gut twisted with sudden fear.

"Believe what you need to, Ryder. But—" Dillon's jaw tightened and he glanced toward the tunnel that led to the underground chamber.

"What?" Krystal gripped his hand, her gaze following his.

"They come," Ryder stated and drew his electro-mace. He gripped the clublike weapon between steady hands. If the spiked tip connected with the enemy's flesh, he could discharge an electro charge that would immediately cause serious harm to the person.

A roar filled the room as a group of men charged through the door wielding weapons.

Krystal made a choked sound and took a quick step backward.

"Stay behind us." Dillon pushed her to the back of the room and drew his own electro-mace.

One man carrying a large knife lunged at Ryder, who swung his mace upward, catching the man in the side. The spike sank deep between the attacker's ribs and Ryder pressed down on the button that would release the electrical charge.

The man's eyes widened and his body began to spasm. Ryder jerked the electro-mace from the man's body and he fell to the floor limp—whether dead or just unconscious, Ryder did not care nor have the time for. He spun around, his blood pounding, ready to face the next attacker.

This one charged, hunched over with the knife in front. Ryder sidestepped him, bringing the mace down into the man's back and setting off the electrical charge. The attacker fell to the ground a second later.

Ryder gripped the mace and spun, seeking the other men. Dillon still fought one, and one lay on the floor.

A scream from the back of the room rang out, and he turned to see the last attacker grab Krystal by the hair. The man pressed the tip of a knife under her breast, obviously in a panic as his gaze moved between Dillon and Ryder.

Krystal's eyes widened, her mouth open as she silently met Ryder's gaze to beg for help. Dillon glanced over at her, though still preoccupied with the other attacker.

*Gods.* Ryder's jaw clenched. He could not get close enough to swing the mace at the man who held Krystal. The man was not stupid; he used Krystal as a shield. He must have realized their weapons were not as sophisticated as the people of Belton's.

"You will come no closer." The man's eyes were wild, spittle flew from his lips. "She will die if—"

The rest of his words ended on a gurgle. A patch of red

spread through his uniform from where the knife lay imbedded in his chest.

"Oh gods," Krystal gasped and broke free to run to Dillon, whose arm was still raised from throwing the knife. The man he'd been fighting a moment before lay in a heap at his feet.

Dillon's arms wrapped around her and then visibly tightened as he squeezed her, his eyes closed, and he murmured something into her ear.

Ryder watched the couple, his own pulse slowing a bit as he came down from the adrenaline rush.

Dillon opened his eyes and his gaze locked on Ryder. Ryder gave a half smile and brief nod.

Easing Krystal out of his arms, Dillon stepped back and spoke to her. "We need to get you to a safe location. If they found us here once, they will find us again."

"I want to stay with you—"

"Krystal." His fingers closed over her chin as he stared down at her. "I will not risk your life again. I should have insisted you stayed in the cabin."

She was silent for a moment and then sighed. "Fine, I will go where you wish. But if you die, I shall be *very* upset."

Dillon gave a soft laugh and then his mouth lowered to hers.

Ryder walked to the edge of the tunnel, giving them the moment of intimacy. Relief flooded through him. It appeared that Dillon had managed to persuade Krystal that they were destined to be together.

Glancing down the tunnel, he listened for any sound of more enemy soldiers, but the tunnel was silent save for the slight dripping of water along the walls.

His gut twisted. Above ground there was a war going on, his people would be fighting for their lives. And somewhere Talia was in a world of trouble. There wasn't a part of him that doubted it.

"Dillon, though I know you would fight strong by my side, I think your destiny lies elsewhere," he stated gravely and turned to face the other two.

Dillon's eye narrowed, but he said nothing.

"I would ask that you gather as many of the women and children possible and take them to safety with Krystal. Will you do this?"

"If you feel that best." Dillon gave a brief nod as he drew Krystal closer to his side. "Then yes. I would be honored."

"Thank you." Ryder looked back down the tunnel. "Then we should go. It is time."

"I don't know, Charles. Ines said Ryder ordered her immediate death."

The voice brought Talia out of a thick darkness and she opened her eyes with a wince. The two men were across the room and had yet to notice her awakening.

"She is a woman. We have never executed a woman before," another voice argued. "And I cannot understand why Colonel Jacobs would issue such a command—even if he lay dying."

*Ryder.* Her chest tightened and she drew her lips between her teeth to keep from whimpering.

"I say we lock her in the maximum security cell and go fight with our brothers," one of the men continued to argue. "We can make the decision about her life later. Belton has regained the stronghold in this war, but we should be out there amongst them."

"I quite agree." There was a brief pause. "All right. Let us put her in the cell and return at a later point."

Talia closed her eyes, just before one of the men crossed the room toward her. He slipped his arms under her body and lifted her.

They would not execute her immediately? She swallowed

hard, uncertain if she were relieved or despondent by the turn of events. Part of her wanted it to be over, to not prolong the horrifying end of her life, which was sure to come.

They walked for a while, before she heard the grating sounds of a steel door being opened.

He laid her down on the cold concrete floor, the chill radiating through her body. Fingers brushed across her forehead and the soldier sighed.

"Gods, woman, I cannot imagine you being the type of woman who would kill Colonel Jacobs," he murmured.

His touch disappeared and she heard him stand up. Then the door scraped shut, a lock sounded, and his footsteps echoed as he walked away.

Talia sat up, opening her eyes. Panic swept through her. She could see nothing; her eyes may as well have still been closed. There was a thin slit in the door to allow in air, but only a tiny bit of light came from outside.

She rose to her feet and lifted her hands. The ceiling was just a bit above her head.

"No." She whimpered and reached her hands to the side, immediately encountering the wall an inch away.

Her high-pitched wail was muffled in the tiny box of a cell. She needed out of here. Oh gods, she needed out!

The cloying pressure of being confined pressed on every inch of her body. Tears ran down her cheeks and she curled herself into a ball and gasped for air.

"Oh gods." The words were a pathetic croak as she rocked back and forth as much as was allowed.

She would go mad in here. A hysterical laugh burst from her lips and she pressed her eyes closed. *Sleep. Just pretend you are sleeping.*

Trying to erase the horror of being in the cell, she pictured the gardens on Belton that she had walked through just yesterday. In her mind she was free again and Ryder was very much alive.

He held her in his arms, smoothing her hair back and kissing her forehead. The pungent smell of flowers tickled her nostrils.

She kept her focus on that image, praying reality would not seep into her vision and bring the unfathomable reminder that Ryder was dead and she soon would be, too.

Ryder switched his electro-mace from one hand to another and glanced around the city. Bodies lay everywhere. Some were his own people, but most were soldiers of Zortou. Smoke lingered in the air, yet the sounds of war and death had ceased.

At present there were talks under way of surrender from the enemy soldiers.

His chest grew tight and he struggled to draw a breath. So much destruction and lives lost in such a short amount of time. And in the past few hours of fighting, he had yet to catch sight of Talia.

It was possible she had found a safe location to hide out through the ongoing battle. Another possibility lingered in the back of his head. The possibility that Dillon had been right. That she had indeed betrayed him and left on a pod hours ago.

The thought did not sit well. His gut protested the likelihood that she was behind this. But if not Talia, then who?

"Colonel Jacobs?"

The voice came from behind him, and Ryder turned to see a soldier standing a few feet away. The man's exhaustion from fighting was evident in his crumpled posture, but his eyes were round with shock.

"Lieutenant?" Ryder raised an eyebrow. "How do you fare?"

"I am well." The soldier did not even blink. "Forgive my behavior, Colonel, but I thought you dead."

"Dead?"

Unease and suspicion ran through Ryder and he stepped closer to the soldier. The only people who would have known about the attempt on his life were Talia, Krystal, and Dillon. And whoever had shot him with the poisoned dart.

"Yes, sir."

"As you can see I am very much alive." Ryder narrowed his eyes. "How did you come about this information?"

"We were informed by Private Ines Santos."

Ines? How the hell had Ines known what had happened to him hours ago? His gut twisted and he tightened his fists at his side. Gods. How had he not seen this coming earlier?

"What else did she tell you?" The question came out harsher than he had intended.

The soldier must have sensed Ryder's change in temperament, because he shifted and cleared his throat.

"Ines instructed us to carry out the execution of a prisoner; said that you had requested it while you were on your deathbed."

The world seemed to tilt and his grip on the electro-mace tightened.

"Which prisoner?" he demanded hoarsely.

"A woman from Zortou—"

"*No!* Gods no!" Bile rose in his throat and his chest grew so tight he could not breathe. *Dead.* They had killed her.

The soldier was speaking, but Ryder did not hear his words. Only the man's hand gripping his shoulder brought him back to focus.

"Sir, I repeat, we did not carry out the execution."

Ryder forced in a breath and stared at the man, letting the words sink in.

"Repeat that, Lieutenant?"

"The execution was not performed. We didn't feel right about it. We put her in the small, maximum security cell."

"How long ago?" The relief spilling through him was not complete, and would not be so until she was in the safety of his arms.

The soldier hesitated. "It was hours ago, Colonel. We placed her in there and came back to fight."

*Damn.* She'd been in that tiny hellhole for hours? His stomach clenched with anger just thinking about it.

"Spread the word that anyone who comes across Private Santos is to take her into custody."

"*Sir.*"

The soldier's urgent tone stopped him as he turned away. He glanced back at the soldier, whose face was now pinched with fear.

"I passed Private Santos just minutes ago. She was on her way to the cellblock."

*Fuck.* Ryder choked in a breath and then turned, sprinting toward the cell house.

# 19

"They did not kill you?"

The high-pitched voice echoed in the hallway, snapping Talia up from the depths of her trancelike state.

Listening carefully, she picked up only one set of footsteps. Ines had come alone.

Talia had suppressed so much horror, pain, and anger over the past few hours that it all reignited with this sudden spark.

*Damn the woman.* Damn the woman for killing Ryder and for betraying her own planet.

"I always knew you should never count on a man to finish a task." Ines's voice was now right outside the door.

The urge to draw blood hit Talia hard. To fight for all she was worth. She may not have a weapon, but she would not go down quietly when Ines unlocked the cell.

"Did Ryder tell you we were lovers?" Ines went on.

*Open the cell door. Just open it, you ice-hearted bitch!*

"And I quite enjoyed myself with the Governing Council when I arrived on Zortou."

She could hear the sound of Ines fidgeting with something. Loading a weapon perhaps?

Talia rose to her feet and stretched her muscles as much as the cramped cell would allow.

"Why do you not speak? You are alive, are you not, Natalia?" Irritation rang clear in the other woman's voice. "I have to say that I am looking forward to plunging a dagger into your heart, then watching the life drain from your eyes."

*Ines had a knife.*

The sound of the lock sliding back rang loud. The cell door jerked open and Talia sprang out, sending her elbow directly into the other woman's face.

Ines stumbled backward with a cry of pain. With vengeance the only thought on her mind, Talia leapt on top of her. She grabbed the hand that Ines held a dagger in, and smashed it against the cold stone floor.

"Let us finish what we started earlier," Talia ground out, her blood pounding with rage as she glared down at the woman's outraged expression. "And we will do it without weapons."

She slammed Ines's wrist again and again into the floor until she heard the satisfying crack of bones and the weapon fell from her limp hand.

"Then again, I prefer using a weapon." Talia reached out and snagged the dagger. "Who will die now, bitch?"

She raised it above her head, ready to plunge it straight into Ines's breast.

"Talia!"

Her hand shook and she blinked, jerking her head to look down the corridor just as someone turned the corner and ran toward them.

*Ryder.* Was it even possible? Had Ines—

"Ooph." Ines's fist jammed into her windpipe, sending pain

through her body and making it nearly impossible to draw a breath.

Talia clutched her neck with one hand and rolled off Ines, attempting to keep her grip on the dagger with her other hand.

"If I die, you die with me," Ines snarled.

The other woman was stronger; even with a broken wrist she managed to wrestle free the deadly weapon. She swung it in an arc. In a blur of motion Talia watched the blade descend toward her own heart.

Just as sudden, Ines's arm went slack. The dagger lost momentum in its course and only glanced across Talia's skin, before clattering to the floor.

Ines's body shook, foam appeared at her mouth, and then her eyes glazed over. Her body went limp on the floor next to the dagger.

"Talia!" Ryder lowered his weapon and closed the space that separated them, kneeling beside her on the floor. "Gods, I thought you were dead."

"No." She reached up and cupped his face, issuing a ragged sob. How was it possible? "Ryder, I was convinced you had the same fate."

"My love." He groaned and lifted her into his arms, crushing his mouth down on hers.

She parted her lips to his tongue, eager to taste him. To assure herself he was indeed alive. His arms tightened around her, his mouth almost desperate as it moved against hers.

His hand reached to cup her breast and she gasped. Lifting his head, his brows drew together in confusion. He glanced down where his hand lay and the air hissed out from between his teeth.

"She cut you."

"I do not think it is a very deep wound." Talia said hesitantly, glancing down at the thin ribbon of red blood that had soaked through her dress.

"Yes ... but ..." His jaw clenched and fear flickered in his gaze. "What if she poisoned the tip?"

Talia's pulse jumped and she ran her tongue over her mouth.

"How do you feel?" he asked and began to walk, carrying her down the corridor.

"I feel ..." She broke off to think about it. Her heart was racing, her body felt alive and tight, but that was just the result of being in Ryder's arms again. "Normal. But a bit horrified to have witnessed the deaths of so many people."

"I am sorry you had to see all this." His grip on her tightened. "To have gone through any of it. If I had not arrived when I did—"

"Then I probably would have killed her myself." A smile played at her mouth and she ran her palm down the stubble on his cheek.

"Yes, I do believe you would have." His gaze held admiration.

"Ryder ..." She licked her lips, her stomach twisting. "The Council is dead."

He paused in his stride, his shock evident by the expression on his face.

"All of them?"

She nodded.

"But how? I did not see any of the members during the battle."

"Franklin killed Ramirez and Victor." She closed her eyes tight, trying not to relive the horrifying image. "And then Ines ... she killed Franklin."

"Ines." The word came out harsh. "I know now that she was behind this. I should have seen it earlier."

"Did you think I betrayed you?" Talia opened her eyes again, wanting to see the reaction in his gaze.

His eyes darkened and he shook his head. "There were others who added up the evidence and wanted to blame you. Yes, it looked bad . . . and yet I knew. Everything within me knew that you were innocent."

"Thank you. To hear you say that . . ." She swallowed hard and looked away. "Oh gods. I never allowed myself to hope to be free of them."

Tears of relief filled her eyes. After years of being their slave, she would never have to endure their touch or temper again.

Ryder stroked her hair and dropped a kiss on her cheek. "Talia, we must get your cut looked at."

She took a steadying breath in. "But surely you are needed on the battlefield. You should not spend your time nursing a prisoner with a small cut."

"The war is over, Talia. Zortou is surrendering as we speak."

Shock swept through her. She stared at him with wide eyes as he carried her out of the building and into the open air.

"Over?" she repeated hesitantly, glancing around. All was silent, though the faint smell of sulfur was in the air.

"Yes. Completely over." He glanced down at her. "Though after I drop you at the medical station, I must meet up with my superiors."

"I understand." She nodded and looked away. Zortou was surrendering? What did this mean for the people of her planet? And most of all . . . what did this mean for her and Ryder?

Ryder rubbed the back of his neck, stifling a yawn as he made his way to the medical station. Gods, it was getting late. The meeting with his superiors had gone on longer than he'd assumed it would.

Keeping focus had been no easy task; his thoughts had always returned to Talia. Switching from concern, to desire, to some sort of soft fuzzy emotion he had no wish to analyze.

He wanted her in his arms . . . in his bed . . . in his life. He just wanted her. His eyes narrowed and he increased his pace, his heart thudding heavy in his chest.

Gods. Was it true? Had he fallen in love with her?

"Ryder."

He paused and turned to see Krystal coming up behind him. He grinned and walked back toward her.

"I was beginning to worry about you, kid. Did you get through all right?"

"Yes, we did fine." She blushed and looked down. "Thank you, Ryder. For knowing what was right for me. For making sure I ended up with the most perfect man in the universe."

"I am glad you two have realized that you are meant for one another. I can think of no better man for you," he said truthfully.

The thought of the love the two had found made his gut twist and the need to reach Talia more urgent.

"If you will excuse me, Krystal, I am on my way to see Talia—"

"To release her? I am so ashamed that I doubted her, for even a moment." His sister stepped forward, her gaze direct. "You are planning on releasing her, aren't you?"

Ryder blinked and glanced away. Release Talia. Gods. Krystal's words were reasonable, yet he had not even considered that option.

"The war is over, Ryder," Krystal argued. "You know she has never been a threat to our planet. She has been far more of an ally to us than an enemy. The time to give her the freedom she deserves is now."

*Release Talia.* His stomach twisted with the thought of letting her go. Gods, how could he not, though? She had been a prisoner her entire life. Who was he to continue to keep her one?

"Yes." He closed his eyes and gave a jagged nod. "Of course I am releasing her."

The words fell from numb lips. She deserved her freedom. He could hardly keep her prisoner here on Belton. Had he really been so selfish to have even considered the idea?

Life on Zortou was about to undergo a dramatic change. In the meeting he'd learned that all citizens of the planet were to be given the option to relocate to Belton and gain citizenship, and that all remaining Rosabelles would be given immediate freedom from their owners.

His throat tightened and nausea gathered inside him. Talia deserved her freedom. Though it would nearly kill him to have to let her go, she deserved the same chance as the other women to start a new life.

"Ryder? Are you well?" Krystal grasped his hand and stepped closer to him.

"I am fine," he muttered and shook his head. "I must go."

"Oh . . . how did I not see it?" His sister drew in a quick breath, her eyes widening. "Do you love her, Ryder?"

He pulled his hand free, before she could notice the slight tremble in it.

"Oh, Ryder." Krystal gave a soft sigh. "What do you intend to do?"

"I will do what needs to be done. What Talia deserves." He drew in an unsteady breath and then set off to find her.

Talia drew in a slow breath, watching her breast rise against the gentle fingers of the nurse who spread ointment over the shallow cut.

"Does it hurt?" the woman, who'd introduced herself as Jammie, asked. She turned away to pick up a small bandage.

"No." Talia shook her head and closed her eyes as the nurse pressed the thin gauze over the wound. "There has been far too much going on for me to notice such a trifle of an injury."

Jammie made a small cluck of sympathy with her tongue. "Indeed it has. The infirmary has been quite busy all day tending to the wounded. Though many couldn't be saved . . ."

Talia's stomach rolled and she bit back a wave of regret and guilt. She whispered a soft, "I feel terrible."

The nurse raised her gaze, surprise in her eyes. "For what, Talia? From what I understand, the situation could have been so much worse had you not warned the Colonel."

Ryder. Warmth stirred through her at the mention of her lover's name. Was he still with his superiors? Would he be returning to her shortly?

"There, the cut should heal in no time and I'd wager there will be no scar." Jammie winked and stood up, handing her a plain cream-colored gown. "Put this on so you don't get a chill."

The sudden knock had both of their gazes darting to the door of the small room.

"Perhaps that is your handsome Colonel now?" Jammie murmured with a wink.

Talia thrust her arms into the gown and tugged it closed over her chest, her pulse pounding and her mouth going dry.

The nurse hurried to the door and pressed the code to open it. The man in the doorway was not Ryder, but he still managed to rip a startled gasp of pleasure from her chest.

Standing from the examination table, tears prickling the back of her eyes, she choked out, "Dane?"

Her assistant from Zortou rushed through the door, the hesitant expression on his face fading into relief.

"Oh my gods, Talia, I've been worried sick about you!"

For the first time in the years he'd worked with her, Dane grabbed her and pulled her into a tight hug.

"I've wanted to do this forever," he muttered and squeezed her extra tight. "You were miserable on that awful planet. I knew it and wished I could help ease your desolation, but my hands were tied. I could not even offer you a hug; those Council bastards would have had my head."

Her lips twitched and a tear spilled down her cheek. "But you can now. You were always so good to me, Dane."

Dane pulled back, his gaze searching hers. "How are you? Have you been treated awful here?"

"No!" Her head shook in rapid denial. "Truly, I have not. And I know it seems insane, but being taken prisoner was likely the best thing that could have happened to me."

Dane's brows shot sky high. "Truly?"

She bit her lip and nodded.

"So, uh, just how attractive was this guy who abducted you?"

Talia's cheeks flamed with color and she lowered her gaze.

"Oh! Well, I see then."

She cleared her throat and tucked a strand of hair behind her ear. "What of you, Dane? How did you fair with the battle? And—oh, no! The soldier you were seeing? Thomas? Did he . . ."

"We faired well. I did not fight in the battle, but was brought along on one of the ships as an extra servant." He hesitated, a dark shadow crossing his face. "As a soldier of Zortou, Thomas had no choice but to fight. I was so damn worried about him. Rightfully so. He was injured, but, thank gods, not critically."

"Oh, Dane." She clasped his hand and squeezed, seeing the sheen of tears in his gaze. She could completely empathize with her friend. "I'm sorry."

"We're okay, though." Dane blinked rapidly, dispelling the

tears. "I had just paid him a visit in the infirmary here, when I learned of your presence. Thomas is well. Though of course worried what will happen to him now that his army has been defeated."

"Belton is a just planet," she murmured confidently. "You will both be treated fairly."

"Yes. I have gained that impression." Dane's gaze moved around the room, past the nurse busy in the corner, before returning to Talia. "Where is this soldier of yours?"

"In a meeting. He should return shortly."

Dane lifted one eyebrow. "And what are his intentions toward you?"

"Dane!"

He rolled his eyes. "I was your servant for how many years? Surely you can not expect me to suddenly drop my tendency to worry?"

She gave him a slight smile. "I suppose not. Ryder and I have not discussed the future as of yet, but he should be arriving soon."

"Hmm." Dane's gaze narrowed and glanced over her body. "Unfortunately, I must leave shortly, but I must say this battle-worn image you have going on does not work for a romantic reunion with your soldier." He turned to the nurse. "Perhaps she could help you?"

The nurse scurried across the room, obviously having had one ear open to their conversation.

"Say nothing more," she murmured and fluffed Talia's hair. "I'm due off work, but will stay late. We'll do something with this hair and I'll have a lovely dress sent in. We'll have you pretty as can be for his arrival."

"Are you certain? Surely I don't—" But the nurse had already left the room, and so Talia turned to Dane with a watery smile. "Thank you, Dane. It relieves me to no end that you are well, and that you sought me out."

"I had to." He touched her cheek. "Be happy, Talia. For once in your life, be happy. You deserve it."

"I will certainly try. And you, as well, deserve happiness."

Dane's gaze warmed and he looked toward the door. "I have found my own happiness, and he is recovering in a room down the hall."

"Then go be with him."

"I shall. Keep in touch, my lovely Talia." Dane drew her into another quick hug.

Talia closed her eyes. "Of course. You do the same."

A moment later he was gone and her stomach jumped in anticipation of Ryder's return. When Jammie came back to help pretty her up, she put herself in the nurse's hands gratefully.

The walk over to the medical unit was agony. Each step Ryder took brought him closer to their good-bye.

A nurse was leaving her room as he entered. She dipped her head and smiled, her eyes twinkling.

Ryder took a deep breath and opened the door.

Talia sat near the window, her back to him as she stared outside. Her hair fell in a shiny red wave down the curve of her back. The globes of her buttocks were outlined through the thin dress she wore.

She turned her head suddenly and saw him, her blue eyes locking on him. Her lips were glossy and parted, her cheeks pinker than usual.

"Ryder." The word was but a breath on her lips.

The air in his lungs stuck and he forced himself to swallow. *Gods, she was so beautiful.*

She stood from her seat near the window and walked toward him. The dress clung to her every curve in a river of gold silk. Her hips swung lightly, her unbound breasts moved with her steps.

Her mouth curved into a smile and she lifted her hands toward him. He took them automatically, his fingers curling around her soft hands.

"You look beautiful, Natalia."

She flinched and the smile faded. Her gaze turned wary. "Why did you do that?"

"Do what?"

"Call me Natalia?"

Gods, had he? His nerves on edge, he released her hand and fisted his hands at his side. If he kept touching her he would never get through this.

"Ryder? Is something wrong?"

"Yes." Damn it. He hadn't meant to admit that. He shook his head and forced a smile. "No. Nothing is wrong. I come with good news for you, actually."

"Oh?" She lifted an eyebrow and he saw a flicker of excitement in her gaze.

*She wanted to leave. She wanted to hear that she would be set free.*

"You are free, Talia." He forced the initial words out, and then plunged on. "We release you as a prisoner of Belton. A pod is leaving in one hour and I have arranged a ticket for you to be on it."

He may as well have plunged a dagger into her chest. Her heart twisted painfully and she could not draw in a breath. The burn of tears pricked behind her eyes.

"Talia?"

"Why?" she choked out.

Gods. If she weren't in such emotional pain, she might actually have been humiliated. She had gone through so much trouble to look pretty for him, had begged the nurse to help her. And they'd giggled, discussing how pleased he would be. Only to find out he did not even want her anymore.

"Why? Because you are free, Talia. Did you not hear me?" His words sounded harsh. "You should never have been a prisoner on Belton. I should never have taken you."

"Should you have made love to me?" she shot back, drawing in a shaky breath.

He flinched and for a moment she saw a flash of vulnerability in his gaze, and then it was once again hard. Confusion took the edge off the pain that ate away inside her.

"I will help you pack."

She shook her head and drew in a painful breath, her mouth tightening. "I brought nothing with me. I will take nothing when I leave."

He stared at her for a moment and then nodded. After a moment's hesitation, he turned away and headed back toward the door.

Knowing it was a gamble, but desperate to keep him from leaving, she blurted, "What do *you* want?"

He froze, nearly to the door. He didn't answer right away, his entire body grew rigid.

"Talia . . ."

"Answer me, Ryder."

"I want . . . you to be happy."

Hope sparked in her heart and she swallowed the thickness in her throat. Her pulse began to pound faster. She licked her lips.

"That is not what *you* want, that is what you want for *me.*" Closing the distance that separated them, she placed a hand on his shoulder. "What do *you* want, Ryder?"

He spun around and gripped her wrist. The torment in his eyes must have mirrored her own.

"I want you to stay, Talia," he ground out, drawing her into his arms. "I want you to stay with me and let me love you like you have always deserved to be loved."

Her eyes filled with tears. Relief spread warmth through her. "Ryder—"

"But I will not ask that of you. I *cannot* ask that of you." His jaw hardened and raw anguish flashed again in his gaze. "It wouldn't be fair of me to ask that you stay with me now that you finally have the freedom to do what you wish."

"And what if I wish to stay with you?" She shook her head and pressed two fingers against his trembling lips. "Are you really such a presumptuous fool to assume that leaving you would make me happy?"

"Sweet Talia . . ." His voice cracked and he kissed her fingers, tilting his head and pressing his cheek into her palm. "Are you sure?"

"Leaving you would condemn me to a fate worse than being a Rosabelle," she whispered, bringing her other hand up so she could cradle his face in both her hands. "I love you, Ryder. And I have never loved anyone. Do not make me leave the only man, the only place, that has made me feel like I am worth something—"

"You are worth *everything*, princess." His mouth closed over hers, cutting off her choked reply.

Talia slid her arms around his neck with a sob and kissed him back, thrusting her tongue into his mouth to find his.

He lifted his head, his breathing uneven as he palmed one of her breasts. "I love you, Talia. Are you certain this is what you wish?"

"More than anything." She drew in her own ragged breath and felt her nipple bead against his hand.

248

He swept her up into his arms and carried her to the couch off to the side of the small recovery room.

He laid her down against the soft cushions and her heart beat like crazy. His gaze ran over her with relief and hunger.

He untied the knot at the top of her dress and the silky fabric fell to her waist, exposing her chest to the cool air.

Her nipples puckered and stretched toward his lips, which were already descending toward them. When his mouth closed hot and wet over one tip she cried out, her legs scissoring on the couch and heat gathered heavy at her center.

The weight of Ryder's body covered hers, delicious and heavy. She moaned softly as his mouth nuzzled the bandage that covered the top curve of her breast.

"I am so sorry she hurt you," he muttered.

"It is nothing." She caught his chin, pulling his head up and seeking his lips with her own. Brushing a fervent kiss against them. "Nothing, Ryder. The only pain I feel is when I think of losing you."

"Never, my love." He gathered her gown in his fists, tugging it up to her waist and positioning himself between her thighs. "You are mine." His cock nudged the damp folds between her legs. "And I am yours."

He plunged into her fast and hard, with no preliminaries. But she didn't need them; she was more than ready, gripping his shoulders as her body welcomed the man who held her heart.

Always when he was inside her, when he held her, she felt so complete. Everything inside of her was at peace. And now, the weight of his body on hers was a tangible reminder that they both had survived today. Survived to love each other.

Tears of relief flooded her eyes and her throat tightened with emotion as Ryder began to move steadily inside her.

She kissed his shoulder, lifting her hips to meet each full

thrust. "Ryder . . . you were the unknown hope in my heart that kept me sane these past few years."

He paused, drawing in an unsteady breath as his gaze sought hers. "And now you will always be mine."

He plunged deeper into her still, stretching her, filling her.

Her heart swelled with love and the tears in her eyes spilled hot down her cheek.

"Always," she whispered.

"Always." He kissed each tear away, before he took her mouth once again.

Turn the page for a sneak peek of "His to Reclaim," Shelli Stevens's novella in SEXY BEAST VII, available September 2009!

# 1

"*Gemma!*" The shrill scream pierced through the woods, filtering past the aged walls of the log cabin. "Oh my God! I can't believe this. *Gemma!*"

The sound of feet pounding down the path mingled with the alarmed whimpers and short breaths of the approaching woman.

Gemma's fingers clenched around the brush in her hand, her pulse quickening as she turned to face the door. *Was it too much to hope that it was nothing more than the caterer having encountered a problem?*

The door flung open, smashing into the wall. Her younger cousin Megan stepped into the room, eyes wild with panic.

"He's really coming."

They were just three words, but they were enough. The brush dropped from Gemma's hand and her body went numb with shock.

This was really happening. . . . No! The room spun, and she gripped the vanity table to keep from falling to her knees. *No.* Was he *insane?*

"There's no time." Megan closed the door, hands shaking. "Shift and then run. Run fast. It's the only way you can possibly escape him."

"How far away is he?" Gemma's voice came out remarkably calm as she fumbled to undo the buttons on her wedding dress.

The cold fear began to subside, and a hot burn of rage blazed through her. How dare he? After five years, how *dare* he?

Megan grabbed her arm and tugged her toward the door. "A mile. Maybe. And he's not alone, Gemma. He's brought friends. You must hurry! There's no time to change out of your dress. Run, and I'll find Jeffrey and tell him what's happened."

"My dress will ruin during transition—"

*Crash!*

The door broke in half and splinters of wood shot into the interior of the cabin like tiny missiles.

Heart in her throat, Gemma retreated, her body trembling as she stared at the man who now filled the doorway. The man who'd just made good on the appallingly dark promise he'd made just days ago in an e-mail. She'd been half-convinced it was a joke—someone toying with her heart—and had told Megan as much.

But it wasn't a joke. The proof was standing in front of her eyes. Maybe a couple of years ago she would have wished for this, but not now. Dammit, not now!

Sweat clung to the hard muscles of Hunter's nude body—it was clear he'd just shifted back to human form. A familiar heat crept through her body and she hardened her jaw, refusing to acknowledge it. The same way she'd refused to acknowledge it for the last five years.

It was hard not to, though. With his dark hair and tan body he was tall and broad, a mass of muscles and ridges. Her gaze dropped and her cheeks burned hot. She swallowed hard, unable to tear her gaze from his hard thighs and the thick cock that rested between them.

The blood raged through her veins, and she closed her eyes to count to ten. When she opened them again, her gaze was firmly back on his face, unwilling to let her eyes shift any lower than his shoulders this time. That would be a guaranteed diversion from finding a way out of this situation.

Unfortunately, five years had done nothing but enhance Hunter's raw sex appeal.

His eyes, burning like dark blue crystals, met hers. And, like the devil come to collect his due, he advanced into the room, his face a mask of fierce determination.

*Oh, God.* She needed to act. Now. Swallowing the thickness in her throat, Gemma glanced around the room, looking for anything that might be used as a weapon. She grabbed the chair from her vanity table and lifted it above her head with a grunt.

Hunter lunged forward and knocked it from her grasp, sending it crashing to the ground behind her. Before she could draw in a startled breath, he'd circled her wrists with one of his massive hands and pulled her body firmly against the rock-hard wall of his chest.

*"No!"* She growled and lifted her knee to tag him in the groin, but he blocked the shot.

Instead he pulled her tighter against him and forced his thigh between hers. His thick cock brushed her hip and she stilled, barely able to breathe as her heart slammed against her rib cage.

His soft laugh feathered warm against her cheek. "You should have listened to your cousin, angel," he leaned forward and said softly against her ear. "You should have run."

The blood drained from Gemma's face and she heard Megan whimper from the corner of the room.

*Megan.* Hope flared.

"Megan, go find Jeffrey!"

Her cousin lurched away from the wall and toward the doorway, but fell back with a shrill yell.

Two more men—though these ones were clothed—filed through the broken entrance.

"It appears we will have to take the younger one with us as well," Hunter ordered with a sigh.

"Me?" Megan squeaked in alarm. "No! You can't—"

Her words were cut off by the hand that slid over her mouth; then the burly man slid another arm around her waist to lift her off the ground.

Panic resumed in her gut and Gemma tugged at her imprisoned wrists, her mouth in a tight line. "Let her go, Hunter. She has nothing to do with this."

"We will, angel. Tomorrow. We don't want her running off to tell Jeffrey the minute we leave, now do we?"

"*Bastard.*"

His smile came slow. "Now, you know my mother well enough to know that's not true."

Of course he would throw that at her. She bit her lip, trying to hold her temper. It wasn't easy as she watched helplessly as the two men carried her cousin kicking and screaming out the door. Megan's muffled sounds were ineffective at bringing them the help they desperately needed.

Gemma drew in a slow breath. "You know, Hunter, I always suspected you were a bit certifiable. Congratulations, you've just confirmed it."

He caught her chin with rough fingers, lifting her face so she had to look at him. A shiver ran down her spine. Unfortunately, it may not have all been because of fear. His eyes narrowed, until the blue irises were just slits of blue. They burned hot as his gaze scoured her face.

"Am I? You were the one about to marry a human." His gaze darkened. "I gave you fair warning. Call off the wedding or I will do it for you."

"I'll *still* marry him."

"I wouldn't count on it."

"Oh! I'll say it again, Hunter. You're certifiable," she repeated. As she tried to twist her chin from his grasp, his hold just tightened. "In fact, I'm sure you won't mind if I just call you Certi from now on."

"Angel, I don't care what the hell you call me." His head lowered, until his mouth was just a breath above hers. "I'll just look forward to hearing you call it when I'm riding you in bed."

Shock ripped through her, widening her eyes and snatching her breath away. Heat rushed through her body, curling thick down through her blood before gathering heavy in her pussy.

His nostrils flared, and she knew his were side meant that he could smell the dampness between her legs that his image had created. Heat flooded her cheeks.

"Like hell that will happen, Hunter."

"You want me, angel." It wasn't a question. And there was no asking when his lips crushed down on hers a second later.

Gemma went rigid in his arms, letting out an outraged feline growl that was all jaguar.

He answered with a deeper growl, plunging his tongue past her compressed lips to take control of her mouth.

There was no fighting him. With each bold stroke of his tongue against hers, a little more common sense got swept away. He plundered her mouth, leaving no inch unexplored, controlling her tongue and mind with ease.

The heat built in her body; her breasts swelled, the nipples tightening to scrape against the lace bustier beneath her dress.

Five years dropped away and once again it was Hunter holding her, kissing her. Making her forget everything but his touch and the way it made her feel.

His cock pressed hard into her belly, a tangible reminder of his promise to fuck her.

With a groan, he released her chin to plunge his hand into her bodice. He cupped her breast in the palm of his hand, squeezing just enough to send another rush of moisture straight to her panties.

Her head fell back, a gasp ripping from her lips. The calloused pad of his thumb swept across one tight nipple, and her knees wobbled.

His mouth lifted from hers, and he pulled her breast above the bodice. His head swooped down and he wrapped his lips around the hard tip. Hot breath and a moist tongue teased her, before his teeth raked against her flesh.

"Oh God." She trembled, minutes away from hiking up her wedding dress and begging him to fuck her.

*Wedding dress? Jeffrey!* The name of the man she was supposed to marry in two hours resounded in her head. *Who's certifiable now, Gemma?*

Hunter reached for the hem of her dress, lifting it over her legs to cup her ass.

*Now, Gemma. Act now!* Knowing she had an advantage—just barely—she grabbed his hair and stepped back enough to slam her knee into his chest.

He stumbled back with a curse, eyes flashing with dismay and rage. It was only a second, but it was the break she needed.

Gemma moved past him and sprinted out the door to the cabin that she'd been using to get ready for her wedding. She leapt off the porch and landed on the dirt path.

Her heart slammed in her chest, her body trembling with

adrenaline. Increasing her pace, she growled and willed the change to speed up. It didn't take long. Her twenty-thousand-dollar designer dress exploded into a mass of pearl buttons and lace as her body shifted into its jaguar form.

Seconds later she was on all fours, charging through the resort in a desperate attempt to escape Hunter. The thrashing of branches and trees behind her signaled that it was going to be one hell of a challenge.

Dammit. How could he have been so stupid to get distracted by Gemma's sweet body?

Hunter snarled and dodged between two trees that appeared on one section of the trail.

He shouldn't have lost focus. As an ESA agent, he was better than that by nature. Their job was to protect and defend all shifter species from threats of corruption, danger, and violence. The Elite Shifter Agency only hired the best of the best. You had to be tough, intelligent, sharp, quick-minded . . . *and definitely not lose your focus over a nice set of tits, you idiot.*

His fellow agents would laugh their asses off if they knew he'd gotten completely muddleheaded by a woman.

He hadn't been able to stop himself from touching her. But it had been a costly delay. He should have had her in the vehicle by now and they could've been halfway to White River. As it was, Joaquin and Brad were probably wondering where the hell he was.

Hunter paused and breathed in the air, careful not to lose Gemma's scent.

She wasn't even following the human-made trail anymore. His gaze darted around the lush forest. His ears listening for the sound of her escape. The sudden flash of yellow and brown between the trees was a dead giveaway to her location. Unlike him, Gemma's jaguar form didn't have the luxury of dark brown fur that hid his spots. Though she was desperate in her attempt to escape, she didn't stand a chance.

His resistance softened a bit with pity before he hardened it again. He couldn't afford such a weakness. He gave a low growl and took off after her. Not that he could blame her for running. Not after what he'd done to her so many years ago. But what Gemma didn't seem to quite understand was the cloud of danger lingering over her life right now. And at the center of that vortex was none other than her husband-to-be.

Jealousy, like a hot brand iron, stabbed sudden and deep, twisting inside him. His paws hit the ground hard as he quickened his pace, jumping over bushes as he gained on her.

She shouldn't have been marrying Jeffrey Delmore in the first place. She was his. She'd sworn it. It didn't matter that she'd been barely twenty at the time. It was one promise he intended to see she kept. Gemma belonged to *him*.

Guilt twisted his gut, that he was completely out of line, but he refused to acknowledge it. Not now. Right now his primal side was in dominance and the chase was on to reclaim his woman.

He was only about twenty feet behind her now and she must have realized she couldn't outrun him much longer. He could hear the agitation in the growls she emitted while continuing to dodge through trees and beneath low brushes.

And then she blew it, giving him the final advantage he needed. Her back legs caught on a tree root protruding from the ground and she stumbled, losing her balance before falling onto her side.

She tried to get back up again, but the damage was done. Hunter used her moment of vulnerability and jumped on her. The weight of his body pinned hers to the ground.

Fur flew as she swiped at him with her claws; jaws snapped

at his neck but missed. They rolled on the hard earth, fighting for dominance.

He locked gazes with her. *"Stop fighting me,"* he said with his mind.

Rage flared in her gaze, and she continued to struggle beneath him.

With a growl of frustration he caught her neck between his teeth, using just enough force to warn her she'd better yield. Relief washed through him when she stilled beneath him.

*Shift back, Gemma. Please, I don't want to hurt you.*

She tried to swat him again with a claw, but he reared back, missing her attempt.

Realizing fighting was futile, her eyes closed. The fur on her face slowly receded to show smooth ivory skin. She had chosen to obey. Quickly, to avoid crushing her, he rolled off her and shifted back to his human form.

"You have no right," she rasped.

When he turned to look at her, his heart clenched a bit. She sat on the ground, her knees drawn up to her chest as she glared at him.

Her pale skin seemed luminescent against the greens and browns of the forest. The tawny curls of her hair—which had always fascinated him—tumbled over her shoulders, shielding her breasts from him.

His mouth pursed. *Too bad.* He hadn't seen her naked in years, and it was quite obvious her body had changed since then. Her curves were bolder, whereas before they'd been slight.

He lifted his gaze to hers, wincing slightly at how her brown eyes condemned him.

"Let's not make this any more difficult than it needs to be, angel."

"Oh, I think it was too late for that the minute you decided to interrupt my wedding day."

His jaw hardened and he stepped forward. "You will walk with me now to the vehicle."

"What's option B?"

"I'll carry you."

Her nostrils flared and the arms around her knees tightened.

"Let me think," she murmured and then continued to watch him for a moment.

Her lips parted a second later, but words didn't come out. Instead the piercing scream she issued was guaranteed to raise the dead. *Or bring her groom running.*